THE MUSEUM OF HEARTBREAK

MEG LEDER

THE
MUSEUM
OF
HEARTBREAK

Scholastic Children's Books
An imprint of Scholastic Ltd
Euston House, 24 Eversholt Street, London, NW1 1DB, UK
Registered office: Westfield Road, Southam, Warwickshire, CV47 0RA
SCHOLASTIC and associated logos are trademarks and/or
registered trademarks of Scholastic Inc.

First published in the US by Simon Pulse, 2016
First published in the UK by Scholastic Ltd, 2016

Text copyright © Margaret Leder, 2016
Interior illustrations copyright © Adam J Turnball, colagene.com

The right of Margaret Leder to be identified as the author of this work has been asserted by her.

ISBN 978 1407 16148 8

Printed by CPI Group (UK) Ltd, Croydon, CR0 4YY
Papers used by Scholastic Children's Books are made
from wood grown in sustainable forests.

1 3 5 7 9 10 8 6 4 2

www.scholastic.co.uk

To Tom Geier, who taught me I could,
and Michael Bourret, who told me I should

Present Day

I DON'T WANT THEM TO GO.

I know I will forget them if they leave now.

I think about running down the 86 flights of stairs of the Empire State Building to the street so I can hold up my hands, block their way, scream, "Don't go!"

But if I do, I'm certain one of them will eat me—probably the T. rex. It'll lift my body with its furious hands, crunch my bones with its massive jaws, chew my tendons with its sharp incisors.

I can't stop them: The dinosaurs are leaving New York City.

Hundreds and hundreds of them in all shapes and sizes, radiating out from the doors of the American Museum of Natural History, walking into the Holland Tunnel, crossing the Brooklyn Bridge, wading through the Hudson River.

They are in groups and alone:

A family of triceratops, the mother nudging a young one with her nose, an impatient stomp of her front foot.

A T. rex angrily swiping its tiny arms at abandoned cars.

A pterodactyl swooping down Broadway.

I watch them from the observation deck of the Empire State Building, popping quarters into the tourist telescope so I can see them up close: the beautiful metallic green-gray glint of scales, the way their chests heave oxygen in and out, the casually powerful swat of a tail.

They take my breath away.

They bump cars and break windows.

Eph was right. They are real.

For a second, I wonder if I should tell my dad that the dinosaurs are leaving. But I can't move, and even though there's no way all those dinosaurs could come from one building, it makes perfect sense to me, and I know then that I'm dreaming.

I still don't wake up.

They're endless and unstoppable, piling up in awkward clumps, spilling against the museum doors in waves, pushing past one another, roaring ferociously, wings beating heavily in the air.

Some of them have luggage strapped around their middles— suitcases piled up in precariously wobbling towers. Others are beasts and beasts only, snarling at one another, at the cloudless sky.

A brontosaurus ducks its long neck, trying not to get caught in telephone cables.

A brachiosaurus splashes into the river, its head bobbing well above the water line.

A giganotosaurus ducks to fit into the Holland Tunnel, scrunching its head down.

They are caravanning on highways away from the city. They leave behind footprints in the melting asphalt, broken-down trees, smashed taxis. Their weight displaces the familiar world: Pylons snap on the Brooklyn Bridge. The Hudson River sloshes past its shoreline. The aforementioned giganotosaurus creates a bottleneck in the Holland Tunnel. (A stegosaurus screams at the delay.)

They fight and growl, plod and stomp, but they are leaving.

And in that moment, I wake with a jolt—a cold sweat in the backs of my knees, my sheets tangled around me, my pillow wet from crying—and feel the familiar empty ache around my heart.

It's 4:13 a.m.

My hand flies to my neck. My necklace is just where it should be, rising and falling against my skin with each slowing breath.

Maybe in real life there aren't happy endings.

Maybe that's the point.

I breathe in and out.

I know what I need to do.

I hop up, click on a lamp. From the end of the bed my cat, Ford, squints unhappily at the introduction of light.

I dig through my desk for a notebook and pencil, then get back into bed, pulling up the covers, a fleece blanket around my shoulders. Ford closes his eyes contentedly, happy to go back to his cat dreams.

I chew on my pen cap, then start writing.

Welcome to the Museum of Heartbreak . . .

WELCOME TO THE MUSEUM OF HEARTBREAK

IN HER JUNIOR YEAR OF HIGH SCHOOL, PENELOPE MADEIRA MARX, age sixteen going on seventeen, experienced for the first time in her young life the devastating, lonely-making, ass-kicking phenomenon known as *heartbreak*.

It happened like this:

She fell in love.

Everything changed.

And just like the extinction event that wiped out the dinosaurs, heartbreak came hurtling at Penelope Marx with the fury of one thousand meteors.

The Museum of Heartbreak (MoH) is the United States' national institution for the documentation, study, and interpretation of that particular heartbreak. It also strives to identify and understand the phenomenon in general, in hopes of preventing and avoiding it in the future.

Founded in New York City, and through the leadership of its curator and staff (the eminent seventeen-year-old feline Ford the Cat), the MoH is committed to encouraging an even deeper understanding of a broken heart by establishing, preserving, and documenting a permanent collection of artifacts and memories related to all aspects of heartbreak.

To achieve its goals, the MoH recognizes:

- That heartbreak is defined by absence: that is, something you love (e.g., a person, place, or thing; your favorite stuffed animal; a firefly-filled summer vacation; the restaurant with the amazing pancakes and fruit butter) is gone.

- That heartbreak is defined by loneliness: that is, not having that thing brings about crippling feelings of sadness and despair.

- That while largely emotional, heartbreak is also a physical phenomenon: that is, it's accompanied by an actual hollow pain in your chest any time you remember what you lost.

- That heartbreak heightens nostalgia: that is, you will suddenly be confronted with remembered sounds, tastes, and memories that will bring you to your knees.

- That heartbreak comes in all shapes and sizes: big, sweeping devastations that leave you reeling; tiny, particular sadnesses that make your bones ache.

- That sometimes the biggest heartbreak of all is letting go of the time before you knew things could ever be broken.

By educating and enlightening the viewing public, the MoH seeks to remind visitors to be vigilant. Because just like a hapless old dinosaur innocently eating leaves or gleefully munching on the bones of its prey, if you have a heart, you too can be flattened by the metaphoric meteor known as heartbreak.

Enjoy your time at the museum.

Sincerely,
The Curator and Ford the Cat

Watchmen, book
Watchmen, liber
Copyright 1987
New York, New York
Cat. No. 201X-1
On loan from Ephraim O'Connor

ON THE FIRST DAY OF MY JUNIOR YEAR, IN THE FIRST TWO MINUTES of open assembly, the most handsome boy I had ever seen in all my sixteen never-been-kissed years sat down and raised an eyebrow right at me.

He had gray-green eyes, cool like a round stone in your hand.

He was wearing a *Catcher in the Rye* T-shirt and a navy corduroy blazer with elbow patches.

He smelled like cinnamon.

If I could have conjured the perfect boy, I couldn't have done better than this.

"Hey," he said, tipping his head my way. "How are you liking it?"

Without thinking, I checked the seat next to me, but no, Eph was sprawled out, doodling intricately on the back cover of a notebook. I checked in front of me, but Audrey was talking to Cherisse, her back to us.

The boy was talking to me.

The boy with the thick eyebrows and the beautiful head of curly brown hair was talking to me.

"Ohhhh?" I said, and the sound came out like someone had stepped on a mouse, and I couldn't help it, I was so flustered: I poked my finger at my chest. *Me?*

He nodded, a wry smile. "Yeah, you, Scout."

My heart shot up and through my ribs to the tip of my tongue, paused for one breath, then plummeted back down even faster.

Like I'd stuck my finger in a socket.

Like I'd been hit by lightning.

Something inside me started, something with fierce, gnashing teeth and adrenaline and bone.

"How am I liking what?" I wiped my palms on my lap, willing myself to be cool, to calm down.

"Your comic book," he said, pointing to the copy of *Watchmen* poking out of my bag. "Do you like it?"

The cute boy across the aisle was, for no apparent reason, striking up a conversation with me, and I had this giddy, fleeting thought: *Wow, maybe it is finally happening.* Also: *Thank you, Baby Jesus, for making Eph lend me his copy of* Watchmen.

And then I opened my mouth.

"Oh, the graphic novel? It's not mine; my friend is loaning it to me. . . ." I nodded in Eph's general direction, afraid to take my eyes off the boy. "Which is cool, because it's a first edition and he's a megafan, probably because he's going to be a graphic artist someday. . . ." The beautiful boy gave an amused nod, so I pushed forward. "Have you read it? I haven't finished it yet, but I saw the movie and it was all right, though Eph said the movie messed a lot of stuff up. . . ."

The boy started to say something, but words were haphazardly tumbling out of my mouth on top of his. "Though I have a hard time following the graphic novel stuff, like do I read the dialogue up to down or left to right . . ." I zoomed my hands in crazy directions like the comic was in front of me. "Or maybe it doesn't matter—I don't know? But I like reading so much."

I stuttered to a stop because I had lost my breath, but also because the boy had this inscrutable look on his face that I could only imagine meant he was trying to figure out the nearest escape route without having to interact with me again.

I winced. "Oh God, I'm sorry."

He shrugged. "I was only making conversation. . . ."

He was only making conversation. He was only trying to be polite.

My neck flushed hot, and a large part of me wanted to get up and scream, *I am terrible at talking to boys! I am terrible at life!* and then run away as far as I could, to some solitary research station at the North or South Pole (whichever one has penguins), where I would never have to interact with another human being for the rest of my life.

(Another part of me—one so very small—wanted desperately to rewind to a minute ago, before I opened my mouth, before I knew he was only being polite, when my heart was all hopeful and electric.)

"Sometimes I talk too much . . . ," I started to explain right as Cherisse—one of my top ten least favorite people in the world (and that list included dictators and people who ran dog fights)—gasped: "Oh my God, Keats!"

The beautiful boy—Keats, evidently—flushed and raised his eyebrows. "Hey, Cherisse. I was wondering when I'd see you."

He pushed his jacket sleeves up and leaned over to give Cherisse a cheek kiss, and I saw one red-and-white-striped sock peeking out from under his cords. The other was a navy blue one with giraffes on it.

Cherisse blushed and flicked her hair over her shoulder, playfully toying with the charm on her gold necklace, leaning close to Audrey, effectively using her back to block me from the conversation.

"Aud, *this* is the guy I was telling you about! His dad and my dad have known each other for forever."

"Wow, that's forever," Audrey murmured politely, meeting my eyes and smiling apologetically.

I shrugged, looking back down at my notebook.

"I've known Keats since before we could even talk," Cherisse continued, smiling coyly at him, and I felt disappointment settle over me like a weary sigh. Even if I hadn't blown it with my epic monologue on *Watchmen*, if Cherisse and her shiny hair and smooth conversational skills were in the picture, I didn't stand a chance.

Cherisse pointed at Audrey. "Keats, this is my bestie, Audrey. You will love her."

I wanted to say, *Audrey's* my *best friend,* but I wasn't seven years old, so I bit down on my lip instead, watching the introductions.

"Nice to meet you," Keats said, reaching across the aisle to shake Audrey's hand, which seemed really gentleman-like and polite, and she shook his hand back and said, "Charmed," and not for the first time I wished I had half the conversational grace Audrey did.

Cherisse pointed at Eph. "And the tall, handsome hottie over there is our friend Eph."

Tall, handsome hottie? Who talks like that?

Eph glanced up from his drawing. "Hey, man," he said, jerking his chin up at Keats, then leaned back over his picture.

Cherisse smiled, evidently done with introductions, and I felt that familiar mix of embarrassment and general badness I got every time it was clear she was merely putting up with me because my presence was a side effect of being friends with Audrey. Why did I care what Cherisse thought? I didn't, right?

I was turning red on the outside and cringing on the inside, because it is terrible to be purposefully overlooked when there is a cute boy in the vicinity, and that, coupled with the previous epic flirt fail—scratch that, epic *life* fail—was making fleeing to the solitary research station at the penguin-friendly pole seem better and better.

But then Audrey placed her hand on his arm and gestured toward me. "Keats, you have to meet my friend Penelope."

If I could have nominated Audrey for high school sainthood right that second, I would have.

Cherisse batted a dismissive glance over her shoulder, so quick I was sure I was the only one who saw it.

I smiled weakly at Keats. "Yeah, we met already," I said.

Audrey raised her eyebrow appraisingly at me, like, *Well, what's this?* and Keats's eyes rested on mine, and my heart fluttered, like it was waking up from an enchanted sleep.

He started to say something to me—so maybe all wasn't lost

after all?—but Cherisse interrupted him. "What classes do you have? You're in AP, right?"

His eyes lingered on mine a second longer as he gave a rueful shrug and turned to Cherisse. "Carroll for chemistry."

I started to say, "I have her too," but Cherisse squealed dramatically. "She is cray! Audrey, didn't she freak out on your biology class last year?"

I shifted back as Audrey started to relay Mrs. Carroll's historic meltdown, one complete with tears and abandoning her classroom after someone sang out the lyrics to "Tiny Bubbles" during an experiment.

There was a nudge on my shoulder.

"You like?" Eph asked, sliding his notebook onto my lap and pushing his hair behind his ear.

He had sketched himself, gangly and knobby, bangs in his eyes, chin-length hair, with a name tag saying HI, MY NAME IS TALL HANDSOME HOTTIE, wearing a clearly bored expression while picking his nose.

At the bottom he'd written, in all capital letters and minus any proper punctuation or actual hashtag symbol, HASHTAG TALL HANDSOME HOTTIE ALERT.

Sometimes the sheer fact of simply knowing Ephraim O'Connor makes me feel like the luckiest girl in the whole Milky Way.

"Fuckin' rad, yeah?" He stretched back in his chair, folding his arms behind his head.

"Language, Ephraim." I took the drawing in, admiring how in such a quick sketch he'd managed to capture the rattiness of his Superman T-shirt and the inked-in bubble tags on the rubber rims of his checkered Vans. "It's pretty frakking rad."

Eph ignored my f-bomb substitution. "*Pretty* rad? Come on, Pen. It's completely fucking rad." He leaned closer, grinning. "You know I'm a tall, handsome hottie. Say it."

I stifled a laugh, which turned into a snort, which tragically morphed into the sound I imagined a seriously constipated (and angry about it) wild boar would make.

No.

My face went cherry red. I couldn't bear to turn around to see if the new boy had heard it.

Eph stared at me, mouth twisting. "*What* was that?"

I decided to pretend that that sound had not come from me. "Sorry to disappoint you, but I can't confirm your tall, handsome hottie status. That's Summer's job."

"Her name is Autumn."

"I get all your girls mixed up," I said, trying to remember if Autumn was the one with the dreadlocks or the one with the nose ring.

Something neon pink shifted in the corner of my vision, and I saw Cherisse taking off her sweater and stretching like a cat in the tiny white T-shirt underneath. She giggled, then leaned over to squeeze Keats's knee and whisper in his ear.

I could never flirt like that. Keats was smiling at whatever Cherisse was saying—and his grin was sly and handsome, like a fox, or a character from a Wes Anderson movie, or that fox character from that Wes Anderson movie, and at that moment, I would have given all my future birthday and four-leaf-clover and stray-eyelash and falling-star wishes to get someone like him to smile like that at me.

I would have given anything to finally be the one someone liked back.

I chewed on my lip—my worst, grossest habit—and glanced at Eph.

He was studying me, his eyes darting between Keats and me, like he knew something I didn't. He raised an eyebrow.

"Nothing," I said, digging in my bag for lip balm, trying to sound all casual and easy-breezy. "It's nothing at all."

Dark chocolate Kit Kat wrapper
Dark chocolate Kit Kat *involucrum*
New York, New York
Cat. No. 201X-2
Gift of Ephraim O'Connor

THAT AFTERNOON, I WAS EMERGING FROM THE FRONT DOORS OF school, hugging my backpack straps against my chest, scanning the crowd for Keats, hoping to "bump into" him, when someone came up from behind me and belched loudly right in my ear.

I smelled Doritos.

Eph stood next to me, his favorite navy-blue knit hat on, straight brown hair tufting out underneath, cheesy orange residue around the corners of his shit-eating grin.

"Did you seriously just burp in my ear?"

He smiled bigger, shrugged, and purposefully chewed Doritos with his mouth open.

"Why would you do that to me? You're disgusting. Apologize."

"Come to the park with me."

"Apologize."

"Come to the park with me."

I turned and started walking down the steps, not in the mood.

"Come on, Pen. It's a perfect day to go to the park with a tall, handsome hottie. . . ."

His skateboard clattered against the concrete, and I heard the wheels whirring right behind me.

I ignored him, pointedly marching ahead.

"So what was up with you this morning? Your neck was kind of splotchy."

Great.

Hands on my hips, I spun around. He jerked his board to the side to avoid running into me, skidded to a stop.

"Apologize."

"Come to the park," he said, giving me his winningest smile.

I frowned, and started walking up Central Park West again.

"I heard Joss is going to be more involved with the next run of the *Buffy* comics," he said.

He was right over my shoulder—I smelled the Doritos and the sweaty-guy stink and, underneath, the other parts of Eph: mint, fresh-cut grass, the ocean.

He needed to apologize.

"I think maybe one of the actors is involved too? And get this: The guy at the comic-book store said he heard a rumor that they're finally bringing back Marcy, the invisible girl. Awesome, yeah?"

I resisted the urge to point out that while Marcy was fine, they should have been bringing back the witch Tara. Now *that* would have been awesome.

Eph continued to talk while I waited to cross Sixty-Ninth, watching a curly-haired woman talking to a bald man, her small black-and-white dog eagerly running circles around his giant gray Muppety one, making me dizzy. Ford would have stood for absolutely zero percent of any of that.

". . . and I'm thinking that now is maybe when they'll finally end the Angel and Buffy crap once and forever."

WHAT?

Eph knew how I felt about Buffy and Angel's cosmic destiny, how they were meant to be. He was 110 percent picking a fight.

I bit my tongue, forced my gaze forward, refused to be baited, and watched the dogs run into the park.

"Because Angel? The *worst*. Mr. Existential Crisis. I'm glad she shoved him into the fucking Hellmouth. Now, Spike? He's her real friend. *That's* who Buffy should be boning."

I whirled around to shoot Eph the stink eye. He kicked the skateboard to his hand, and I could tell he was being all purposefully tall, looking down at me with the sun shining behind him so it was right in my eyes and making me feel like I needed to squint.

I refused to grant him the satisfaction.

My index finger was pointy against his ribs. "Buffy shoved Angel into the Hellmouth to *save the world*. And don't be vulgar. It's *frakking*."

He stood one foot on his board again, rolling it back and forth. "She wouldn't have had to save the world if he hadn't turned all evil, thanks to her sleeping with him."

His figure was dark in front of me, and the sun spots floating all around him made me dizzy. He was ruining my afternoon. "Stop slut-shaming Buffy," I said, pushing against his chest for emphasis.

I pushed harder than I planned.

With a look of surprise on his face, he toppled backward, the board shooting out from under his foot, and crashed hard on the sidewalk, his elbows slamming against the concrete, his half-zipped backpack spilling open.

"Eph!"

I dropped to my knees and leaned forward, too anxious to touch him in case something was broken.

"I'm so sorry," I said under my breath, mentally counting the three freckles across the bridge of his nose, his Orion's belt, scanning his arms and legs for anything that seemed jagged and broken, counting his freckles again, the bridge of his nose crooked from when I punched him in fourth grade for lifting up my skirt on the playground.

What if he'd broken something?

"Are you okay? I didn't mean to push that hard, I . . . I'm sorry."

His eyelashes fluttered, like he was dreaming, but the rest of him was dead still.

What if he had a concussion?

"Eph . . ."

He slowly opened one eye; the other one stayed scrunched, shut tight.

"Pen," he whispered. "Do you . . ."

I leaned closer, so I could hear him.

"Do you admit you're wrong about Buffy's one true love now?"

Wait. WHAT? I straightened as he opened both eyes and pulled himself up, examined his elbows (both skinned), and smiled his infuriating cocky smile.

A few of the onlookers (because we had onlookers *plural* now,

20

as if the whole thing weren't embarrassing enough) started clapping, while a short, dowdy, disapproving woman murmured loudly to her friend, "*She* pushed *him*."

Right then a super-tall, thin, strawberry-blond-haired, willowy girl, who probably had traveled on a unicorn straight from some mystical elven city to this particular moment, kneeled down next to Eph, handing him his skateboard like she was paying tribute to some king, and I barfed a little in my mouth.

"Are you okay?" she asked; even her high cheekbones were all concerned. "I'm Mia."

"Ephraim," he replied. "And I am now."

"Oh, for God's sake," I muttered.

She smiled, all eyelash batting and lip puckering, and I felt my hackles rise in protest, full of self-righteous indignation. She was hitting on him right in front of me. What if Eph and I were together? Was that so hard to imagine? I was of dateable age, wasn't carrying around a stuffed cat in my purse, didn't have a third arm growing out of my forehead.

She held out her hand—I swore I had seen the elf queen do the same move in *Lord of the Rings*—and he took it, smiling his stupidest, charmingest Eph smile, and stood up, one perfect inch taller than her.

Several of the old ladies watching actually cooed.

Whatever.

I scooted around on my knees and began gathering the papers and crap that had spilled from his bag: his old copy of *The Hobbit*—the one he brought everywhere—a brand-new calculus textbook, a jumble of keys on a skiing carabiner, a Moleskine journal . . .

Without giving it a second thought, I opened the journal, expecting to see more comics like the ones he'd always drawn: crass and cartoony, plenty of fart jokes, with renderings of his favorite comic-book villains thrown in for good measure.

But these pages were different.

These were pages and pages of intricate city scenes: tiny metropolises, blue-inked lines intersecting at sharp angles, with small people moving their way through the world.

I recognized major cities—London with Big Ben and the Eye, Paris with Notre Dame and the Eiffel Tower. And then there were cities that defied logic: skyscrapers sprouting from clouds, waterfalls pouring under streets.

I snuck a glance over my shoulder. Eph was deep in conversation with Elf Queen Girl.

I rested back on my knees, flipped to the next page of Eph's sketchbook.

The scene was Times Square, frantic and chaotic, a giant *Phantom of the Opera* sign, stock-exchange prices rolling by on an electronic ticker, the discount TKTS booth with a winding line, a little Naked Cowboy in the corner eating a hot dog, an Elmo impersonator scowling at the world around him.

I peered closer. There, in the corner of the page, waiting at a traffic light, was a stegosaurus wearing an I ❤ NYC T-shirt. Tiny spines poked through the back of the shirt.

It was so weird and incongruous, but so absolutely perfect at the same time, that I felt goose bumps rise up and down my arms. I met Eph the year I started first grade, right when my family moved to New York City for my dad's new job at the American Museum of Natural History. Eph's dad worked there too, and our parents introduced us in the lobby, a looming T. rex next to us. Despite Eph's parents' objections, at the time he only answered to Superman (and constantly wore the cape to prove it). He also swore that there was a real live dinosaur, a T. rex, living in the museum and that it wandered the halls at night.

The cape was long gone now, but it seemed like the fascination with dinosaurs and Superman had stuck around.

On a hunch I flipped back to a previous spread: Paris. I scanned the page, and there, wrapped around the base of the Eiffel Tower, was a brontosaurus, its long neck winding up but not high enough, trying to get a glimpse of the top.

In a roller-rink scene, crowded with people skating under a disco light—couples with linked arms, children sandwiched between parents, a small boy clutching the railing—there, in the middle of it all, a triceratops with oversize skates hunched down for balance or maybe to fit in better with the crowd.

At the Delacorte Theater in Central Park, actors participated in the *Romeo and Juliet* balcony scene, and behind the stage, by the turtle pond, a little T. rex pressed against a tree, its face pure longing.

They were the most magnificent things I'd ever seen.

"Did you find your surprise?" Eph asked.

Startled, I twisted around.

The Elf Queen was gone, but he was grinning, pleased with himself despite the presence of two skinned elbows, and I figured he must have ended up with her number.

"These?" I asked, holding up his notebook. "Eph, these are phenomenal. How long have you been drawing them?"

He looked up, a blush spreading from his neck to his cheeks. If I didn't know better, I almost would have thought he was embarrassed.

He yanked the notebook out of my hands (I immediately felt the loss of its magic, my palms left open and empty). I watched wordlessly as he snatched his bag up and shoved the notebook deep in there, followed by the books I'd stacked neatly on the sidewalk.

"I've never seen anything like that. . . ." I stood up, brushed off my knees, tried to straighten. I was three degrees off balance, the whole world tilting slightly. Eph never kept stuff from me. "It's amazing. You're so good."

"That's what she said," he replied, so automatically and smugly and insufferably that I remembered why I had just, albeit accidentally, pushed him over.

"You are the worst, Ephraim O'Connor."

"I'm not the one who tried to kill me." He zipped and shouldered his bag, effectively ending the dinosaur conversation.

"Hardly."

He squinted, pushing his hair off his face and back under his hat. "Come to the park with me."

"Apologize."

He let out this long, aggrieved sigh, dug in the outside pocket of his bag, and tossed me a small, red-orange-wrapped square.

"Your surprise."

I barely caught it.

"Holy cow, where did you get this?" I breathed, holding it reverently in both hands.

Dark chocolate Kit Kats were my favorite candy in the entire

24

world, nectar of perfection, the candy of the gods, rarely found in stores in the US and usually enjoyed only when my dad brought them back through customs at Heathrow. Finding them in person in New York City was like finding the holy grail.

"Bodega in the West Village. Now come to the park with me?"

I thought of the tiny dinosaurs I'd seen in his notebook, imagined them standing on his shoulders, protecting the secret parts of him, the parts that still believed in dinosaurs.

"Okay, apology accepted," I said, turning toward the park. "For now."

Anne of Green Gables, book
Anne of Green Gables, liber
Copyright 1908
New York, New York
Cat. No. 201X-3
Gift of Jane Marx

"SO FRENCH CLUB IS SPONSORING A MONTHLONG TRIP TO PARIS this summer," Audrey said, sitting cross-legged at the end of my bed.

"That's cool." I tossed her the giant bag of M&M'S we'd grabbed at the bodega and dropped my book bag on the floor.

"I *have* to go. My dad said if I can save half, he'll chip in the rest. I figure an August spent immersed in everything French will be killer on my college applications. Besides, it'll help take my mind off not being at Gram's."

I sighed, flopping down next to her. After Audrey's grandfather passed away peacefully last year, her grandma Mary had decided she'd spend one more summer at their house on Lake George before moving to a retirement community in Pleasantville, making the past August that Audrey, Eph, and I had spent there with her our last.

"What am I going to do without you for a whole month?" I asked.

"You'll survive." She opened up the bag and leaned over it, inhaling deeply. "Oh man, never disappoints."

She handed it to me, and I sighed, smelling the chocolate too. Her grandmother had taught us the trick during one of our summer trips—how smelling an entire jumbo bag of M&M'S was *almost* better than eating the candy itself.

"Or better yet, why don't you come with me to Paris?" Her face brightened as the idea started to take shape. "You and me and Cherisse can share a triple. All you have to do is join French Club. And start saving."

"Aud, I take Spanish," I said, not mentioning that if Cherisse was going to Paris, I'd rather spend next August on NYC garbage patrol. I hugged a pillow against my chest. "French Club *no es bueno*."

"But you don't *have* to speak French to join French Club. It's more about the culture and food and movies—next week we're watching this classic black-and-white French film about a girl who drives all around Paris on a Vespa with her cat in a shoulder bag. Doesn't that sound fun?" She flopped down on her stomach next to me, propping an elbow up. "Besides, it's a good way to meet cool people."

Like Cherisse, I thought with an inner grimace.

"Like Cherisse!" Audrey said brightly.

"I don't need to meet new people. I have you and Eph," I reminded her.

She started to say something, thought better of it, and started again. "It can't be the three of us forever, Pen."

"Sure it can!" I narrowed my eyes at her. "Wait a minute. Are you telling me we're breaking up?" I folded my arms in a mock huff.

"No, I'm trying to say—" she began earnestly.

"It's been great getting to know me, but you want to spend time with other people?"

She ignored me. "That expanding our social circle is really important, and I—"

"Our social triangle isn't fulfilling all your needs?"

"I love you and Eph, but sometimes—"

"It's you, not us?"

"Shut up!" she yelled, scooping up Barnaby, my favorite stuffed animal of indeterminate species origin (Dog? Bear? Unknown) and winging him right at my head.

"Ow," I said. "I would have thought by now you'd have learned firsthand the dangers of toys around heads, young lady."

She grimaced. "Tom and George *ran* that Tonka truck up in my hair. They didn't throw it at me. Besides, if they'd never done that, you and Eph might not have been my friends," she said.

She was right. When Audrey joined our class in third grade, she was immediately known for four things: her sparkly silver shoes, her crazy-good double-Dutch jump-rope skills, the fact that she owned four American Girl dolls, and her beautiful, long, shining hair. None of which interested Eph or me very much. That is, until week two, when two boys in our class ran the spinning wheels of a battery-powered Tonka truck into her hair. Her sobbing was what brought Eph and me over to the crowd of gathering students. But it was the fact that she seemed so lonely, standing there in the center of the circle, that made me go over and say hi and, with Eph's help, lead her to the school nurse (who made short work of Audrey's long locks, hacking out the truck with blunt scissors).

Even though Eph and I thought dinosaurs trumped dolls, Audrey fit with us somehow, or maybe it was more that she stuck with us, and had ever since.

"Okay, I know you don't speak French. But listen for a second, okay?"

I nodded, resting my head in my hands in mock excitement. She ignored me.

"It's just that at French Club . . ." Her voice lowered. "There are guys there too, Pen. Hot, *dateable* guys."

Oh.

Oh.

"Yeah?" I tried to tiptoe casually around the elephant suddenly sitting in the middle of my heart. "Is Cherisse's friend, that new guy, in French Club too?"

Audrey wrinkled up her pert little nose, a gesture I, owner of a "nose with character," was desperately envious of.

"Wait, who? Keats? No. But there are other guys. . . . Come on, say you'll at least try it."

I folded my arms against my chest. "You know peer pressure doesn't work on me, *mi amiga*. Besides, do you remember what I'm like with new people in general? I'm socially inept."

"Pen."

"I'm like the personality equivalent of . . ." I racked my brain. "Of crusted Norwegian scabies."

Audrey groaned, hiding her head in her hands. "We should have *never* looked at my dad's issues of *Journal of Dermatology*."

"Worst. Dare. Ever."

"Worst. Dare. Everest."

I reached over to hook pinkies with her.

"Seriously, though, Pen. You are *not* crusted Norwegian scabies, not even close. It's never as bad as you make it out to be."

"It's *always* as bad as I make it out to be," I said.

"Such as . . . ?"

"Me trying to start a conversation with the coffee guy at Grey Dog who was all greasy-dirty hot, the one I had been crushing on, oh, for no less than a year, only to discover I had a booger on the outside of my nose in the middle of asking him what music was playing?"

(I was so mortified that I ran outside, leaving my purse behind, but then Audrey found me and made me cry-laugh by insisting that boogers were in the new issue of *Vogue* as *the* fall accessory, and I decided I wouldn't run away forever after all.)

She flapped her hand. "No changing the subject. Think about French Club."

"I will," I lied, mentally crossing my fingers. "But before I forget, I was going to see if you and Eph wanted to come over tomorrow for a David Lynch marathon?"

She wrinkled her nose again. "Um, David Lynch? Please tell me you're not talking about the guy who did that movie we watched last month, the one that gave me nightmares for four straight nights after? I hate that movie more than goatees or mashed potatoes or men wearing sandals."

"Mandals," we groaned together, before I added, "I still can't believe you hate mashed potatoes."

"They're like big piles of tasteless mush. Disgusting."

"Sometimes I wonder how we're friends."

"You know you love me," Audrey said, giving a charming, beaming smile.

I snorted. "I was thinking we could do a *Twin Peaks* Season One marathon. It's totally the best season, and it's only eight episodes, so if we start early, I think we can do the whole thing in one night. It's the same director, but I swear it isn't as terrifying. The main guy, Agent Cooper, is crazy hot, I promise," I said, crossing my heart.

"Well, as much as I like crazy-hot guys . . . ," Audrey said.

I started to clap. She held up her hand.

"I promised Cherisse we'd go dancing tomorrow night. You should come with us!"

The only thing less appealing than going dancing was going dancing with Cherisse. I had eight left feet—I was literally an octopus of awkward movement when it came to music—and I could only imagine how terrible it would be to try to fit in while Audrey and Cherisse whirled around, sexy and glamorous, next to me. The fact that Cherisse was willing to go dancing with Audrey was maybe the only thing I liked about her—it made me feel less guilty every time I said no. I wasn't quite sure why Audrey kept asking.

"I don't think I can . . . ," I started.

Audrey's phone dinged, and she was immediately distracted, fingers typing a fast response.

I picked up Barnaby and ran my fingers over his soft worn ear.

I hadn't spoken to Keats since the first day of school, just a week ago. I had, however, spent each chemistry class since obsessively studying the rebel curl on the back of his neck, the one that went the opposite way. I always imagined twisting my finger around it, hooking him to me.

My heart flushed.

I had to stop.

"Put your phone down," I demanded.

She ignored me.

I winged Barnaby back at her so he thunked against the side of her face.

"Hey!" Audrey dropped her phone and rubbed her neck.

"Oh my God." Before she could stop me, I sat up and pushed her hair back. The bruise on her neck was mottled red and purple, the size of a plum.

She leaned away and slapped at my hand. "Stop it, Pen."

Scenes from every single teen cancer movie and book flashed through my mind. "Are you okay? Maybe you should go to the doctor. What happened?"

"I think you mean *who* happened," she finally said.

"What do you . . ." I stopped, understanding settling uncomfortably over me. My insides cringed in embarrassment.

I was probably the only sixteen-year-old in the entire Milky Way who didn't recognize a hickey when she saw one.

"Duh." I gave an exaggerated smile and smacked my forehead, felt the sting of slap on skin.

Audrey smiled gently, squeezed my knee. "It freaked me out when I saw it this morning too."

I tried to push past the inner mortification of being hopelessly, abnormally inexperienced, but every molecule in me felt whiny and monumentally terrible. Ever since I met her in third grade, Audrey and I had gone through pretty much everything together: learning there was no Santa (she told me and I told Eph), the horrors of puberty and zits and cramps, swooning over *Titanic* marathons on cable, scoping out all the boys in our class yearbooks. Yet somehow in the past year her life had merged onto the sleek highway of making out and hickeys, and I was still on the slow back road of never-been-kissed.

"Don't you want to know more?" Audrey asked, gently bumping her shoulder against mine.

"Um, yes." I straightened and tried to put on my best friend smile. "Okay, who was it, when did it happen, when are you going out next, what's his name, how old is he—"

"Whoa, slow down there, Delphine."

I felt a smile creep onto my face, and I tried to appear stern. "Not fair. Vivien tells Delphine everything. Besides, you know Vivien is always making foolhardy decisions."

"Foolhardy. Nice one."

"It's a good Delphine word, yeah?"

"Most definitely," Audrey said.

I eyed my bookshelf and the old copy of *Anne of Green Gables* that my mom had given to me in seventh grade. The pages were yellowed, and there was a picture of the actress who played Anne in the miniseries on the cover. The spine was so cracked from multiple reads that pages 48 through 103 came out in a separate chunk. After I read it, I made Audrey read it. We fell in love so hard, so fast with that book, we decided to write our own series—not the story of an orphan girl on Prince Edward Island but rather the story of *two* orphan girls in New York City in the late 1800s. Totally different, right?

I was Delphine, a bookish and shy, dreamy girl who wanted to be an English teacher; Audrey was Vivien, an outspoken, scrappy tomboy who wanted to be an actress. Of course we were kindred spirits and bosom friends. Of course we had myriad adventures—many, I'm sure, plagiarized straight from the adventures of Anne Shirley. And of course, more than anything, we each wanted to find our own Gilbert Blythe.

"So, what does the real-life Thomas Flannery look like?" I asked Audrey, referring to Vivien's one true love, a rakish troublemaker who later became a World War I pilot. (Of course Vivien nursed him back to health when he lost his leg.)

Audrey made a dismissive hand flap. "Nah, no Thomas Flannery. This was just some random guy from Saint Ignatius. Cherisse and I met him and his friend when we were at the smoothie bar near Union Square, *after French Club*." She glanced at me significantly.

I gently rolled my eyes.

"By the way, Cherisse had me try this kale smoothie, and it was divine. I want to take you there. Plus, the guys from Saint Ignatius *all* hang out there after school. Maybe if not French Club, we could meet someone there. . . ."

"Kale?" I asked, unconvinced that anything associated with kale, let alone Cherisse, could ever be enjoyable.

"Hot guys, Pen."

"But what about the guy who gave you that? What's *his* name?"

"Mark? Or Matt? Maybe Mike?"

"You don't even remember his name?" I asked, dismayed.

She blushed. "Gregory! It was Gregory!"

I resisted the impulse to point out that Gregory sounded *nothing* like Mark, Matt, or Mike. "Okay, okay. Here's how it's going to go: Gregory's totally going to grow on you. What started out as a casual hookup is going to turn into true love, right when you both least expect it. You're like Molly Ringwald and Judd Nelson in *The Breakfast Club*, or maybe, even though you didn't know each other beforehand, Monica and Chandler in *Friends*, and before you know it, you'll be totally head-over-heels smitten with each other."

"I don't even know who those people are. You and your old movies and television shows . . ."

"You know *Friends*! Besides, John Hughes's movies are classic!" I said.

Audrey looked unconvinced.

"Okay, think of Eph's parents' meeting instead. It's like a happy *Wuthering Heights*! The way they were both rushing across campus during a thunderstorm, and the leaves were falling and whipping all over the place around them. And then they fell into each other— literally!—and Ellen dropped all her sketches in a puddle, and George stopped to help her pick them up, and they huddled under George's umbrella and dashed into a coffee shop where they talked for hours and hours."

I sighed happily. I loved that story.

"I'm not sure things usually work like that, Pen . . . ," Audrey started.

"Listen." I gripped her arm. "Someday, you'll tell your and Gregory's kids, 'Once upon a time, I was drinking this splendid kale smoothie'"—I mimed gagging and continued—"'and over the top of my glass I locked eyes with this handsome boy across the room, also drinking a kale smoothie, and I didn't know it then, but it turned out to be your father! And so we had kale smoothies at our wedding and they were disgusting but we lived happily ever after!'"

Audrey started to reach for Barnaby, but I got to him right in time, clasped him dramatically to my heart.

"Oh, Jesus," Audrey muttered, starting to laugh.

"Remember, Vivien, we're settling for nothing less," I said grandly, reminding Audrey of Vivien and Delphine's vow. "Nothing less than absolute, one hundred percent, soul-stirring, Anne-and-Gilbert-meant-to-be, Jack-and-Rose-forever-and-ever, one true love. Nothing less."

Dinosaur sketch
Adumbratio dinosaur
New York, New York
Cat. No. 201X-4
Gift of Ephraim O'Connor

THE NEXT NIGHT, I HOPPED DOWN OUR WOODEN STEPS, ADMIRING my new silver striped socks. While having an uninterrupted eight hours for our *Twin Peaks* marathon hadn't panned out (Eph wanted to get in some skating "while the weather was still nice," a reason I said made him sound like an old man), his family was coming over for dinner. I smelled garlic and tomato sauce, bread baking in the oven.

"Mom? Do you need help?"

Eph's mom, Ellen, peeked around our kitchen door frame instead, a glass of red wine in her hand. Her red hair actually rippled, and even though she had this artist thing going on, she wasn't dippy; instead she was wearing a cool black dress and clunky motorcycle boots and an amazing chunky bright orange-and-red beaded necklace.

She always reminded me of a Pre-Raphaelite painting. She was the most beautiful person I knew.

"Penelope! Hello!"

"Hi, Mrs. O'Connor! I didn't know you guys were here already."
I gave her a hug. She smelled light and flowery, but not in a way that
made you sneeze.

"Your mom says dinner will be ready in about ten minutes."

"Eph here?" I asked.

"Setting the table. I'm sure he could use some help."

In the dining room Eph was staring intently at a place setting,
picking up the knife and putting it on the right, outside the spoon,
then picking it up and placing it on the left again.

"Hopeless," I said, reaching around his waist and placing the
knife back on the right, nudging the spoon out.

He handed me the rest of the silverware, then man-spread in a
chair while I rearranged all the place settings he got wrong.

"So, you try to kill anyone new today?"

"A whole week and still that joke hasn't gotten old, yeah?" I
asked.

"Killing is never a joke, Penelope," he said sternly.

"You get any new girls' numbers today?"

"Thirty-seven," he said.

I pointed at the pitcher of water. "Get up. Get to work."

He sighed and stretched like he was waking up, then bumped
around me, filling the glasses, water sloshing off the top onto the
tablecloth. How could someone so uncoordinated create those
beautiful drawings? Speaking of, maybe this was finally the time to
broach it . . .

"You draw any more of those pictures with the tiny dinosaurs?
I really liked them."

"No," he said, an ornery expression on his face, his shoulders

40

bunched up in an irritable shrug. Okay, then—subject dropped.

"Did I tell you Audrey wants me to join French Club with her and *Cherisse*? She thinks we need to 'expand our social circles.' I think Cherisse would rather burn the whole school to the ground than include me in her social circle."

He snorted.

Emboldened, I continued. "Remember that time she scolded me for using the phrase 'killing two birds with one stone'?" I mimicked her prim reprimand: "'Um, as a vegan, I prefer the phrase "feeding two birds with one seed." It's more humane.' Whatever. Doesn't stop her from wearing her stupid expensive suede boots."

I was just getting warmed up.

"Or that time she was grossed out because there was cat hair on my coat and she said it was unhygienic?" I said, reflexively wiping my clothes for any stray cat hair before continuing. "As a *vegan*, you think she'd be a bit kinder about animals."

On fire!

"Remember that time she brought a whole box of fancy chocolate back from Paris, and then as soon as I had a second piece, she lectured us on the dangers of fat and the virtues of willpower? Who does that?"

I was unstoppable!

"At least she finally knows my name now. I think Audrey had to introduce her to me like eleven times before she could remember it. But I'm still convinced she knew it and was pretending not to remember. . . ."

Eph wasn't saying anything.

"Why aren't you saying anything?" I demanded.

He shrugged. "I don't know . . . maybe Audrey's right."

"What? About Cherisse?" My voice came out in a disbelieving squeak.

He scoffed. "No fucking way. I meant about the circle socials."

"Social circles."

"Whatever, you know what I mean."

"I like my social circle! I have you and Audrey. Why would I need anyone else? We make a perfect social triangle, right?"

He didn't respond.

"Wait a minute, are you guys trying to dump me?" I tried to sound jokey, but I hated the note of vulnerability that crept in.

"That is the most ridiculous thing I've ever heard," he scoffed. "Stop being absurd."

Even though he was actually saying something nice, his response was so simultaneously dismissive and patronizing, I immediately wanted to burst into tears and kick him in the knees.

Luckily for all parties involved, at that second my mom called out, "Time to eat!"

As our moms entered the room, I fell into a seat across the table from Eph, scowling.

Every time he and I made eye contact, he'd laugh quietly to himself, like he thought it was hilarious how absurd I was being, like I was the biggest absurd person in Absurd Town, like I was the freaking President Emperor Queen-Elect Grand Absurd of Absurd Town.

Jerk.

Ellen began spooning pasta onto everyone's plates, while my mom brought in a big steaming bowl of tomato sauce.

I settled back in my chair, pointedly ignoring Eph, watching as our dads entered the dining room, deep in museum talk.

As usual, my dad had this distinctly Nutty Professor–like vibe, running his hand nervously through his thinning hair, scattering more dandruff on his black cardigan, his glasses crooked on his nose.

Eph's dad, George, however, was all handsome, restless, long-limbed energy. I had a crush on him when I was in first grade—a crush that lasted until I asked Eph if I could be his mom when Ellen died. That didn't go over well. My crush was kaput now, but on occasion he was so debonair, so much like an old-time movie star that I had to avert my eyes, like he was the sun.

"Penelope, so nice to see you," he said, leaning around and giving me a kiss on the cheek. I dropped my head, trying to hide my blush.

"Mrs. Marx, can I have some bread?" Eph asked, and Mom handed me the bread basket. I took my time choosing a slice, then waited until my mom wasn't looking and passed it the opposite way.

He rolled his eyes.

"Ellen, how is your new glass studio? It's in Bushwick, right?" my mom asked politely. She had already confided to me no less than a dozen times that she was worried Ellen would get mugged, going that far out in Brooklyn.

"It's amazing," Ellen replied. "I have so much more space . . ."

At that point I became aware of the table vibrating, a slight rattle of silverware, drinks shaking, drinks sloshing, and my mind immediately went to an earthquake or huge alien-overlord ship hovering above the city. Eph met my eyes and nodded his head toward my dad, the source of the kinetic energy. He was shaking his leg so hard under the table I thought the whole room was going to start inching itself out of its foundations.

I could tell Mom was trying to suss out the source of the vibrations while still pretending to listen to Ellen, so for my mom's sake (but *not* for Eph's, who'd called me absurd), I bit the bullet.

"How was your day, Dad?"

He exhaled deeply, relieved to let out all that bottled-up energy. "Willo's coming, darling daughter!"

As if the declaration freed him, he reached for a hunk of bread and began happily gnawing on it.

"Who's Willo?" Ellen asked.

"I'm glad you asked, Ellen," my dad started, his mouth still full of half-chewed bread. Mom patted him gently on the leg, shaking her head.

"If I may, Theo?" George asked my dad. My dad frowned, eager to expound further but reluctantly held back by my mom's good table manners. George spread his napkin over his lap with a flourish. "We're mounting a major exhibit on dinosaur physiology. Were they fast, were they sluggish? Were they closer physiologically to birds or reptiles? Willo was—"

There was a buzz and George paused, grabbing his cell phone out of his pocket and lowering his dark-rimmed glasses to squint at the number. "Oh, I have to take this." He pushed his chair back.

"George," Ellen said, touching his elbow, inclining her head at the rest of the table.

"It can't wait—I'm sorry." He leaned down and kissed her on the cheek, then turned to my mother. "Jane, please excuse me. I

44

promise I'll be back for more of this amazing meal," he said, winking at her before he left the room.

Ellen grabbed her glass of wine and put the whole thing back in one gulp.

My mom's face knit in disapproval, whether from the wine or George's departure I couldn't tell. I knew she wasn't crazy about these dinners: I had overheard her telling my dad more than once that she worried that Ellen drank too much, that she didn't like the way George got all handsy at the end of the evening, that she thought George and Ellen shouldn't leave Eph alone for so long when they traveled for George's exotic museum-curating trips.

I loved her, but I wished she wouldn't worry so much.

"Who's Willo?" Ellen asked.

My dad gulped down a mouthful and leaned forward, chewing as he talked. "Willo was a dinosaur. And what's remarkable about him, you may ask?"

"Funny, I *was* going to ask that," I said.

"Actually, he's *not* remarkable!" My dad laughed at his joke, officially reaching Peak Dad Humor. "But here's where it gets interesting." My dad leaned forward, his voice lowering to a moderately loud whisper. "Back in 2000, scientists in North Carolina began to examine Willo's remains more carefully. They peeled away all this dirt and fossilized bone in his chest, and they made what at the time they thought was a huge discovery. Can you guess what it was?"

"A baby dinosaur?" my mom said.

"A second brain?" Ellen said.

"Amelia Earhart's remains?" I said.

"A heart?" Eph said.

45

"Ephraim for the win!" my dad yelled, high-fiving Eph while holding a fork full of pasta, splashing red sauce on his own shirt in the process.

Eph mouthed *I win* at me. I stuck my tongue out at him.

"It was the first dinosaur heart anyone had ever found! I mean, they had all but given up on finding one. Can you imagine actually *seeing* the organ that pumped blood through those creatures? God, it's amazing. And I haven't even gotten to the big part yet. Are you ready? Their findings suggested it was *four-chambered*! Can you believe it?"

We all stared at him.

"That would mean that dinosaurs were closer to us than we ever thought, that they were *like* mammals! A four-chambered dinosaur heart!" He grinned at us.

"Wow, that's really something, Theo," Ellen said graciously.

Eph turned to my dad. "So is Willo's heart going to be here?"

"Well, you see, Ephraim, that's the funny thing. After all that press and hubbub, another group of scientists took a look at Willo. And much to everyone's chagrin, they've suggested it's not a heart—it's a deposit of sand instead," my dad said, sitting back, his eyes bright.

Mom straightened up, familiar with that posture and tone of voice. He was settling in for a lengthy story—one that would probably run longer than the Triassic, Jurassic, and Cretaceous periods combined. She held up her hand. "Honey, we haven't even had a chance to ask the O'Connors about their last trip. Why don't we save this for another time?"

My dad, visibly and instantly deflated, muttered, "Sure, sure."

"Mr. Marx, maybe next time I'm by the museum you can show me Willo," Eph said, and just like that, my dad's demeanor swung to cheery again.

"The exhibit is opening later this fall, Ephraim!"

I was still feeling grudgy about our earlier conversation, but I had to admit: Eph was infinitely more patient with my dad than anyone else I knew.

George strolled in, smoothing his hair back, his face flushed, and I wondered how much he'd drunk already.

"So, guys, tell us about Kenya," my mom said, passing the bowl of salad around for seconds.

"Jane, it was glorious," George said. "You should see the sunsets there, the way the whole sky is on fire. And you should see this one standing in front of them." He put his arm around Ellen and stroked her hair. "More beauty than a man deserves."

Eph let out an irritated sigh, so quick I might have missed it if I didn't know him better. "Excuse me," he said. "I'll be back." He dropped his napkin on the chair and stalked out of the room.

Ellen ducked out from under George's arm and reached over for more wine.

"The fossils we found—prime, undamaged specimens. One of the best trips we've had in years. Oh, and the people were so welcoming."

Ellen chimed in. "You should have seen all the arts and crafts! I found some bead workers—simply stunning. In fact, I keep forgetting . . ." She leaned down to get her purse and took out two small bags. After peeking in one, she handed it to my mom, the other to me.

"Ellen, this is beautiful," my mom said, holding a delicate blue beaded bracelet up to the light.

"I thought you'd like it," she said.

Mine was a chunky red-orange beaded bracelet, matching the necklace Ellen was wearing.

"It's awesome," I said, trying to fasten the clasp.

"I've got it, Penelope," George said, leaning over, and my heart fumbled around. A wave of his cologne made me feel swoony.

"So, Penelope, are you starting to think about college? Going to follow in the footsteps of your dad, another museum genius in the family?" George asked.

I shoveled some spaghetti around on my plate. "I'm thinking more English or journalism. Words, I like them?" I ended uncertainly.

Dad looked proud but vaguely confused, but I saw Mom smiling gently at me.

"Ephraim told us the other day he's thinking of art school. Art school." George scoffed. "He's going to have to get a lot more serious about his work if that's what he wants to do. And being an artist is hardly a way to make a living. Ellen knows that."

She smiled uncomfortably, knuckles white on her wine glass.

"More salad, anyone?" Mom said abruptly, holding out the bowl.

"About Willo . . . ," my dad started.

I frowned at my plate and fiddled with my new bracelet, feeling protective of Eph's drawings.

"What'd I miss?" Eph asked, rounding the corner.

"Theo and I have to get going," George said, holding up his watch. "We're going to be late for the staff meeting."

Dad groaned and dramatically pushed his chair out, grumbling under his breath about budgets and morons, stalking out of the room even more disheveled than when he came in, bread crumbs up and down his sweater, the red sauce stain on his collar.

Mom sighed, a weary but affectionate sigh full of years of displaced crumbs and dinosaur lectures.

"See you later, Mr. Marx," Eph called out.

Meanwhile George slid on his blazer, bent down, and whispered something to Ellen in French, followed by "See you at home, El?" She nodded stiffly, and he gave my mom a kiss on both cheeks, and the smile on my mom's face was all weird and awkward.

"Thank you for the amazing dinner, Jane."

"You're welcome," she said in a too-loud voice.

Eph grunted toward his dad, and I waved.

After another half hour of Kenya talk (safari stories) and reports on my mom's class of fourth graders (sixteen boys and only five girls this year) and brownies (my specialty, with extra chocolate chips baked in), Ellen seemed more at ease and definitely tipsier.

"We should head out soon too," Ellen said, reaching over to ruffle Eph's hair.

"Mom," he groaned, ducking under her hand.

Ten minutes later I was handing Ellen her vintage green pleather coat (also totally badass and amazing), and my mom was giving Eph two packed Tupperware containers.

She hugged him and moved to Ellen. Eph, meanwhile, looked at me and scoffed again. "Like I'd dump you. Absurd."

"I'm not being absurd."

"By the way, you've got something back here," he said, balancing both pasta tubs in the crook of one arm and leaning closer.

"If you belch in my face, I will murder you," I muttered.

But instead I felt the touch of his hand in the soft spot behind my ear, like he was going to pull out a magic quarter, the calluses rough against the unknown parts of me—and all the hair on my arms stood up, an involuntary shiver, blood singing.

He placed a folded-up paper square in my palm.

"Later, killer," he said.

As my mom walked them out, I unfolded the paper, its edges torn.

My breath fled, a startled swoop of birds taking flight.

Eph had drawn a tiny T. rex holding a heart, and in small capital letters underneath he had written, apostrophe missing and all: DONT BE ABSURD.

Nevermore flyer
Nevermore libellus
Saint Bartholomew's Academy
New York, New York
Cat. No. 201X-5
Gift of Grace Drosman

"SO, ON SATURDAY . . . ," I STARTED TO SAY.

I tried to sneak a glance at Eph's notebook, wondering if he was drawing his dinosaurs. I hadn't brought them up since family dinner at our house last week, but I was dying to know if he was working on more. That afternoon, however, he was hunched over on his Chipotle chair in a way that prevented any peeking.

". . . what time are we leaving for Saint Bart's Fall Festival? Four?"

Without taking his eyes off his notebook, Eph made a fart noise, his de facto response anytime anyone mentioned a word that rhymed with fart—a habit honed to perfection since we'd attended Saint Bartholomew's Academy since kindergarten.

"You're disgusting. Audrey?"

Audrey started slurping her Diet Coke hard, avoiding my eyes.

"Wait a minute, we're going, right?"

Audrey raised her eyebrows at Eph.

He shrugged, mouth still full of chips. "I thought you were going to tell her."

"Tell me what?" I asked.

The three of us had gone to the Saint Bart's Fall Festival since we met Audrey back in third grade, not because it raised money for our school, though there was that. When we were little, we went because everyone in our class went. We'd get our faces painted like Spider-Man and eat so much cotton candy and caramel apples that our teeth felt tingly and rotten in the first half hour. We won goldfish in water-filled bags and instant grade-school cred by riding the Scrambler. I loved it so much, I actually looked forward to it during summer vacation.

Sure, it had gotten less cool as we got older, but we had still gone every single year. It was tradition, history.

I glanced between my two best friends, waiting for someone to crack.

"I'm going to Saint Ignatius's homecoming dance," Audrey blurted out.

"With Gregory?"

Her face scrunched in confusion. I pointed at my neck—you know, now that I was completely familiar with the world of hickeys.

"Oh God, no. It's with this guy named Ethan. Cherisse is going with his friend Hunter. Wait a minute . . ." She chewed her lip thoughtfully. "You know, maybe I could see if one of their friends needs a date. . . ."

"No, that's okay," I said quickly, the thought of going on a blind date in front of Cherisse less appealing than eating those bug-egg beads in tapioca pudding.

"Are you mad? Please don't be mad."

Last week's conversation about French Club and social circles came ricocheting back. "No, not at all," I said, my voice going artificially cheery.

"I'm sorry, Pen. I meant to tell you earlier this week. I figured we had outgrown the festival and weren't going to go anyway. I shouldn't have assumed."

She didn't mean it as an insult, but I immediately felt like a giant baby-faced baby for still wanting to go to the festival.

I remembered last year, how Eph and I finally talked Audrey into riding the Ferris wheel, how even though she was sandwiched between us, she was terrified the whole excruciatingly slow way up—white-knuckled, slightly green-faced—but when we got to the top, she let out this sweet little exhalation of wonder, surveying all the flashing festival lights below. "Why didn't you ever tell me it was this lovely?" she asked indignantly.

I shook my head, making myself return to the present moment, trying to seem breezy and okay, like their bailing on tradition was not a big deal. For some reason deep inside me, *that* was important—that no one know how my insides were sinking faster by the second, how I felt completely alone.

"So you're out too, I'm guessing?" I asked Eph, my mouth twisting into this phony super-gracious smile.

He gave me a weird look. "What's wrong with your face? And why are you getting all splotchy again?"

"Are. You. Going."

"Sorry. Autumn got us tickets to this interactive *Macbeth* thing in a warehouse."

"That sounds awesome," I lied.

"Trust me, I'd *much* rather hang out with you. Autumn's in a constant hand-holding phase. It makes my hands sweat."

He held up his palms, as if to prove his point.

"Okay, okay." I chewed on my lip, brainstorming. I could fix this. "Maybe we can hang out next Saturday instead. I know, let's go to Coney Island! It'll be like the Fall Festival but a little tackier. And with the ocean."

There. Totally natural, breezy. Nice recovery, self.

Audrey's face fell. "Next Saturday? I promised Cherisse I'd go to that new guy Keats's First of October party with her."

Oh.

Keats was having a party.

"First of October party?" Eph snorted.

"I would bring you guys, but it's invitation only . . ."

(Of course it was.)

". . . and Cherisse has been crushing on Keats forever . . ."

(Of course she has.)

". . . and it's this fancy costume party . . ."

(Ugh, so cool. Of course, of course, of course the beautiful new boy would have a fancy costume party.)

At that moment I was seconds away from having a crumbly meltdown about hickeys and festivals and French Club and social circles and the fact that my life was an open book but Audrey's and Eph's lives had chapters I wasn't cool enough to read.

My melodramatic subconscious started playing "One Is the Loneliest Number" in my head.

My subconscious is the worst.

"I'll go to Coney Island with you, Pen," Eph offered. "I heard last week that people got stuck on the Cyclone and had to walk down the hill. How rad would that be?"

"So rad," I said hollowly.

Without all three of us there, it wouldn't be the same thing. It already wasn't the same thing.

Plus Keats was having a party.

Forget Coney Island.

I was pretty sure that everything I ever wanted, that everything I was currently missing out on, would be at that party.

A small and terribly traitorous sigh escaped my lips.

At the sound of it, the three of us halted all interaction. Eph frowned and turned back to his notebook, and Audrey tugged so hard on her hair I thought she might pull it all out. Meanwhile, my face was frozen in some uncomfortable, phony lunatic smile.

This was not how our afternoon at Chipotle was supposed to be going.

Be the better person, Pen. You love these people.

"Do you know what you're wearing?" I asked Audrey, forcing my voice to be positive, willing us all to change the conversation.

"To Keats's party?" she asked, face confused.

"No, to homecoming!"

Her face broke out in a relieved smile, and she whipped out her phone and flipped through pictures before pointing one out. "Here.

Cherisse and I found it at this new vintage shop downtown called Hong Kong Eight."

The dress was beautiful—a pale, silvery-pink beaded sheath. "Very Audrey Hepburn. Living up to your namesake, yeah? That'll be gorgeous on you."

"Sweet," Eph muttered after giving the phone a perfunctory glance.

Audrey relaxed, explaining how she was going to do her hair (a professional blow-out so it was straight and shiny) and what shoes she was going to wear (silver Mary Jane wedges) and the boutonniere she was buying her date (a deep pink peony).

For the rest of the afternoon I tried to pretend everything was normal.

But after I waved good-bye, I rounded the corner where they couldn't see me and slumped against a building, relief rushing through me, my toes uncurling, my fists unfurling.

The feeling was terrifying.

I had never felt so out of sync with Eph and Audrey.

For the new few days, I worked on convincing myself that missing out on the festival wasn't a big deal, that our disastrous Chipotle interaction had been a hiccup.

I wasn't very persuasive.

Instead I became 100 percent absolutely positively convinced that the Fall Festival was a harbinger of doom, my friends were ditching me, and I would be alone for the rest of my life.

It didn't help that eleven chemistry classes after our initial meeting on the first day of school, there had been no discernible progress regarding my crush on Keats. There had been no lab partner assignments, no random encounters in the hallways, no meet-cutes outside a coffee shop.

In fact, one could argue (if one were feeling really contrary and down on oneself) that I had actually made *negative* progress with Keats. On Wednesday of the second week, there had been a potential half wave sent my way, and my heart started to burst out in song, but when I waved back (too fast, too eagerly, too *everything*), I saw that the dude in front of me was returning a subtle cool-guy wave to Keats and realized that the initial greeting had not been for me after all, so I tried to make it seem like my wave was only a stop on the path to running my hand through my hair, that that had been my intention *all along*. But then my oversize amber flower ring snagged in my hair, so I had to run to the bathroom with my hand on top of my head to untangle it.

Insert definition of "hopeless."

By the time Saturday, the day of the Fall Festival, rolled around, I felt lower than the rats that live in the subway tracks and eat garbage. I trudged into the kitchen wearing sweats, yesterday's mascara smeared under my eyes, my hair flat in the back but aggressively bushy in the front.

Dad lowered the *New York Times*, scanning my attire.

"Rough morning, darling daughter? Or maybe I should say afternoon?"

I looked at the clock—it was almost noon.

"I'm fine," I said, the prickliness in my voice an unfortunate giveaway that I was anything but.

"Well, if you want to talk—"

"I don't."

"Hmm. The darling daughter is distinctly lacking in darling today." He chuckled to himself.

I rolled my eyes, wishing at least for the five billionth time that there was a moratorium on dad humor on the weekends.

"Your mother was looking for you, by the way."

I wanted to point out that our apartment in the brownstone was only so big, that there were only so many places to look, but I bit my tongue instead.

Boy oh boy, was I was feeling ugly on the inside.

To cheer myself up, I pulled out my favorite glass—the one with the illustration of the boy holding his nose underwater—filled it up with skim milk, and added chocolate powder.

Sitting down next to my dad, listening to him hum along with classical music, I decided I needed to change my frequency. Sure, I wasn't going on a date with Keats or anyone else, and sure, I didn't have people to go with me to the Fall Festival. But I had a delicious glass of chocolate milk and a full Saturday afternoon ahead of me in one of the best cities in the world. Maybe I'd go to the Met and read by the pool at the Temple of Dendur. Or perhaps I'd pick up a sandwich at Chelsea Market and read on the High Line. Who needed boyfriends? Who needed friends? I had New York City and the e-book of the Complete Works of Jane Austen at my fingertips. What more could a girl want?

"Pen! There you are." My mom stood in the doorway holding her cup of tea against her chest. She's always cold—even on sunny eighty-degree September mornings. "When you go to the Fall Festival today, can you make sure to bring the bag by the door? It has the afghan I knit for the silent auction. Did you see it? It turned out nice."

"That afghan could go for at least eight hundred dollars, Jane," my dad suggested, totally unrealistically, right as I declared, "I'm not going."

"Why aren't you going?" Mom asked.

My teaspoon clinked against the edge of my glass as I stirred the chocolate powder about two minutes longer than needed.

"I don't want to."

"Aren't Eph and Audrey going to be disappointed?" she asked.

"They've got other plans," I said, feeling sour again.

"Ahh," she said, as if that explained everything, which okay, it totally did, but I wasn't in the mood to throw her a bone. In fact, I wasn't in the mood to throw anyone any bones—possibly ever again. I imagined myself as a ninety-five-year-old spinster, living in a decrepit old rest home with puke-yellow walls, whiskery and wrinkled and ornery, hollering at anyone who deigned to talk to me: *No bones for you!* That seemed about right.

"Can't you drop it off?" I asked.

"Your dad and I are going bird-watching in Long Island."

The meanness in me yawned and stretched, waking up.

I bet Eph's parents weren't going boring old bird-watching. I bet they were going gallery hopping in Chelsea or checking out the new costume exhibit at the Met.

"There's no reason you can't go on your own. I'm sure you'll see people you know."

I heard both helpfulness and hopefulness mingling in her voice. My mom loved me more than anyone on earth, probably even more than my dad, but at that moment her concern made me feel pathetic, which made me feel angry, which let the ugly full-on out, growling and tearing off faces as it went.

"I said I don't want to go!"

Mom flinched. Dad dropped the paper.

"I don't want to . . ." I trailed off. Both my parents were staring at me like I was four years old again, which granted was probably the last time I had raised my voice at either of them.

The monster disappeared and shame settled, all patronizing and prim in its place.

"The bag's at the door?" I asked quietly.

"Yes," Mom replied curtly. "Thank you for dropping it off."

I stomped upstairs to shower, in an attempt to make myself somewhat presentable.

Four hours later I dropped off the bag from my mom in the school lobby. (The PTA president: "We can start this bidding at at least seventy-five dollars!") I walked outside, hearing the traces of the carnival carry through the fall breeze.

At the wafting scent of funnel cake that came along with it, my heart did a giddy little hop, awakened by the possibility of fried dough and powdered sugar.

Maybe I'd go in for a quick spin around the length of the festival—it only ran across one block—and *then* I'd go to Central Park and read for a little bit. I was still feeling guilty for yelling at my mom, and this seemed like a bearable penance. I could tell her I went and had a nice time.

As I entered, two little girls with matching red gym shoes tore past me, their moms simultaneously telling them to slow down.

Another boy ran around me, the edges of his mouth pink with cotton-candy sugar. A dad pushed a stroller in one hand and held an oversize stuffed lion in the other. The kid in the stroller was sound asleep, head sprawled back, mouth open, face streaked with tears.

I wandered past a ring-toss booth offering goldfish as a prize, and a booth selling an excess of USA-labeled socks. I thought about the year when we were nine and Eph barfed after riding the Scrambler (two pre-ride hot dogs too many), and then Audrey and I vomited sympathetically, and my parents had to take all three crying kids home. And then there was the year when I won at Whac-A-Mole, earning us a certificate for dessert at Serendipity. My mom took me and Eph and Audrey, and I pretty much thought I had died and gone to best-friend hot-fudge heaven.

Right then, amid happy kids and carnival songs, I missed Eph and Audrey both so much that I felt like a haunted house, all hollow echoes where they used to be.

I patted the weight of my e-reader in my bag, trying to reassure myself, and turned around to cross the street to leave, when my eyes fell on a small folding table in between a face-painting booth and an informational display about the ski team. Taped to the edge of the table was a neatly lettered sign:

DEAD POETS PHONE
$1 per call
SEIZE THE DAY!
CARPE DIEM!
TALK WITH GREATNESS!
(all proceeds go to *Nevermore*)

I stepped closer. In the middle of the table sat an old beige rotary phone and a glass bowl with two lonely dollars in it.

I thought I recognized the two people behind the table from school. I was pretty sure they were seniors. The girl was short and curvy with a definite rockabilly vibe: hair dyed fire-engine red, a *Schoolhouse Rock* T-shirt, and super-dark Buddy Holly glasses. The boy had a pointed Mohawk, the tips spiked up, and a rich, haughty expression that reminded me of some minor scheming character from *Masterpiece*. He was reading an old beat-up copy of E. E. Cummings's poetry.

The girl caught me checking out their setup and brightened. "Want to talk with a dead poet? All proceeds go to the Saint Bart's literary magazine, *Nevermore*. By the way, I'm coveting your shirt," she said, pointing at my CONEY ISLAND CIRCUS SIDE-SHOW T-shirt.

I flashed back to last year, when Audrey had ecstatically introduced me to Cherisse, who had just transferred to Saint Bart's. Cherisse had given me a once-over and winced out a pained smile that immediately put her in the running for any superhero movie that ever needed a frost-queen villain.

The girl in front of me had the exact opposite energy. She was sunny and warm, and maybe it was because I was already feeling so needy, but I immediately wanted her to be my friend.

"I'm Grace. And this is Miles," she said, pointing to the Mohawk boy.

"Are you a junior?" Miles asked, his voice drawling out the *u* sound.

I nodded, unsure about him. His eyes were the softest gray, but the tips of his hair were gelled sharp enough to draw blood, and he looked a little bored watching me.

"I'm Penelope," I said. "But everyone calls me Pen."

Miles slouched in the chair and tapped his upper lip, sussing me out. I stood a little bit straighter, putting on my Cherisse armor.

And then he sat up. "Oh my God, you're the one who always hangs out with that tall dreamy boy." He flopped back, fanned himself once with the book. "He is hot."

It took me a full ten seconds.

"Wait. You're talking about Eph? You think *Eph* is hot?" I asked.

"We both do," Miles said, gesturing eagerly to Grace and himself. A mortified look crossed her face, and, blushing, Grace smacked him on the arm.

"Ow!"

"So how does the phone work?" I asked, eager to stop thinking about Eph and his alleged hotness. I pulled out my wallet and handed Miles a five. The phone was plugged into a big fat empty space of nothing.

He dug in his pocket and started counting out change.

"Keep it," I said.

"A generous literary patron! Thank you!"

I couldn't tell if he was making fun of me, but when I eyed the near-empty bowl and heard him muttering to himself, "Worst fund-raising idea ever," I figured maybe it was genuine after all.

At that second Grace abruptly picked up the phone, saying, "Hello . . . yes, hi! . . . Uh-huh, okay, she's right here," and handed it to me. "For you! It's Walt Whitman."

I wasn't sure what to expect when I took the receiver. A

recording, perhaps, or maybe Miles throwing his voice so it sounded like it was coming from the receiver. What I didn't expect was complete silence.

They both waited expectantly.

"Ummm . . . ," I said.

Miles folded his arms. "Is he talking about Oscar Wilde? I heard they did it, you know." He elbowed Grace. "Scandal!"

Grace still looked terribly earnest. "Is he yammering on about blades of grass? He had me on the phone for at least twenty minutes one day, going on and on about how beautiful they are." She made a chatterbox gesture with her fingers.

I wasn't sure what to do. I kept the phone up to my ear and racked my brain, trying to think of what I had learned in last year's American poetry class.

"He's . . . he's . . ."

Grace waited eagerly, and like a bolt of lightning from Zeus, I had a mini epiphany.

Grace was having fun.

She hadn't outgrown the Fall Festival either.

And I wasn't completely sure, but it seemed like Miles might have been enjoying himself a little bit too, unsuccessful fund-raiser and all.

I covered the receiver with my palm. "Walt's talking about a stranger who passed him on the street."

Grace turned to Miles. "It's your Starbucks Guy poem!"

I was surprised to see Miles's neck redden. That wasn't very *Masterpiece* villainy.

"Yeah, Walt, I totally get it. I crush pretty hard too," I said, feeling

64

completely ridiculous. But Grace's face was lit up all bright like carnival lights, and Miles seemed pleased that a passing couple was curiously watching my exchange.

"I don't know what to do, Walt. But I guess it helps to know I'm not alone. . . ." I mimicked Grace's previous nonstop-talk hand motion.

"I know, right?" she whispered.

Finally, after a few more seconds of pretend conversation, I said good-bye and handed the phone back to Grace.

Miles immediately grabbed it, listened for a second, and held it out to the couple. "For you. Emily Dickinson doesn't just call anyone, you know?" he said. "This is an honest-to-god once-in-a-lifetime moment. Only one dollar!"

Grace slid a neon-green flyer across the table to me. "You should check out our journal, *Nevermore*. . . ."

Miles nudged her. "Gracie, Gracie, tell this guy Emily is worth one hundred million dollars, let alone one."

She waved good-bye to me, and I smiled, folding the flyer carefully and placing it in a safe spot in my bag. Maybe I would check out the literary magazine. Maybe I could write something, or maybe they needed readers.

I could do things without Eph and Audrey.

I thought of Audrey on the Ferris wheel, her face glowing, her surprise that something so terrifying could be so lovely.

Party invitation
Convivii invitatio
Saint Bartholomew's Academy
New York, New York
Cat. No. 201X-6

THE NEXT MONDAY AFTERNOON, THE MIRACLE HAPPENED.

I opened my locker, and there, on the top of my Spanish book, was a small, folded white square.

I read it, and read it again.

Sunlight burst through the ceiling and illuminated the hall, in certified angels-singing-above-a-manger miracle style.

It was an invite to Keats's First of October party that Saturday.

The invite was on smooth white card stock, and the instructions—address, time, **BRING ONE GUEST ONLY**, **COSTUMES MANDATORY**—were perfectly minimal, crisp capital letters stamped into the paper. Only the top left corner was dinged up, like it had gotten snagged in my locker slot, and there was a smear of blue ink on the back. But it had found its way to me.

Keats had invited me to his party.

I'd won the Willy Wonka Golden Ticket.

Keats invited me to his party.

I wanted to hug the acne-ridden freshman passing by; I wanted to dance with the football dude laughing at a dirty joke across the hall. I wanted to burst into a full musical number, complete with a choir of singing unicorns and my cat, Ford, tap-dancing across the hall with a top hat and a cane. I wanted to kiss a baby on the cheek, draw chalk tulips on the sidewalk, and buy grape Popsicles for everyone in the city of New York.

Keats invited me to his party!

My veins were filled with tiny carbonated bubbles, joyfully rising, making my throat tickle not unpleasantly. I wondered how he knew where my locker was. I wonder if he'd asked Audrey or Eph.

Shoot.

Eph.

Saturday.

Coney Island.

But Eph would understand; he'd have to. We'd been to Coney Island a few times already during the summer. And when I told him how much this meant to me, how fate was finally giving me a chance, he'd get it. In fact—stroke of genius—why not bring him? The invitation called for a plus one. Problem solved! Everything was turning up roses. Acres of roses without thorns, the smell so heady it made me dizzy.

I sprinted to Eph's locker, hoping to catch him before he left for the day.

When I rounded the corner, I skidded to a stop.

A tiny girl with white-blond dreadlocks and clunky steel-toed combat boots was standing across from him, pointing aggressively at his chest. "You knew I wanted to go to that!" She stopped and saw me, folded her arms defensively in front of her. "Is this her?"

"Oh, sorry," I said, backing up, raising my hands in front of me.

Eph was leaning against his locker, his slouch a mix of irritated and resigned.

"Autumn," he said. "There is no *her*."

The girl was still shooting me a stink eye, but her eyes were also welling up. I remembered meeting her briefly in Central Park a few weeks ago, how she was sitting in Eph's lap, her legs tangled in his, her laugh like bells. Now she looked both furious and broken, wiping her sleeve across her face.

"I'll leave," I said quickly.

"We're pretty much done here anyway," Eph said wearily.

She whirled back around, trying to stifle a sob. "You don't know a good thing when you see it, Ephraim O'Connor. And one of these days, you're going to end up"—and here she pointed at him with each word, like she was holding a sword—"totally fucking alone."

She picked up her backpack and hugged it to her chest.

"Autumn," Eph said, trying pull her back toward him.

"Don't fucking touch me!" she shrieked, and I cringed; people around us were stopping to watch. She pushed her way through them, and everyone started to move again like nothing had been going on.

I waited for Eph to say something.

"Well, that could have gone better," he said dryly, resignation on his face, his jaw jutting out stubbornly.

"I'm guessing *Macbeth* wasn't a hit," I said lightly.

He shrugged, turning to his locker and starting to slide books in his bag.

69

"Do you want to talk about—"

"No fucking way," he said, shutting his locker and sliding his bag onto his shoulder. "What's up with you?"

To say that Eph is bad at showing his emotions is an understatement. His heart is pretty much a quadruple-locked vault encased in concrete dropped in the part of the ocean where all the blind bug-eyed monsters live. At that second he had this awful grimace on his face, like he was trying to forcefully pretend the entire moment out of ever existing.

It reminded me of the expression on his face when I found his dinosaur notebook.

I wanted to ask, *Are you okay?* and *Why do you always break girls' hearts?*

I wanted to say, *You don't know how lucky you are.*

I wanted to say, *I don't want you to end up alone.*

I wanted to say, *Tell me about the dinosaurs.*

Instead I chucked him lightly on the shoulder. "Now I know where you picked up your excessive use of the *f* word."

Eph snorted. "You're never going to let that drop, are you?"

"No. And guess what we're doing on Saturday?" I hopped a little in place.

"The Cyclone and the Wonder Wheel."

"Wellllll . . ." I pulled out the invite and held it in front of him. "Want to be my plus one?"

Eph scanned it quickly, met my eyes. "This sounds like a douche fest."

I moved to slug him in the arm, and he backed up.

"Easy, killer."

"Don't call me that. Say you'll go with me."

"On one condition."

I did a fist pump, which was probably totally uncool, but whatever, I did it. "Name it."

"I'm not dressing up."

"No, you *have* to dress up. It says costumes mandatory."

"What, is he going to turn me away at the door or something?"

"Eph, please."

He rolled his eyes. "Well, I'm not dressing up as half of the periodic table," he said. I cringed, remembering our spectacularly dorky fourth-grade Halloween costume, one suggested by our parents.

"Fine. But no raptors, either," I said, referencing another year's ensemble. We'd ended up looking like garbage bags with wings.

"The things I do for you," he muttered under his breath,

I resisted the impulse to seize his shoulders and jump up and down in sheer glee, and instead looped my arm through his, pulling his elbow close as we started walking down the hall.

"It is going to be awesome. I promise."

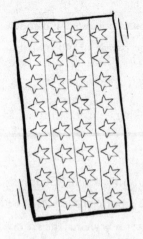

Star stickers
Stella stickers
New York, New York
Cat. No. 201X-7
Gift of Jane Marx

FIVE DAYS LATER, THE DAY OF THE PARTY, OCTOBER THE FIRST, I was 100 percent freaking out.

"Nothing is awesome right now," I said to Audrey as she brushed out her long hair. She looked perfect: flared polyester pants, a plunging plaid shirt, big shiny hoop earrings, brown high-heeled boots.

"I told you—we only have two Charlie's Angels. You should be our third."

"Bosley would be more like it," I mumbled under my breath, glancing briefly in the mirror at the unruly mess of my hair next to Audrey's shiny mane, before heading across the hall in a funk.

It was four short hours before party go time. I was costume-less, pacing the empty space in my room—a pretty limited pacing zone, considering the clothes I had thrown in frustrated piles on the hardwood floor. I shoved items on the rack in the closet and pulled down an old vintage blue dress, holding it up and assessing its potential. Alice in Wonderland? But it was polyester, and showing up at Keats's house stinky with anxiety sweat would probably not help my already terrible flirting skills.

I tossed it over my shoulder.

"Watch it!" Eph said from the bed, looking up irritably from his comic and throwing the dress on the floor.

"Sorry," I said.

He shook his head and turned back to his comic, mouthing the words to himself as he read, a habit I'd noticed soon after we first met. When I told my mom I thought it was weird, she sat my six-year-old self down and explained about reading disabilities. A week later, when Wayne Pinslaw teased Eph about it on the playground, I kicked him in the shin, drawing blood and earning my only visit to the principal's office. I had to apologize to Wayne, but Wayne had to apologize to Eph, making the whole thing totally worth it.

I stared at Eph, envying the fact that he already had a costume, though whether it actually qualified as a costume was debatable. He was dressed in all black—black jeans, black knit hat, black boots, long-sleeved black T-shirt, black thermal on top of it.

"I'm the dark night of the soul. Or a black hole. Or something like that," he'd said when I'd asked him earlier.

"You're copping out," I said.

"How is being in more than one costume copping out? I'm actually so invested in this, I am in an infinite number of costumes. It's meta and crap."

I rolled my eyes and resumed scanning the Internet for costume ideas.

That was an hour and a half earlier, when I'd still had five and a half hours to create the perfect costume, the one that would get Keats to notice me at his party. Now it was seeming like there might be another black hole wandering around with Eph.

"I'm so, so glad you guys are coming," Audrey called out from under the noise of the blow dryer across the hall. "I told Cherisse she should get Keats to invite you. I'm so glad she did!"

I was willing to bet the gold charm bracelet my grandma gave me—my number one thing to grab in a fire after my parents and Ford the Cat—that Cherisse had *not* talked to Keats on our behalf. Divine intervention from Zeus or Thor or Buddha or the patron saint of single, unkissed sixteen-year-old girls seemed more likely.

"I think it's great you guys can hang out with Cherisse more . . . ," Audrey continued.

Eph pointed at himself and in a low voice said, "Tall. Handsome. Hottie. Right here."

I tried to smile, but it came out all grimacey. I had no costume.

"Your neck is getting all red and splotchy again."

"Telling me that doesn't help anything." I rubbed at my neck.

"Audrey, Pen is panicking." He flipped lazily through his book.

"I'm *not* panicking!"

Audrey's voice was calm but forceful from across the hall. "Pen, stop panicking. You're not going to think of anything if you're running around like a rooster with its head cut off."

"Chicken," Eph and I both said simultaneously.

I flopped down on the bed next to him, hoping that if I rubbed my forehead hard enough, the magic idea would simply arise.

"Eph, what am I going to be?"

"High School Junior."

"Eph," I said.

"Girl Without a Costume?"

"Eph," I repeated more insistently.

He sighed, put his comic book down, and propped his elbow up, head on his hand, and studied me. I saw a stray eyelash on his cheek, Orion's belt across the bridge of his nose.

"If you give me one more bad suggestion, I'm going to sic Ford on you."

"That cat hates me." He frowned, contemplating Ford's inexplicable disdain for and fury toward him, before resuming. "No, what I wanted to say was fuck them. If anyone gives you a hard time? Fuck them. We'll leave, okay?"

That wasn't what I was expecting.

I stared at his face until it blurred, everything behind him sharpening: the glow-in-the-dark stars on my ceiling, the white Christmas lights I had strung around the edge of the room.

"Whoa," said Audrey when she saw Eph leaning so close over me.

I scrambled guiltily up, even though there was nothing to be guilty about, and in the process knocked my skull squarely into Eph's nose.

"Ow, fuck!" he yelled, falling back and covering his face with both hands.

"Oh, I'm sorry! I'm so, so, sorry!"

"Why do you keep trying to kill me?" he moaned from behind his palms. "You already broke my nose once."

"God, it was fourth grade! Besides, you instigated that one," I couldn't resist reminding him, thinking back to how he lifted my skirt in front of half the class.

Eph pushed himself up, still cradling his nose, and Audrey leaned down and pulled away his hands.

"You're not bleeding, so that's good."

The bridge of his nose was a little red, but aside from the cranky expression on his face, he seemed pretty much unharmed.

"Eph, I'm so sorry. I didn't mean to . . ." I hid my head in my hands. "You know, this whole evening is a mistake. I don't know what to wear; I hate parties; I nearly killed Eph. We should have gone to Coney Island."

"Too late," Eph said. "Besides, I only saw stars for like four seconds. It's probably only a minor concussion."

"Wait, what'd you say?" Audrey asked him.

"Only a minor concussion?"

"No, before that."

"It was an accident, I only saw stars—"

"That's it!" Audrey yelled.

Eph and I flinched.

"Pen, does your mom still put those little gold stickers on the papers she grades?"

"Yeah?"

"Get them!" Audrey said. She checked her watch and frowned. "I have to leave in like five minutes. I'll meet you in the bathroom." She started digging through my dresser, held a navy tank up, frowned, and discarded it on the floor.

I checked Eph to make sure we were okay, and he spun his finger, making a cuckoo motion in Audrey's direction.

"Go, go, go, Pen!" she shouted over her shoulder.

I burst out into the hall and halfway down the steps, yelling over the banister, "Mom, can I borrow some of your teaching supplies?"

Once I had a packet of stickers, Audrey met me at the bathroom door. She shoved my black boatneck pocket tee, short pleated black skirt, black tights, and maroon-but-so-beat-up-they-were-practically-black Docs into my arms, while somehow pulling her jacket on at the same time.

"Here's what you're going to do," she said, grabbing the stickers and starting to put them over the skirt.

"Can't you stay a little longer?"

"I wish I could! I told Cherisse I'd head over with her. But you can do this."

She leaned over and gave me a quick kiss on the cheek.

"You're the best ever, Vivien," I said to her.

"You're the best Everest, Delphine," she replied.

We hooked pinkies before she ran out the door, yelling, "See you at the party, Eph!"

Fifteen minutes later I emerged. Eph was sitting up on my bed, drawing, and from where I was standing in the doorway, I could tell he was working on one of his dinosaur cityscapes.

"Eph?" I asked.

He looked up from his drawing, his eyes going wide.

Picking up where Audrey left off, I had stuck gold and silver star stickers all over me. Stars on my boots, a few stars on my cheek, stars over my heart. I was covered in constellations, like Eph's and my ceilings. I had three stars in a row on my sleeve, like the freckles across his nose, like backup. My hair was twisted up into crazy knots with sparkly bobby pins.

"The planetarium?"

"Or the Milky Way. Or Van Gogh's *Starry Night*. It's an infinite number of costumes," I said.

He nodded appreciatively, shutting his notebook and offering me his arm.

New York City subway token
New York City subway *tessera*
New York, New York
Cat. No. 201X-8
Gift of Ephraim O'Connor

I SHOULD HAVE ENJOYED THE JOURNEY TO KEATS'S WEST VILLAGE
brownstone. I was going to a party, a party thrown by the potential love
of my life. Several people, not counting the man on the corner muttering to himself about pork rinds, had already stopped to compliment
me on my costume. Eph was in a good mood, chattering most of the
way there about comic books and skateboard decks, and when we got
out at West Fourth Street—"Holy crap, check out the moon!" And the
moon was luminous: big and oddly, precisely circular, like it was a space
hole-punched out of the sky. People in sweaters and boots were smiling
pleasantly around us, all the frustration of the summer humidity suddenly forgotten.

Like I said, I should have enjoyed it.

The climate inside my head, though, was distinctly terrible.

My lip gloss was tingling unpleasantly, and I was pretty sure
I was having an allergic reaction and would end up with lips that

were swollen but not in an appealing Angelina Jolie way.

My Docs suddenly felt like the heaviest shoes in the world, like I was a fat horse clomping on the sidewalk.

A few stars had fallen off, and I felt bad about littering, but I was too busy second-guessing my costume to stop, thinking of how I'd appear amid all the sexy vampires and slutty Dorothy Gales and at least two hip Charlie's Angels who'd be there.

Dinner was not sitting well in my stomach. I was heading to possibly the most momentous event of my sixteen years to date, and my breath reeked of the Chipotle that Eph and I had shoved down thirty minutes ago. Things were gurgling ominously down below.

Two doors from the address, I flat-out froze.

He looked back at me.

"Let's go home."

He waited.

I gnawed on my lip and bit at the sore spot on the inside, tasted the iron tang of blood, and wiped my clammy palms on my skirt. A few more stars fell off. I imagined a giant white hand hurtling through the universe, wiping out entire galaxies.

"I'm sorry for dragging you out. I'm sorry I made all this stupid fuss."

He sighed, patiently exasperated. "You want to go. You dig Keats."

"No, I don't," I said automatically.

He raised his eyebrows. "Oh, so you're a total party animal now—that's why you wanted to go in the first place?"

I sighed and shook my head, trying not to meet his eyes, trying not to be all weird and watery-eyed, and totally failing.

"God, you really like this guy, don't you?"

I bit my lip so hard it almost bled. "I do."

I waited for him to joke how it was about time I got a boyfriend or to make a loud fart noise or something else terrible, but instead he nodded, studying me carefully, his eyes taking me in like I was something new.

"All right. I was saving this for myself, but . . ." Eph pulled his wallet out from his back pocket and dug through the billfold. His hand emerged with a small, round piece of metal, the center cut out.

"An old subway token?"

He nodded, pleased with himself.

"Thanks, I guess?"

"You 'guess'?"

"Sure?"

"Pen, I won that in a game of cards with the Bearded Lady at the Coney Island freak show. It's full of totally sick magic."

"The Bearded Lady? Oh, please." I studied the token in my hand.

"It's true! We were playing a round of five-card draw, and Rufus the Sword Swallower and Serpentina had already folded."

"You are so full of it."

"My sketchbook was up for grabs, and now that you've seen my latest stuff . . ." He raised an eyebrow. "You *know* it's worth millions."

"Um-hmm. So now we get to talk about it?"

He ignored me. "So the Bearded Lady had her lucky subway token on the table—the one you currently have in your clammy hands. Turns out she had never been beat, thanks to that very token.

And of course she was winning—she was crushing me. I thought me and my dinosaurs were toast. And I was convinced she was fucking stacking the deck. Her beard? Huge. There could have been a whole deck of cards hidden in there. But no way could I accuse her with Rufus there—I mean, his lady's reputation was at stake. I would have ended up with a sword through my spleen."

"The Sword Swallower and the Bearded Lady were a couple?"

"Totally head over heels in love with each other."

"Really."

"Yeah, and to be honest, I probably could have gone home with Serpentina. She was giving me sex eyes." He wiggled his tongue, snakelike, at me.

"Gross."

"Occupational hazard of being a tall, handsome hottie. Anyway, so she puts down a straight flush, all smuglike, and I can see her, practically reaching for my notebook, when *bam*, I crush it with a royal flush."

"I don't know what any of this card stuff means, you know."

"The Bearded Lady was mega pissed, couldn't believe I had won, especially with all her cheating, and I grabbed the token, right as Rufus shot his sword down into the table, only fucking millimeters from my hand. My life flashed before my eyes—sort of like when you pushed me off my skateboard? Or tried to give me a deviated septum by ramming your skull in my face? Or broke my nose?"

"I was ten!"

"But Serpentina held up her hands. 'Rules are rules; the wager was made; promises must be kept.' Damn, she was hot." He sighed wistfully. "So I shoved the token in my pocket and got the fuck out of there. And now I'm bestowing it on you. I mean, the Bearded Lady landed Rufus with the magic in that token, Pen. That's some powerful shit there."

I unfurled my fingers, studied the totally average-seeming old subway token.

"Not that I'm comparing you to the Bearded Lady," he added hastily.

Eph was so full of it.

But he was waiting, expectant, and I felt a trace of the things you can't hold glowing around me: glimmer and potential and maybe.

"Okay, let's do this," I said, and slid the token into the pocket over my heart.

As we climbed the stoop to Keats's brownstone, I patted the token against my chest for reassurance. The thump of the bass on the other side of the door was so loud I felt it in my ribs. I reached for the doorbell, but Eph pushed in.

The first person we saw? Cherisse.

Not an auspicious start.

Her blond hair was curled in feathery seventies waves, held back by a terry-cloth headband, and she was wearing a white tennis dress—the pleated skirt so short I worried about potential hygiene issues for her lady parts. Nestled deep in her cleavage was a gold charm on a gold necklace, all glittery in the light.

"Ephraim!" She pulled him into a hug, giving him a kiss on each cheek.

She squinted at me. "Are you an arts-and-crafts project?" The drunk slur in her voice made it sound like she had called me an

85

arts-and-*craps* project. Though it was Cherisse we were talking about—maybe she actually had.

"Hey, Cherisse," I said, edging around her. "No, I'm the night sky."

"Oh my God, Penny, that's so cute!"

Okay, she called me Penny, but had she actually complimented me? Maybe she wasn't so bad.

"I could totally see my little cousin in kindergarten rocking that!" No, she was indeed still the worst.

"Is Audrey around?" I asked, stretching on my tiptoes and scanning the immediate crush of partiers in the front room, searching for Audrey but also for Keats. I saw scantily clad nurses swaying their arms overhead rhythmically to some electronic music, two big guys dressed in drag sitting wide-legged on the couches, sweaty beers in hand, eyes glazed over appreciatively, crowds of people bouncing to some loud music. It was pretty much my idea of hell.

Cherisse stumbled off and Eph pumped keg beer into a plastic cup.

"Can you get me one?" I asked him above the noise.

"You don't like beer."

I shrugged, holding my hand out until he gave me a cup.

I didn't like beer. Or any alcohol, for that matter. But even more than that, I hated the idea of being the only person in the room not holding one.

I scanned the crowd again, and then I saw, like a lighthouse on the shore, Grace and Miles of Dead Poets Phone fame huddled in the corner of the room. She seemed kind of miserable, and he looked totally bored. Across a group of guys dressed as zombies, Grace met my eyes and raised her hand.

"Penelope, over here!"

Maybe that token was lucky after all.

"I'll be back," I said to Eph, and took the first step in Operation Social Circle: trying to make my way to Miles and Grace's corner without bumping into anyone and spilling beer on anything expensive. It wasn't going to be easy. From what I could tell about the parts of the room that weren't obscured by drunk partygoers, Keats's parents liked expensive-looking art—there were some modern pieces on the walls, paint spattered and bright, as well as a few striking angular metal sculptures on either side of the fireplace.

When I got there, proud of being neither spiller nor spillee, Grace pulled me into a hug. She was dressed like a Mexican Day of the Dead woman, her face made up like a skeleton, bright red roses in her hair. "Nice art, eh?" She held up her plastic cup for a toast and we smushed glasses.

"Wine?" I asked when I saw the contents of her cup.

"No, Diet Coke. I had to dig through the fridge to find some."

"Penelope," Miles said, giving me a small, careful smile. I smelled his beer breath from where I was standing, three feet away. His hair was gelled into a spiky mullet, and he had a lightning bolt painted on his face.

"Harry Potter?" I asked.

"Ziggy Stardust," he said.

For a second I thought about pretending I knew who that was. But Grace was drinking Diet Coke, and Miles's smile had seemed genuine, and my nerves were too frayed to hold back.

"I don't know who that is. And I hate beer. I mean, really, really hate it. I think it tastes like urine and green olives got together and had a baby. And I saw my archnemesis at the door and it sounded like she told me I was an arts-and-*craps* project. And I'm probably dying from an allergic reaction to my lip gloss, even though I now own a lucky subway token from a bearded lady. And I hate, hate, hate parties."

They both stood there for a second with unreadable expressions.

Miles took my beer. "That was a lot to handle. But I like that you have an archnemesis." He took a big swig and handed it back to me. "The love child of green olives and urine? I could see that." He licked his lips.

Grace leaned in confidentially. "I hate this party too." She sighed and said, more to herself than anyone, "It makes me miss Kieran so much."

I raised an eyebrow.

Miles snorted. "Kieran is Grace's totally perfect boyfriend who says totally perfect things all the totally perfect times they're hanging out and who makes anyone else's boyfriend look like the worst because Kieran is literally a totally perfect superhuman being. They're all ick."

Grace slugged him in the arm, and Miles shrugged, nonplussed. "What? You know it's true," he said.

She pointedly turned her back on him. "We're only here because Miles found an invite in the cafeteria and was hoping maybe by some coincidence the hot Starbucks guy he's been crushing on would be here. No luck . . ." She made a sad trombone "wah-wahhh" noise.

"Gracie, why do you tell everyone my secrets?" Miles asked.

"Which doesn't really matter anyway, because if Miles would just open his eyes and give the new guy Oscar a chance . . ."

Miles scowled at her and grabbed my beer, then drank half of it in one gulp.

". . . he could have a totally perfect boyfriend too."

"I told you, Oscar's too quiet. He has no edge. He plays Dungeons and Dragons," Miles said, as if that explained everything.

"You and your standards," Grace muttered.

"It's called not settling!" Miles hollered.

"Okay, you're cut off, Drunky McFerguson," Grace said to Miles. She turned to me. "We're bailing and getting churros at this all-night Cuban diner on Fourteenth and Seventh. Want to join?"

Hanging out with new people sounded a little terrifying, but that was what Audrey and Eph had been going on about: hanging out with new people. *Yes* was on the tip of my tongue, when I saw Audrey waving at me from a crowd of people down the hall.

I didn't know if I felt more relieved or disappointed.

"I should probably say hi to my friend and stick it out a little longer. I'm sorry."

"No problemo," Miles said, pulling my cup closer and sipping more beer from it.

I laughed as Grace pushed the beer back in my hands.

"Take my details, in case you change your mind," she said. I handed her my phone and she typed in her number.

"Later," Miles said, his smile hazy.

"Eat some churros for me!" I called out, watching them leave.

I started to weave my way to Audrey, but being short in a crowd makes finding particular people pretty impossible. I stood on my tiptoes, my boots straining to give me some height, and wished I could transport myself by clicking my heels three times.

"Pen!" Audrey said, ducking under some guy's armpit and bursting into my space. She pulled me into a hug. "You look incredible, starry girl! Isn't this amazing? Let's find Eph!" She grabbed my hand and began tugging me through the crowd.

"By the way, what was that with you and him earlier?" she yelled over her shoulder.

"What?"

"On the bed. I thought you were going to start making out or something."

I stopped, grimacing. "No way. It was *Eph*."

"But you're getting all weird and blushy."

"No I'm not!"

"Whatever you say."

"Not whatever I say—what you're suggesting is just wrong. Take it back."

She rounded the corner to the dining room, turned back, and wiggled her eyebrows suggestively.

"Take. It. Back."

Eph's arm was balanced against a door frame, and he was leaning over a girl dressed as Annie Hall, wearing a men's vest, tie, and fedora. Wisps of long strawberry-blond hair trailed out from under her hat; a tiny nose piercing sparkled from the light of the dining-room chandelier. Her hand was resting on Eph's elbow and she kept laughing at whatever he was saying.

It was the Elf Queen.

"Guess who's interrupting one of Eph's many hookups . . . ," Audrey sang under her breath to me as she swept us in between the couple.

"Hey, Eph," I said, more than a little embarrassed that we were cutting in.

"Pen, Audrey, long time no see," he said, reluctantly dragging his eyes away from the willowy girl.

Audrey's theory was clearly ridiculous.

The Elf Queen leaned over, stretching out her hand to us. "I'm Mia."

"Yeah, I know—I was there when you guys met," I said, irritated that she hadn't registered my existence.

"Ohhh, you were the one who pushed Ephraim over!"

So she had noted my existence.

"It was an accident."

"Hmmm, okay, whatever you say?" Mia said in a voice as sweet as perfect tiny pink flowers, all honey and lightness, a tone I personally thought was inappropriate to adopt when you were clearly implying someone was officially a shover-over-er.

"Nice to meet you," Audrey said, extending her hand in return.

"Ephraim talks about you guys all the time," Mia said eagerly.

"Mia's an artist too," Eph said.

"Ephraim's an aaaaamazing artist," Mia said, tilting her head up at him, touching his elbow lightly again.

"Oh, for God's sake," I muttered to myself. "Why are *you* here?" I asked her.

Audrey elbowed me, whispering "Rude!"

Mia either ignored or totally missed my tone. "Keats and I know each other from grade school," she said brightly.

Was Keats childhood friends with *everyone*?

Right then, from behind, a body slammed into me, and I spilled what was left of the beer down my shirt.

"Crap!"

"Penny! I'm so sorry!" Cherisse slurred, and tottered in front of me, swaying so far to the right I thought she might keep going. Eph grabbed under her arm, straightening her out.

She belched. "Ooops!"

"Nice one," Eph said.

Mia handed me napkins, and I started to blot the beer across my chest.

Cherisse grabbed Audrey's shoulder. "I can't find Keats!" she said, giving a pouty frown. "He was just next to me."

"Where is he?" I blurted without thinking, and clapped my hand over my mouth.

Audrey glanced over at me, confused.

"Um, I think he's right over there?" Mia said, pointing over Cherisse's shoulder.

I couldn't help it: I spun around as fast as Cherisse, only to see what seemed like the back of Keats's head as he pushed through the people in the living room toward the steps.

Simply seeing him made me feel all pinprickly and warm, my heart clumsy and oversize.

Cherisse swayed tipsily. "Where? I donna see him."

"I could have sworn he was right over there . . ." Mia craned her neck.

"Pen, can you help me with Cherisse?" Audrey asked pointedly, inclining her head toward the kitchen.

I was losing my chance with Keats. My eyes darted to Eph's, and in that moment I knew he could see the secret parts inside me, the token over my heart, the fleeting lives of the stars in my sky.

"Mia and I'll help," Eph said immediately. He wrapped an arm around the other side of Cherisse's waist and started walking toward the kitchen. Cherisse belched again, eliciting another admiring "nice one" from Eph.

"I'll get her some water," Mia said, rushing ahead.

Audrey opened her mouth like she wanted to say something more, but at that second Cherisse nearly plowed into the wall. Audrey grabbed her more firmly, moving toward the kitchen, as Eph met my eyes, patted his hand to his heart.

Good luck, he mouthed.

I put my hand to my heart like he did, feeling the Bearded Lady's token glowing warm.

Time to find Keats.

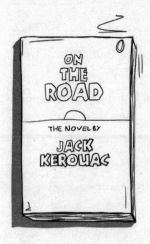

On the Road, book
On the Road, liber
Copyright 1957
New York, New York
Cat. No. 201X-9
Gift of Keats Francis

I SMELLED CHERISSE'S SPILLED BEER ON MY SHIRT, AND MY LIPS still felt weirdly throbby, and all the drunk, sweaty people were making me feel claustrophobic. But the token was beating against my heart, powering me forward.

Unfortunately, the second-floor hallway was as crowded and socially challenging as downstairs. There was a line of people waiting distractedly in front of a door—the bathroom, I guessed. A guy with nerdy art glasses stared right through me with bloodshot eyes, and feeling bold, I scowled right back. He blanched, and I felt momentarily pleased and then guilty.

I didn't see Keats. This was terrible.

I turned to the first door in the hall and opened it like I knew where I was going, slid into the dim room, and shut the door behind me with a satisfying click.

I leaned against the door, taking in my surroundings.

The bedroom had hardwood floors, and there was cool silver light from the big full moon spilling across an unmade bed. I saw a book poster for *On the Road*, and a bunch of sports trophies on a shelf. I was guessing it was Keats's room. But the most intriguing thing in it? The far wall: a floor-to-ceiling bookshelf packed with books and only books, books with wrinkled and cracked spines, books filled with thousands and thousands of words. I walked over and picked a random one from the shelf—*Franny and Zooey* by J. D. Salinger.

Someone cleared his throat. "What book found you?"

Busted.

"Oh, I'm sorry! I shouldn't be here—I'm sorry, I just . . ." I tried to shove the book back on the shelf, but my hands had suddenly lost all normal functioning skills, and I fumbled it onto the floor, hastily picked it up, tried to shove it back in, failed, and then spun around and faced the voice, smiling like I wasn't some random uncoordinated book-thieving person.

Sitting on the floor in the dark corner across from me was Keats, disheveled in a twenties-style gangster suit, tie loosened, a silver flask in hand.

He wrinkled his eyebrows. "Huh. You're here? It's you."

If this were a cartoon, my heart would have pounded out of my chest, all *AOOGA!* Instead my fingers sprang open and the book thunked on the floor. Again.

"Easy there, Scout."

I picked it up and hastily and unceremoniously jammed it in a new spot. "I'm sorry. I'm a klutz. I'll go," I said, heading to the door.

"You don't have to leave, you know," he said, and oh God, his

96

smile was deep and dark, like a thousand books begging to be read, like the doorway to Narnia. "Come over." He patted the wooden floor next to him.

I blinked three times. This was happening.

I took careful steps through the moonlight over to him, thinking *be cool* thinking *don't fall* thinking *don't blow it* thinking *seize the day,* and slid down against the wall, pushing aside a stack of books and papers and folding my skirt and Docs under me.

He offered me his flask.

"Sure," I said, and took a small sip, and it burned a river so far into me, I felt it in my fingertips. I tried not to cough and mostly succeeded, stifling a throat tickle when I handed it back. "Thanks."

"Of course."

He took a swig, and I saw his eyelashes silhouetted in the moonlight. Long. He was wearing two different socks again: the left a black sock with tiny Christmas trees, the right a tan one with alphabet letters all over it.

"You're the girl with the comic book, right? I'm the worst, but remind me of your name again?"

"You're not the worst," I said. And then, "Penelope."

"Penelope," he echoed. "The girl who reads comics."

He studied me, moving closer, his face inscrutable, inches from mine, and I felt my breath catch inside me.

He smelled like red hot candy, things that burned your tongue.

"I don't always read comics," I started to say, when he held his finger up.

"Wait." He turned and started rooting through a pile of books next to his bed, then passed me a weathered paperback. My fingertips

97

skimmed his and I felt the hundredths of millimeters of possibility between us, and my whole body shivered.

"You should read this instead," he said. "It's fucking incredible."

I held it in my hands: *On the Road* by Jack Kerouac. The cover was wrinkled like someone had spilled something on it, and the pages were covered in black ballpoint underlined phrases with exclamation points in the margins.

"Okay, yeah, I will."

I wasn't sure what to say or do next, but since I didn't want to leave, I sat there, my chest rising and falling with his, studying the books in the room, the book in my hand—anything but his eyes. I was pretty sure if I started reading those, I'd . . . I didn't know what I'd do, but it would surely end in tears.

"So tell me, are you having a good time at the party?" he asked, his voice strangely vulnerable.

"Of course, it's really . . ." I tried to think of a word that wouldn't betray how much I hated parties. "It's fun."

His head fell back against the wall. "'Fun'? Oh man, that's no good."

"But fun is good. It's an awesome party!"

"Good." He smiled sleepily and closed his eyes.

This was totally weird.

My gaze fell upon a framed picture on his bedside table: Keats in a prep-school blazer, standing in front of the fountain at Central Park, his arm around a reed-thin girl, long shiny model hair blowing across her face. She was mid-laugh, face raised to the sun, and Keats was gazing at her, and his face was reverent, his eyes wide open and alive, clearly in awe of the girl he had his arm around.

I was 100 percent certain that no one had ever looked at me like that.

And for that second I felt it in me—how badly I wanted that, how I was so hugely envious of that girl that I almost cried out from the unfairness of it all.

"That's my ex."

I glanced over at him, startled he'd seen me looking, startled to realize he was watching me.

"She broke up with me this summer. After three years."

"Oh," I said.

"She insisted I was cheating on her. With Cherisse, you know her?"

My heart stood still.

"I wasn't, though. Cherisse is just an old family friend."

My heart exhaled.

"I think Emily, my ex? I think she was scared." He paused. "She burned me bad, made me feel like I was the worst person on the planet."

I felt myself wanting to challenge this Emily to a duel, to fight for Keats's honor, to reassure him he wasn't anything close to the worst anything at all.

"I'm sorry," I said instead.

He made a small noise of surprise. "Yeah, me too."

I practically felt his eyes as they traced my face, the over-pronounced slope of my nose, the curve of my cheekbones, the tips of my eyelashes. And then, like a miracle, he lifted a hand and skimmed my cheek, and millions of tiny stars burst into being.

"You had an eyelash there."

I shivered.

"Thanks . . ."

Something loud crashed downstairs, and Keats pulled away, staring irritatedly at the door. "Shit. I hope that wasn't one of Mom's sculptures or something. I should never have thrown this party. I hate parties."

"I really, really hate parties too. In fact, I almost didn't come tonight. I mean, I don't hate your party, because, well, I don't. But I hate most of the others, not that I go to many, and pretty much . . ."

He studied me, wry smile curling from the corner of his mouth, and I slowed my words, slowed my heart, tried to calm my anxiety.

"Pretty much, I'm really glad I came tonight."

"Me too," he said. He offered me his hand, and I took it, and he pulled me up.

I thought, *I'm holding Keats's hand.*

I thought, *I will remember the feel of his hand around mine for the rest of my life.*

I thought, *Thank you, Bearded Lady.*

I thought, *Holy crap, the moon.*

Luminous luminous luminous moon.

I smoothed my skirt with the copy of *On the Road* in my hand, and a few more stars drifted off, their tips curling. "This costume was better at the beginning of the night."

I started to pick them up, but Keats pulled me closer to him. He swayed, smelling like whiskey. Every nerve in my body was a solar system, stars and explosions and light and luminous moons.

"It's okay. I like your stars with me. Come on," he said, tugging me gently to the door.

When he opened it, the hallway was too bright, and I squinted. But Keats towed me through the crowd and it parted for us, and even though he seemed a little crooked with booze, he didn't let go.

We maneuvered down the packed steps, and when we got to the bottom, it seemed like the party had gotten even more crowded, as if the room was filled beyond normal capacity, like people couldn't move even if they wanted to. There was another loud crash, this time from the kitchen, and a group of people burst into cheers.

"Shit," Keats muttered.

I didn't see Audrey or Eph anywhere.

"My neighbors are probably five minutes away from calling the police if they haven't already," Keats said, his eyes scanning over the crowd. "I need to shut this down."

He let go of my hand.

I tried to smile gamely, but inside, I wished I could rewind four minutes, back to the moonlight in his room. "Yeah, yeah, of course—I should head out anyway, curfew and all . . ." My voice trailed off, and I started to turn away.

Keats reached out, tugging my shoulder.

I blushed and bloomed and brightened; I couldn't help it.

He pulled me close, studying me like I was something strange and marvelous, something he was holding up to the light. He took a stray strand of hair off my face, tucked it behind my ear.

That wry half smile. "See you soon, Scout."

He had a nickname for me, something charming and just my own. Swoon.

He let go, stepped back, still grinning, and pushed his way through the crowd and out of sight.

I didn't move.

Part of me wanted the world to end right then.

Because it was perfect, that moment.

But the muscles in my legs walked me down the last step and into the foyer, and my arms grabbed my coat from a pile on the couch, and my left shoulder bumped a cowboy, and my mouth murmured an apology. I slid past the people smoking on the stoop, and smelling of spilled beer but floating two feet off the ground, I stepped out into the cold, good luck emanating like warmth from the token over my heart.

Gray sweatshirt
Tunica canus
New York, New York
Cat. No. 201X-10
On permanent loan from
Ephraim O'Connor

THE NEXT MORNING I KNOCKED GIDDILY ON AUDREY'S DOOR,
the smell of the doughnuts in the bag I was holding already making
my mouth water, and slid Eph's good-luck token back and forth on
the thin silver chain I had pilfered from my mom's jewelry box.

No answer.

The sky grumbled ominously behind me, irritable with rain.

I counted to ten and pressed the doorbell, cringing at how loud
it was. But Audrey's parents were always up early, so if I was waking
anyone up, I doubted it would be a parental unit.

A shadowy shape moved behind the frosted glass, and locks
unclicked.

Audrey squinted at me, shielding her eyes from the sun. Her
face was still made up from last night, but one side of her hair was
sticking straight out.

Shrugging off my denim jacket, I squeezed past her, holding

up the bag, grease spots shining through. "Vivien! A vanilla-with-raspberry-jam doughnut for you, a crème brûlée for me."

"Awesome," she mumbled.

I hung my jacket on the front rack and she followed me toward the kitchen, yawning loudly. In the kitchen, gray light was filtering in through the windows, dust motes moving lazily. "Where are your mom and dad?"

Audrey wiped sleep out of her eyes. "Visiting my grandma in Pleasantville."

"How's she doing in the new retirement community?"

"Eh. Not great. She's missing my grandpa a lot. Keeps insisting he's talking with her at night."

"That's hard. I'm sorry."

"Yeah, thanks. Me too."

"How late did you stay last night?" I grabbed two clean glasses from the dishwasher and poured us each a glass of orange juice. "I tried to find you before I left."

"Not late." She pulled out one of the stools and slouched over the island, yawning again. "Cherisse was too drunk to go home, so she crashed here. She's still asleep." She pointed at the ceiling.

The doughnuts waited for us: one for Audrey, one for me, none for Cherisse. "Oh."

She waved her hand at me. "She won't eat those anyway. Not vegan. Fried. Too many calories." I slid her plate over and she scooped a big glop of jelly out of the center into her mouth. "Perfect."

I took a huge bite of my doughnut, feeling totally content, even if my archnemesis was one floor away.

"So last night," I started, my mouth full of chewy doughy heaven.

"I'm sorry we didn't get to hang out more. I totally wanted to, but even though Cherisse got some water in her, she still barfed all over the backyard and was so mortified and worried that Keats would see her getting sick, I spent most of the night trying to sober her up."

I glanced down at my hand, the one Keats had held, stretched my fingers, fully expecting it to be glowing with leftover moonlight.

"That's okay. I was actually with Keats," I said, trying to keep my voice calm, but really wanting to stand up and sing it, the hills being alive with the sound of music and whatnot. My sticky doughnut fingers were not exactly helping with the vision, but still.

Audrey stopped, mouth halfway open.

"You were with Keats?"

My beaming smile spoke for itself.

She put her half-eaten jelly doughnut back on her plate and started tugging on a front lock of hair. "I didn't know you knew him all that well."

"I didn't. Until last night. But, Aud, it was amazing. He's amazing. He loves all these awesome books and gave me one to read. The moon was shining in his room and it was only the two of us. And at one point . . ." I chewed my lip.

"Please tell me you guys didn't hook up," Audrey said.

I looked at her, surprised. "No, but he held my hand. It was so romantic. I think Delphine has found her—"

She buried her head in her hands. "No, no, no, this is not happening."

I frowned. "What does *that* mean?"

She tapped the table and spoke slowly, as if trying hard to choose the right words. "Pen, I don't know if Keats is the best guy for you."

"Wait. What? Why?"

She rubbed her hands against her forehead, like she was trying to work away a migraine. "It's, how do I put this . . . Cherisse and Keats . . ."

Relief flooded through me. "Oh, it's okay! Keats doesn't like Cherisse like that; he told me. So it's all good. He even gave me a book—"

"No, it's just they've got a really complicated history."

"So? It's history—in the past." I tried to smile.

Audrey let go of her hair, rested both palms on the table, and took in a deep breath. "Pen, you liking Keats isn't like having a crush on some character from a book or lusting over some random from a distance. Trust me: He's not Prince Charming. Listen . . ."

Without knowing why, my body braced itself, like it does when you get on the Cyclone roller coaster at Coney Island, trying to minimize the bruising and shaking before the ride kicks into action.

"I'm really happy you finally like a real person, but Keats isn't a good one."

A real person?

At that moment everything around me got really still, except for my heart thud-thud-thudding in my ears. My vision tunneled inward, the edges black. I realized that something terrible had unfurled. That mere seconds ago I had lived in a world where I didn't know Audrey could hurt me. That now I lived in a world where I did.

"Listen, I can't go into the details because she swore me to secrecy, but he *really* messed up Cherisse. He lies and he's manipulative and acts down on himself so other people will build him up, making you feel like crap in the process . . ." She reached her arm across the table and squeezed my still hand. "I don't want you to misinterpret anything and get hurt."

I physically recoiled, yanking my hand out of her grasp. "You think I'm so pathetic that I can't tell if someone likes me?"

She straightened, dismayed. "No, that's not what I meant."

"You're happy I finally like *a real person*?" My voice broke at the end.

Her face was awake now, alarmed.

"Of course that's not what I meant!"

"You think I'm pathetic," I half said to myself, processing the words.

I grabbed the bag, shoved my half-eaten doughnut in, and stood up. "I need to go." My voice was shaky, not brave.

"Wait, Pen, let's talk about this." Her voice was desperate, pleading.

"I need to go," I repeated.

"Penelope!"

I walked hurriedly down the hall, crumpling the paper bag edges in my hand. As I passed the stairwell, Cherisse was coming downstairs, last night's blond curls flat. She stopped mid-stretch and stared at me, and I resisted the urge to give her the finger.

"Pen, wait!" Audrey yelled, her voice close.

I pushed the door open and didn't turn back.

The wind outside had picked up, and it was starting to rain

sideways—sharp daggerlike drops. I thought about the first time Audrey slept over, how I woke up early in the morning to find her watching me intently, eyelashes fluttering.

"What are you doing?" I whispered.

She pointed solemnly at the wall behind me. Evidently a black spider had decided to camp out there.

"You sleep with your mouth open," she said. "I didn't want the spider to fall in. I saw it at five twenty-three."

It was 7:02. She had been keeping watch the whole time.

I rolled up, away from the spider. "Not counting Eph, you're my best friend ever," I declared.

"You're my best friend Everest," she said, holding out her pinky, crooked. I hooked mine in hers, believing then, unquestioningly, that it was true.

I tried to get back last night: the moonlight in Keats's room, the way he was surprised to see me, and his hand holding mine, soft brown curls of hair on the nape of his neck, how he brushed an eyelash off my cheek, the way I felt pretty, noticed. But now everything felt ruined—the person I was ten minutes ago suddenly pathetic and childish, the magic from last night as dead and gone as the dinosaurs.

I tried to button up my jacket, when I realized it was not on me because I had left it on the coatrack at Audrey's, which was terrible not only because it was insult upon injury or the temperature was dropping with the storm, but because it was my favorite jean jacket, the one I got from a stoop sale, perfectly worn in and soft, and it was lost to me forever because I was never going back to Audrey's house, not ever, not if it was the last best jean jacket in the entire stinking world, not if my life (or evidently my body temperature; my teeth were clattering in my skull like they weren't my own) depended upon it.

What if I *had* misinterpreted everything with Keats? I couldn't contemplate that possibility one second longer without it crushing me completely.

I hunched my shoulders against the wind and huddled into the rain, becoming more wet and more cold with each step. I headed up Columbus and over to Eighty-First, stopping at the front door of a beautiful old brownstone. Using the door knocker, a brass fist, I tapped away, my fingernails tinted purple from the chill.

"Got it!" someone called from inside.

Eph swung open the door, the soft edges of his grin a contrast to the sharper parts of him, the elbows and cheekbones, angles and points.

"Good day for a walk, eh?" He pointed at his nose, slightly swollen from last night's head smash. "Come to finish off what you started?"

But I hugged myself, biting my lip so I wouldn't cry, teeth chattering, and his face shifted instantly into protective concern.

"What happened?"

I didn't know how to say that in the twelve hours since I'd seen him, a boy had brushed an eyelash off my cheek, the feel of his hand making my whole body shiver, but that now hurt was seeping through me like octopus ink, that I didn't know what to do with myself in that second, in that minute, perhaps ever again.

"Can we watch a movie?" I asked instead, my voice small.

He motioned me in.

"Who was it, Eph?" George called from the other room.

"Pen. We'll be upstairs."

"Hi, Pen!" voices called out in unison.

I followed Eph, envying his warm-looking wool rag socks and missing my jacket all over again.

"Give me the word and I'll kill him," Eph said, pushing open his door and kicking a pile of dirty laundry off the floor to make room.

"Who?"

"Keats. Prince Masturbate Theater. The reason we went to that shitty party."

"No, no," I said, trying to rub warmth into my arms. "Keats was really nice."

Eph snorted in genuine surprise. "I didn't see that one coming."

He dug through a drawer and tossed a gray sweatshirt my way. It smelled detergent-y and seemed clean, so I figured it was safer than the navy pullover at my feet or the thermal tee hanging on the back of his desk chair.

The sweatshirt bristled with static, and when I pulled it on, the sleeves fell past my wrists, and I imagined it swallowing me up in grayness.

He left and came back with a blue towel, handing it to me as he dropped to the floor and leaned back against his bed, knees up. I dried my hair, and I slid down next to him, cross-legged, letting as much of the sweatshirt pool around me as possible.

"So, you wanna talk about it?"

"Audrey and I got in a fight. About Keats."

He waited, not saying anything, while I fiddled with the cuffs.

They were soft and worn, gray clouds losing their edges.

"It's . . . She thinks . . ." I debated how much to tell him. "Cherisse and Keats have some kind of history, I guess, and she doesn't want me 'misinterpreting' things with him." My finger quotes felt hollow.

"Oh." He picked at the floor.

"What? Tell me."

He shrugged uncomfortably. "Last night, near the end of the party, I saw Cherisse and Keats going into a bedroom together."

I dug my fingers into my palm, small red half-moons. "He doesn't like her like that! God, why is it so hard to believe someone might actually like *me*?"

He held up both hands, surrendering. "Whoa. Relax. That's not what I'm saying at all, Pen. I only thought you'd want to know. I'd want to know."

"Sorry," I mumbled. I took a breath, refusing to look at him. "I would want to know, I do want to know."

"Okay, then."

"Okay."

Eph huffed, and when I looked over, I saw his eyelashes, longer than you'd think. I'd told him once they were pretty, and he had refused to talk to me for the next two days.

"So the thing with Audrey." I made myself push the words out, hoped Eph wouldn't look at me. He couldn't look at me when I said them. "She pretty much implied that I'm kind of pathetic. That up to now I've only wasted away, harboring unrealistic crushes and living in some loser fantasyland, and that I'm in over my head with Keats."

I snuck a glance at him. He was grimacing, but it wasn't exactly pity—it was more like empathy, an echo resonating back from the deep caverns of him.

"That's really shitty, Pen," he finally said.

Neither of us said anything more for a while, so long that when I turned toward him next, his head was resting back on the bed, his eyes closed. I couldn't tell if he was asleep, but it didn't matter. The stillness waited.

I began a mental list of all the *real* people I currently liked or had liked in the past: Keats, of course, and the dirty hot guy who worked at Grey Dog. I wasn't going to count Eph's dad, because gross. But there was Ryan Kurtz, who transferred into our class in third grade and who had just overcome some tragic childhood illness and had black hair and black eyes and who I liked so much, I pushed his desk over (obviously) with him in it (maybe not so obviously). And then there was . . .

I chewed on my lip.

Okay, so I guess I'd count Eph's dad. And that left . . .

The sweatshirt sleeves hung limply over my wrists. Eph's breath started to whistle, his chest rising and falling.

He'd fallen asleep.

I didn't have anyone else to add to the list.

I hated to even think it, but it was there, stark and ugly, unavoidable and unwanted: Audrey was a little bit right.

I let out a huge sigh and let my head fall onto Eph's shoulder, let it rise and fall with his soft breath, the way his eyelashes did in his sleep, and hoped on my subway token that Audrey wasn't right about everything.

Handwritten note
Chirographum
Saint Bartholomew's Academy
New York, New York
Cat. No. 201X-11
Gift of Keats Francis

THE NEXT MORNING, BY THE TIME CHEMISTRY CLASS ROLLED around, I was 100 percent *Alexander and the Terrible, Horrible, No Good, Very Bad Day* miserable. I had woken up that morning with a hangover of sadness—not that I knew what a hangover felt like, but I imagined it'd be something like this: a headache, a stomachache, sadness emanating like a stench from my pores. The Sweet Truck, which parked in front of school in the morning, was out of carrot-raisin muffins, and despite my best efforts with the blow dryer, my hair insisted on looking like butt.

To top it off, a small dumb part of my heart kept beating *maybe maybe maybe—maybe* I hadn't imagined the spark with Keats—but then Audrey's words would boom through my brain on loudspeaker: *I'm happy you finally like a real person . . . I don't want you to misinterpret anything . . .*

I hated that small part of my heart.

As I reached for my chemistry book from my locker, I saw a hole in the armpit of the shirt I was wearing—my favorite, a vintage They Might Be Giants T-shirt—the perfect crescendo to the morning's symphony of crappiness. I picked up the subway token from the chain under my shirt and rubbed it between my thumbs, praying to the Bearded Lady: *Please, let me spontaneously combust like some boring old Dickens character (Note:* Bleak House, *you are the worst). Right now, in the hallway, before I have to go to chemistry.*

I waited.

Nothing.

Instead I heard an anxious voice say my name.

I turned and Audrey was standing there, hugging her books against her chest. She met my eyes and shifted from foot to foot anxiously. Her brown eyes were big and watery, like she was a deer caught out.

I broke eye contact, pretending to be really focused on putting the books from my bag in my locker.

"Hey, Pen, can we talk?"

I shrugged.

"I'm really sorry about yesterday. Everything I was saying was coming out wrong, and I hate that things are weird with us—it feels really, really terrible."

Inside me I felt something small and invisible relax just a little bit.

"I feel pretty terrible too," I admitted, meeting her gaze this time.

She brightened slightly, her face cautiously opening, tentative sun after a storm.

"I'm so glad I found you this morning. Cherisse told me I should give it some time, but I didn't feel right waiting—"

"Wait, you talked to Cherisse about us?"

"Well, yeah, she was there when you left yesterday . . ."

"Did you tell her about me and Keats?"

She nodded carefully, but her voice was steady. "She's my friend, Pen. I was upset about our fight. Of course I talked with her."

I turned back to my locker, chewing on my lip and feeling a mortifying impulse to burst into tears.

Instead I said, "I wish you weren't friends with Cherisse. I wish you'd just pick me."

I immediately wanted to take it back. I hated how pathetic I sounded. It wasn't fair. It wasn't nice. It wasn't who Audrey and I were. But before I could say anything, Audrey shook her head at me.

"God, it's really hard to be your friend sometimes. You know that? I can be friends with more than you and Eph! You can too! You have this stupid set of expectations and rules about how everyone should act and how life should be, and they're so damn impossible, you shut out everything." She choked back an angry sob, her face red. "You know what? Cherisse doesn't make me watch David Lynch movies. Cherisse likes to go dancing and try new things. Cherisse called my grandma to see how she was doing in her new home. And you know what else? Cherisse isn't fixated on some stupid unrealistic Leonardo DiCaprio movie we watched in seventh grade."

I clapped my hand over my mouth. "If it's so hard to be my friend, then maybe we shouldn't be friends anymore," I said, my eyes stinging.

Her face went stunned and white, like I'd slapped her, like I'd pulled out her heart instead of mine. I turned toward chemistry, leaving behind Tonka trucks and Vivien and Delphine and M&M'S.

I waited for her to call my name.

The first bell rang.

I listened.

The second bell rang.

I felt Eph's subway token against my chest.

At that point the Bearded Lady sent me a little gift. It wasn't the bursting into unexplainable flames I'd been hoping for, but it was a spark.

I was angry.

Yesterday Audrey should have been excited for me, not judgmental.

And Cherisse was mean and terrible and I didn't want to be around her at all, and if she was such a good friend, Audrey could keep her.

Maybe we shouldn't be friends anymore. Maybe that was just better.

And I was going to talk to Keats, today, right now—bad morning, Cherisse history, armpit hole be danged.

When I stepped inside the classroom, I saw him sitting by the window, so I sucked in my breath, made sure I held the sleeve with the armpit hole close against my side, and slid into the desk in front of him.

Talk to him. Talk to him.

"Hey, Keats," I said.

He met my eyes and I held my breath, and oh man, there it was: that half smile, that slight turn up of one side of his grin.

"Hey, Scout."

The fire sparked further, bolder, encouraged.

"So, how'd the rest of the party go?" I asked, making myself talk slowly, trying to ignore the way all the blood in my body was rushing to the very tips of me.

He rolled his eyes. "There was puke in the backyard and two busted wine glasses, but I got everyone cleared out by four and no cops, so all in all, not so bad."

"Oh, good, good. It was a really good party, good and all, um . . . ," I said, thinking, *Don't be pathetic—stop saying "good"!*

Mrs. Carroll entered the room and began handing out quizzes.

He cleared his throat. "So, how's *On the Road* going?"

"Thanks for that, by the way! I haven't started yet, but I'm planning to tonight."

His face fell. "You hate it, don't you? First I forget your name at the party, then I give you a book you hate . . ."

"No! I honestly haven't started it yet. I'm sorry, I didn't mean to give you the wrong impression, honestly."

He shook his head. "Really? You don't hate it? Because my ex, Emily, hated it."

Turns out Keats was a little bit nervous too.

"No, I haven't even cracked the spine. I'm sure I'm going to fall totally in love with it."

His eyes widened at the phrase, and I clamped my mouth shut and turned around.

A big bucket of water fell on the little spark that couldn't.

What was wrong with me?

From the front of the room Mrs. Carroll cleared her throat. "Let's start with last night's reading. Who wants to tell me about covalent bonds?"

I am pathetic, I thought, the words cold and final.

But then, from behind, someone took my hand and pressed something into it, something small and square, folding my fingers over it one by one.

A shiver ran up my arm.

A small miracle.

I slid my hand into my lap and opened the tiny square as the girl in front of me raised her hand and started reciting facts about electron pairs and valences.

COFFEE ON SATURDAY? I WANT TO HEAR MORE ABOUT KEROUAC.

2PM, CAFE GITANE, SOHO?

K

Sunshine exploded in my heart and out my mouth and my ears and from my chest, and it blinded everyone in the class, setting the world on fire.

I turned my head slightly over my shoulder.

"Yes," I whispered.

"It's a date, Scout."

My heart was a goner.

I left chemistry ablaze with miracles and luck, waving good-bye to Keats as he walked down the hallway, then waving again. I hated the word "squee," but at that second I couldn't think of a better description for what I wanted to do.

I had to find Audrey. The note was in the palm of my hand, like a talisman, like an honest-to-God real-life miracle, and I wanted to show her Keats's handwriting—proof *it* was happening—so we could erase the fight, so everything could go back to normal, the way it always had been.

But when I got to the cafeteria, PB&J and Diet Coke in hand, she was sitting across from Cherisse.

I stopped, watching them.

Cherisse was making funny faces at Audrey, and even though Audrey clearly had been crying earlier—her face was puffy and her makeup streaked—she was currently laughing so hard she was holding her stomach like it hurt.

Backing up, before Audrey could see me, I turned and walked down the hall. It was too chilly to sit outside. Eph didn't have the same lunch period as me. As far as I could tell, Keats wasn't in my lunch period, but even if he were, how weird and stalkery would that be? *Hey, you asked me out but I don't have anyone else to sit with so can I sit with you?* And forget a bathroom stall—every time I saw someone do that in movies, I couldn't stop thinking about how gross it was.

I was so busy freaking out about where to eat, I didn't realize I had stopped in front of a doorway until someone said, "You joining us for *Nevermore*, Penelope?"

Mr. Garfield, my English teacher, was waiting behind me, holding a lunch tray, beard crinkled around his smile. He was my favorite teacher, despite the aforementioned *Bleak House* assignment.

"I didn't know you did this," I said.

"I'm their advisor, though they can handle it without me. I'm only here for tiebreaker purposes, which happens more than you might think." He motioned me in. "Come on . . . it'd be nice to have another neutral party."

When I entered, Grace grinned hugely.

"Hey, Penelope! So happy to see you! You joining us? Grab a chair."

The room we were in was tiny, with crowded bulletin boards, a giant poster of a raven, and a mess of papers on a round table.

"Guys, this is Penelope, the most generous donor from the Dead Poets Phone Drive, as well as a fellow attender of parties. You remember Miles?"

Miles's Mohawk was currently tipped green, and he was wearing a Joy Division T-shirt. "Nice one," he said, nodding appreciatively at my They Might Be Giants shirt.

I blushed. "Thanks. You too."

"This is Oscar," Grace said, pointing to the short guy with close-cropped black curly hair, and wire-rimmed, dadlike glasses. "He's our new art director."

"Hey," he said.

"And May," Grace said, as the tall girl across from me stretched her hand out, "is our esteemed copy editor."

"Hi," I said, shaking her hand, admiring the several dozen chunky silver rings she had on.

"You know Mr. Garfield, I'm guessing?"

He was at his desk, settling back with a stack of blue composition notebooks.

"Yeah, I'm in his junior English lit class."

"Oh God, *Bleak House?*" Miles asked.

"You'll thank me during the AP test," Mr. Garfield said sternly, lowering his glasses.

Hated it, Miles mouthed to me.

"So this is how this works. We all have copies of the same stuff to read, so each submission gets at least four people reviewing it," Grace explained.

"Five today with you," Oscar added.

"And each submission is numbered—no contributor information—so you can read without knowing who wrote it," Grace said. "That way the entry can stand on its own merits, whether the creator is your best friend or your archnemesis from third grade."

"Misty Cooper," Miles said. "Asked me why I didn't wear dresses."

"Pete Franklin," I replied without missing a beat. "Asked me why my nose was ugly."

"Bastard person," Miles said disgustedly.

"All right, enough talking, people," Grace said.

Miles wiggled his eyebrows at me. "I think she means us."

"Sorry," I said to Grace, as she handed each of us a stack of submissions. She smiled, shaking her head. "It's not you."

"I can hear you, Gracie."

She ignored him. "Remember, check 'publish-worthy,' 'not sure,' or 'nope' on a reader report after you finish an entry. And anything you want to talk or share or ask about, feel free to bring up now, though we'll also leave the last fifteen minutes to go over stuff."

Thirty minutes later I was in a groove. I loved everything about the process: reading the overwrought, melodramatic heartbreak poems and the words in a short story that took my breath away, Oscar's appreciative nods over a beautiful black-and-white photo of a tree, May pointing out humorous typos, even Grace and Miles arguing passionately about whether or not to run a collage featuring hundreds of Miley Cyrus faces—small and big, upside down and cut apart, glitter in between.

"It's rad," Grace said.

"Hate it," Miles said.

"I don't know," May said, chewing on the edge of a pencil.

"Who's Miley Cyrus?" Oscar asked without looking up from the photos he was shifting back and forth on the table.

Miles's pen clattered on the table. "What? You're kidding, right?"

Oscar looked up and seemed surprised to see the entire staff looking at him.

"*Hannah Montana*? 'Party in the USA'? 'Wrecking Ball'? Billy Ray Cyrus's daughter?" Miles asked.

Oscar scrunched his face. "Is Billy Ray Cyrus that Republican guy from Texas?"

Miles threw his head in his hands, muttering, "How is this even possible?"

Oscar glanced at Miles and shrugged, then winked at the rest of us, something sly and secret and unexpected.

Grace burst out laughing. "You are totally messing with us, aren't you?"

Miles looked up, confused, while May leaned across and high-fived Oscar. He raised an eyebrow archly at Miles.

"Third row at Madison Square Garden last month," he said.

Miles opened his mouth to say something, shut it, opened it, and shut it again. When he was flummoxed, all his villainous looks disappeared, and his face got super red.

"I say we vote," Grace said. "All for including it?"

She and Oscar raised their hands.

"Nos?"

May raised hers reluctantly, and Miles, starting to recover, shot his arm straight up.

"What d'you think, Penelope?" May asked, turning to me, her long hair shadowing the desk, and I could tell she genuinely wanted to know.

"Well, it could just be fan art," I said.

Miles nodded vehemently in agreement, his Mohawk bobbing. "See?" he said to Grace and Oscar, lingering a little longer on Oscar's face.

"But you can also read it as a commentary on celebrity, and how there are so many images of things, we lose who the real person is."

"Exactly!" Grace said.

"So, I think yes. Sorry, guys."

"Ugh," Miles said, burying his head in his hands.

"Overruled, Miles and May," Mr. Garfield called from his desk, as Grace added the image to the yes pile and Oscar looked quietly triumphant. "And it's about time to wrap up . . . ten minutes till first bell."

I started gathering the extra copies for the recycling bin.

"So how was the rest of the party on Saturday? Did you find your friends?" Grace asked.

"Actually, I got to talk to the guy throwing the party for a while."

I tried to keep my voice nonchalant. "He's pretty nice."

Miles shoved a stack of submissions in Grace's arms. "Pretty nice? Please. I can tell by the way you're all sparkly. You like him."

I blushed and my smile got all big.

"How did you know?"

"Psychic."

Grace laughed. "I think it's more the fact that he recognizes a fellow romantic when he sees one. You guys are like a club."

Miles rolled his eyes at Grace, but when she turned back to what she was reading, he winked at me. Little bluebirds of happiness danced around me, making me dizzy.

"Speaking of, Miles, any sighting of Starbucks Guy?" May asked.

Miles let out a weary sigh. "No. But I forgot to tell you he was wearing those awesome double-laced black leather Converse last week. He has the *best* taste in footwear."

"Converse are supposed to be really bad for your arches," Oscar called out nonchalantly.

For the second time that afternoon, Miles opened his mouth and shut it, speechless.

May wiggled her eyebrows at us, pointing in Oscar's general direction and giving him a thumbs-up before following him out the door.

"Holy Batman, he's knocked all the infinite words right out of you," Grace said.

"No, he hasn't!" Miles burst out, then blushed. "God, that was loud, sorry."

"You were saying about Starbucks Guy . . . ," I prompted.

He gave me a grateful look. "I'm not asking Starbucks Guy out yet because I have to wait for the perfect moment."

"No such thing as the perfect moment in real life," Grace said. "If I had waited for the perfect moment with Kieran, he would never have asked me out!"

Miles narrowed his eyes at her. "Ick."

"I'm with Miles on this one," I said.

"I forgive you for the Miley vote," he immediately offered.

"Don't encourage him," Grace said sternly.

"I think . . . ," I started, thinking of Eph's parents, of Mr. Darcy and Elizabeth Bennet, of Jack and Rose, of Keats. "I believe in meant to be . . . that when you find the right person, it's a little bit like opening the door to Narnia—it's all lampposts and snow and Turkish delight. It's meant to be."

Miles grinned and clapped his hands.

Grace smacked her forehead. "Pen, Edmund has to be a slave to the White Witch. Mr. Tumnus gets turned to stone. The lion *dies*."

"Okay, bad metaphor," I said, right as Miles said, "Willing suspension of disbelief, Gracie. Remember from sophomore English class?"

"That doesn't even make sense," she pointed out.

Miles glared at her and grabbed his stuff. "Good-bye, Pen. I will miss you and you alone in this room."

"You know I love you, Miles," Grace called out at his retreating form.

"Um," I started sheepishly, chewing on my lip, suddenly nervous even though everyone had been so nice. "Can I join you guys again?"

Grace grinned. "Of course! Every Monday, Wednesday, and Friday—and on Fridays Mr. Garfield gets us pizza."

"Thanks!"

"See you around, Penelope," Mr. Garfield called from behind a stack of papers as Grace waved.

As I walked to World History, I couldn't stop smiling.

I tried, literally, but the corners of my mouth kept pulling up and my Docs felt like they had coils on the bottom, like the potential for springs in my step was now infinite.

Red cowboy boots
Cowboy *calcei ruberi*
Goodwill Store
New York, New York
Cat. No. 201X-12

THAT FRIDAY—THE NIGHT BEFORE MY *DATE WITH KEATS!!!*—I knock-knock-knocked on the O'Connors's brownstone door.

"Penelope, hello!" As I walked in, Ellen grabbed me in a warm hug, holding a glass of red wine to the side. "Eph'll be down in a minute. Come on in and have a seat."

"Thanks, Mrs. O'Connor."

"The bracelet is lovely on you!" she said, examining my wrist, the orange and red beads bright against my paleness.

"I really love it," I said, as George jogged down the stairs.

"Ah, if it isn't the lovely Penelope!" George said. "How are you this fine Friday evening? You here to hang out with Eph?"

"Um, yeah, yes," I said, totally ineloquently. "We're going to see Frank Miller at the comic-book store. He's giving a talk at eight."

"Enjoy yourselves," George said, bending down and giving his wife a kiss on the cheek, cupping his hand lightly behind her neck.

Agh, so romantic it made my heart hurt. I studied my Converse, trying not to seem like a creeper.

"Don't wait up for me tonight," George said as he zipped up his jacket. "It's going to be a late one. Tomorrow, too."

Ellen sighed, not so gently. "Again? And on a Friday *and* Saturday? They've got you working too much."

George grimaced, picking up his keys with a violent jangle. "I don't know what you want me to say, El. It is what it is."

"I'd like to see my husband more, that's all." Ellen flushed red, crossing her arms in front of her, her fingers white-knuckled on the wine glass.

Uh-oh.

What was happening?

No, no, no.

Were they fighting?

I felt a sudden desperate panic to stop the scene unfolding in front of me—to burst into a tap dance, to scream fire, to hide behind the couch . . . anything not to witness this.

"Well, it's not that easy. And it's even harder when my wife is being—" George said, his voice getting louder. I recognized the defensive jut of Eph's chin when someone was mad at him, and I knew nothing I wanted to hear was going to be at the end of that sentence.

I stood up.

George and Ellen both startled, like they'd forgotten I was there.

"I'm . . . I'm going to go find Eph," I said.

"Of course, of course," George said, shaking his head.

Ellen brushed her hair off her face, and for a split second there was an expression there I didn't remember seeing on her or any parent before, something very raw and vulnerable.

"Penelope, I'm so sorry. I'll get Eph." She pushed off the couch and left the room, her feet moving hurriedly up the steps, the wine sloshing precariously in the glass. I heard her call Eph, her voice loud and uneven; then a door slammed upstairs.

George gave a hefty sigh and stepped outside without saying good-bye, a draft of cold wind sneaking in as he left.

The door closed with a resounding click.

The room around me felt haunted with their absence, as if by leaving the way they had, they had left George- and Ellen-shaped empty spaces in the room. I shifted uncomfortably, kicking the curling edge of the oriental rug.

Eph walked slowly down the steps, frowning.

"Is my dad gone already?" he asked.

"Yeah."

"My mom's pretty pissed," he said under his breath, glancing over his shoulder up the stairs.

"We don't have to go out if you don't want."

He frowned. "Nah, I think she's going to go to her Bushwick studio, and she doesn't want company anyway."

I followed him outside, pulling the collar of my denim-jacket-replacement fleece coat up against the chill of the evening. Eph was silent, his shoulders hunched against the wind, which had picked up considerably since the sun went down.

"You need a coat," I said, scanning his tee-thermal shirt combo.

"Whatever, I'm fine."

"Soooo . . . ," I said, trying to gauge his mood and deciding to plunge in anyway. "That was kind of intense seeing your parents fight, like ten levels of awful. Is that something new?"

He pushed his hair behind his ear, moved to the side for a jogging mom with a stroller, shrugged at me without making eye contact, and walked ahead of me again. I ran to catch up with him, fiddled with a gum wrapper in my coat pocket, and waited for him to say something.

Nothing.

"Would you mind if we stop at a vintage shop in the East Village before the comic-book store? We have time to walk over after, right? I need to look for something." I thought of Audrey's beautiful homecoming dress. Maybe I could find something equally cool. "Keats and I are going out tomorrow—did I tell you that?"

"Yeah, we have time," he said, ignoring my news. I decided to let it lie.

"So I've been thinking more about your dinosaur illustrations. The world should get to see them—not just the Coney Island Sideshow poker crew," I said, nudging his elbow, hoping to call him back from the surliness threatening our evening.

The result was a halfhearted grunt.

I chewed my lip, debating my next move. "I think they're good, Eph, really good. Like Pratt Art Institute good." I waited for him to open up to me, to share that he wanted to go to art school, to tell me that his new drawings were from all the secret parts of him, the parts that woke up sweaty and racing in the middle of night or that put unwarranted big hope in fortune-cookie predictions or that still believed, like he had when he was six, that there were real dinosaurs living in the museum.

Instead he jogged down the subway steps, sidestepped a used condom, and pulled out his MetroCard.

"Hey, I'm talking to you, if you didn't notice," I said, grabbing his hand. It was bone cold. "Jesus, you're freezing."

I clasped both my hands around his, trying to warm him up. He jerked away, scowling and shoving his hands in his pockets.

"I'm fine, Pen, okay? Drop it."

My insides curled up, like they had been kicked.

Jerk.

When our D train finally arrived, it was crowded but not impossible, with Friday night energy pulsing through the car— the couple sloppily making out in front of us, the kids in basketball uniforms good-naturedly shoving each other in the aisle, the old woman with lavender hair smiling benevolently at everyone around her.

When we transferred to the F at Rockefeller Center, Eph flopped down in a seat across from me, eyes closed, his head leaning against the wall, which was fine because I didn't much feel like continuing to try to elicit conversation when he was clearly being an a-hole. Oblivious to Eph's Mr. Hyde mood, a small boy decked out in Yankees regalia plonked down next to him, his mom standing watch overhead, and after scoping Eph out, the little boy leaned back and closed his eyes too, mimicking Eph.

After no less than one stop he was sound asleep, his tiny crew cut resting against my Eph's shoulder as if he'd always known him.

I swayed with the movement of the car on the tracks.

My parents fought. But their fights weren't fights—more like tiffs or disagreements—small irritations discussed and bickered over until one or both of them got past it.

But Ellen . . . Ellen was shipwrecked. Like it was about so much more than George working late, like the very fate of her heart was at stake. And George's frustration had boiled to the surface so quickly, so angrily, it scared me.

I couldn't imagine seeing my parents fight like that and *not* talking to Eph about it. I talked to him about everything.

A mariachi band got on at the next stop, playing loudly, but the little boy's mouth stayed open and he snored slightly. The kid's mom smiled gently at me while a guy with a guitar plinked out "La Cucaracha."

Finally, when we reached Fourteenth Street, the small boy leaning against Eph sat up and screeched, "Mom, I'm hungry!"

Eph startled awake and I stood, gathering my bag and grabbing Eph's, too. Some Batman comics poked out from the top.

"Exactly how many did you bring to get autographed?" I asked.

He ignored me, grabbing the bag and saluting the little boy, and we headed up the station steps. Outside, kids were break-dancing on the sidewalk, a crowd watching and cheering, tourists filming it on their iPhones. I smelled charred meat from a halal vendor, wove around a drunken bachelorette party debating whether or not to get tattoos. The city's weekend energy was creeping into my bones.

I was going on a date with Keats tomorrow! My first real date!

Eph must have felt the energy too, because as soon as we came aboveground, he seemed lighter, his parents' fight behind us, taking in the movement and the people around us, pointing out a man walking by with a cat standing on his head.

"Ford would murder me if I tried that," I said.

"You'd at least lose an eye," Eph said. "Nice necklace by the way."

I held up the token. "This may surprise you, but when you gave this to me, I thought you were full of crap."

He raised an eyebrow.

"But I'm happy to say it has brought me endless luck," I said gleefully.

"I might need that back," he said.

We walked east on Thirteenth Street, and when we got to Hong Kong 8, I was surprised how crowded it was on a Friday night.

Eph inclined his head back toward the guys' section. "Heading that way. Meet you back here in a bit? We're going to have to leave here by seven thirty if we want to get to Forbidden Planet in time for the talk."

"Sure," I said, already hopefully scanning the rack nearest me for something to wear.

I grabbed a bright red polyester shift covered with garish orange flowers and headed to the dressing room, laughing when I saw the strategic placement of the two biggest flowers right over my boobs. Instinctively I grabbed my phone to take a picture and text Audrey, but then I remembered we weren't talking, and like in some Japanese horror film, the badness started creeping in like a dark stain.

Twenty minutes and at least six outfits later, I was beyond irritated, each click and slide of a hanger along the rack the mark of something that was wrong with me.

I was lost without Audrey's opinion.

I had tried on an old *High School Musical* T-shirt and jean-skirt combo, but worried the irony would backfire and Keats would think

I was a sixteen-year-old Disney fan. I tried to squeeze into a black cocktail dress that looked *Breakfast at Tiffany's*–ish, but after studying my mess of thick hair and how the dress hit at the point that made my calves extra stumpy, I determined I was not very Audrey Hepburnish, plus that reminded me of Audrey, which made me sad. I rejected a wispy poet-girl Anthropologie dress (too pregnant milkmaid) and a preppy fitted navy blazer with olive khakis (too young Republican).

My hands felt dirty and my clothes felt dusty and my body felt dehydrated.

What if Keats and I didn't have anything to talk about?

What if the sweater I was holding was infested with bedbugs?

What if Keats spent more than a half hour with me and determined I was a weirdo?

Why were they selling T-shirts with visible sweat stains?

What if Audrey and I never talked again?

Did I even want to know what that was wadded up under the dressing-room stool?

What if I sweated the whole time and grossed Keats out with my clammy palms?

Did anyone even wash these clothes before they put them up for sale?

Was Ellen okay? Was she crying in her studio right now?

SCABIES.

The oppressively loud techno music in Hong Kong 8 was making me more jittery, and I left the women's clothing section in search of Eph.

I found him in the T-shirt corner, talking with none other than Mia. God, she was everywhere. Her strawberry-blond hair was arranged in a braided crown, and with her sequined silver cardigan she seemed even more like elven royalty than she had the previous two times I'd seen her, which was saying something.

"Oh, hi, Penelope," she said brightly as I approached Eph.

I tried to smile, but by that point I was so worked up that I was pretty sure if I tried one more outfit that didn't work, I'd burn the whole place down.

Eph raised an eyebrow at me.

"We should go. We're going to be late for your comic-book thing." My voice, I knew, was too loud, but I couldn't help it. It came blurting out of me that way: uncalm, uncool, probably the way I'd sound with Keats tomorrow. The guy next to Mia gave me a snotty hipster eye roll and headed to a different rack of clothes.

Eph turned to her. "See you tomorrow, yeah?"

She smiled, and I tugged on his sleeve. He followed me out of the store.

When I got outside, I stood on the sidewalk, jiggling my leg, then stopped when I realized it was exactly what my dad did.

"So that place kind of sucked. Eighty dollars for a vintage Led Zeppelin shirt when I can get the same thing for a buck at Goodwill? No thanks, amigo," Eph said.

I didn't say anything.

"Did you find something for tomorrow?"

My bottom left eyelid starting twitching, the energy from my leg needing another outlet. "Let's go to Forbidden Planet. Tomorrow's not a big deal anyway."

"Huh," he said, a little surprised. He kicked the sidewalk for a second before turning decisively, like he knew exactly where he was going to go.

135

"Forbidden Planet is that way," I called.

"I know."

"We're not going to get to the talk in time."

"I know."

I was tired of myself. I wanted to be the kind of person who didn't freak out when she was going to a party, who didn't want to vomit when she saw a guy she liked at school, who was able to find the perfect first-date outfit without having an anxiety attack.

If I didn't move now, I'd lose Eph in the crowd. I thought about the way Keats had handed me the note, the way I'd seen his hair curl on the nape of his neck, and I sighed, jogging to catch up.

Eph was moving ahead of me like he was on a mission, beat-up boots kicking stray leaves along the sidewalk. I bet he was cold again. I sped up to match his long strides, and out of the corner of my eye I saw him slowing down to match my shorter steps, and after a few seconds we found an even rhythm.

The thrift store we entered was regular and unglamorous and old. No hipsters or hipster music here, only an old lady with a cart full of sweaters, some elevator music, weird bluish industrial lighting, and a musty rest-home smell.

I followed Eph as he browsed a section of old T-shirts and pointed out a few, in his words, "dope" ties.

We ended up in the shoe section, weaving around a tall drag queen who was admiring a pair of silver leather knee-high boots.

"Sweet," Eph said. "Kind of old-school *Star Trek*."

"Thanks, darling, that's what I think," she said, taking the boots and heading toward the counter.

The bench in the middle of the aisle was calling my name, so

I sat cross-legged on it, watched him scan the rows of worn shoes.

Eph grabbed a pair of old green-and-yellow neon Nikes, checked the size, frowned, and assessed my feet.

"No. Absolutely not. Stranger foot sweat," I said.

He pointed at a pair of battered combat boots splattered with paint, and I shook my head.

"Too clunky." I paused. "Eph, why aren't we at Forbidden Planet?"

"You need something for tomorrow. That last place sucked." He held up a pair of bright orange stilettos with marabou puffs at the vinyl base.

"I don't think I'm going to go tomorrow." As soon as I said the words, the anxious questions buzzing around in my chest disappeared, leaving behind stillness. And maybe a little disappointment.

He put the shoes back on the shelf. "What? That's fucking ridiculous."

"I was thinking more about it. Maybe Audrey's right," I said. "I couldn't even go to that party without freaking out. Every time I think of Keats, my heart gets all fast and my hands get all clammy, but not in a good way. There's something wrong with me. I should be over the moon. And I am, but . . .".

Eph wordlessly held out a pair of cherry-red cowboy boots that were scuffed at the tips, the outside parts of the heels worn down to an angle.

I automatically untied my high-tops, kicking them off, sliding one boot over a rainbow sock, then the other, continuing. "I mean, what do I do if he kisses me and I mess it up and he laughs at me? I'm almost seventeen and I can't even find an outfit for a date without freaking out."

"If he laughs at you, he's an asshole," Eph said.

"But . . . ," I said, exhaustion with my own anxiety making my voice crack. I buried my head in my palms, rubbing my eyes with my hands so hard I saw stars.

The bench shifted as Eph sat next to me.

"Pen?"

"Yeah?" I mumbled.

"Will you look at me?"

"No."

"Will you at least look at the boots?"

I spread my fingers and opened one eye, then the other.

The boots were, in a word, magnificent: beat-up but still bright, the fit so perfect it was like the previous owner had been me in an earlier life. I stood, walked up the aisle and back, testing the feel of them on me.

The boots reminded me of a picture book my parents had read to me when I was little—a book about a mouse with red cowboy boots and a purple purse. I adored that book. The mouse was spontaneous and outspoken and sometimes interrupted people, but even back then I knew that she had something I didn't have: That mouse had spunk.

"Pretty damn sweet," Eph said.

I imagined walking into the coffee shop the next day, the boots peeking out from under a pair of jeans, one of my vintage tees (minus an armpit hole) and some sparkly earrings on top, Eph's subway token over my heart and Ellen's bracelet on my wrist.

It was a start.

"So you're not going to wuss out, right? You'll go?" Eph asked.

138

I looked at him, Orion's belt, the flecks of gold in his brown eyes, leftover bits of sun.

"I've never been kissed before," I finally, finally blurted out.

I had never said that aloud to anyone. Ever.

He raised his eyebrows in surprise, and I immediately wanted to pull the words back in, but I had let them go and they were already out of my reach, miles away.

Mortified, I turned the other way, frantic for the closest exit, but I still had the boots on. Maybe the lady at the register would let me leave with them if I threw all the money in my wallet at her on my way out the door.

Better yet, she could have the whole wallet.

"Pen, turn around."

I looked slowly behind me, and Eph was standing there, and even though I was an inch taller with the boots on, he was still so tall, I had forgotten how tall he was, and my cheeks reddened, hot with embarrassment.

"I'll kiss you," he said offhandedly, as if he'd offered me some of his Sno-Caps at the movie, as if he'd told me he could watch Ford when we were out of town.

"Wait. What?" My heart started going *thud-thunk, thud-thunk*.

"Yeah, why not?"

"Here? Now? Shut up," I said nervously, waiting for him to yell "Punked!" or to belch so loud people two aisles over would hear or to take a call from the Elf Queen—something, anything other than what he was proposing.

Instead he reached down, tilted my chin gently up toward his, rested his hand on the small of my back. He was so tall, it was like craning your neck at a skyscraper with clouds moving behind it, and everything felt weird and dizzy.

"Is this all right?" he asked.

My breath caught and I nodded.

"You sure?"

"Yeah," I said.

"Yeah," he echoed.

And then, before I could process what was happening, Eph was leaning down, his lips meeting mine.

I didn't turn away.

He kissed me, and I thought of tearing mint leaves, of licking salt water off my lips, of the mornings you wake up heart alive, no alarm.

I stood on my tiptoes, my body stretching to meet the length of his.

His lips were gentle against mine.

Eph's lips.

Eph's.

I pulled back, my legs shaky, and practically crumbled onto the bench.

"Whoa," Eph said, and his voice was pure wonder, dinosaur bones bigger than the both of us, muscular tails knocking over cities, roars that made your ears ring, fossil hearts. "That was . . ."

"Weird," I answered without thinking.

He took a step back, and his face fell.

"Eph, I'm sorry, I didn't mean . . ."

But I did mean it, because it *was* weird, because this was Eph, the boy I'd known since I was six, the boy whose nose I'd broken, who broke girls' hearts as regularly as it rained, who made fart noises during all of the digitally remastered rerelease of *Casablanca*, who said things like "Exsqueeze me."

A kid with a red-lollipop-smeared face and lips ran down our aisle, and the fluorescent lights were twitching above us, and an old man yelled at the lollipop kid from two aisles over, and the kid was laughing maniacally like he was secretly a demon.

"I'm so sorry."

His face was flushed, like the day I'd punched him, but he laughed. "Sorry? It was just a kiss, Pen. Not a big fucking deal."

"Oh, okay," I said, confused.

"Okay," he echoed a bit more quietly.

A wavery voice started speaking on the store intercom, static punctuating each space: "Store's closing in five minutes. *Five minutes.*"

Eph shifted. "You getting those? I'll save you a spot in line." He didn't even wait for me to answer before jogging away, so desperate was he to get to a Penelope-free zone.

I slid off the boots and shoved my feet back in my Converse, knotting the laces once, then twice, desperately trying to brainstorm topics to ramble about to Eph on the subway ride home—anything to avoid the dinosaur in the room.

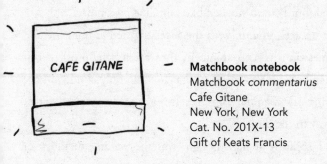

Matchbook notebook
Matchbook *commentarius*
Cafe Gitane
New York, New York
Cat. No. 201X-13
Gift of Keats Francis

THAT NIGHT I DREAMED I HAD A PET DINOSAUR.

The dinosaur was little and he was cute. His teeth were sharp, yes, but he was a baby, so he only gave my arm or bare leg light nips when he was hungry. Sort of a *Hey there, remember me? I need some eats, stat!* His eyes were big and his scaly skin was a shimmery green and brown. I had never seen that color in nature, and it sort of took my breath away.

But because it was a dream and dreams are weird, the dinosaur got bigger—fast. His tail started knocking things over: Mom's rosebud tea set. Dad's transistor-radio table. My dollhouse.

He trembled then, that dinosaur, his eyes wide and watery, scared and hungry and too big for the walls around him, claws clicking, panicked, among shattered pieces on the floor.

And then one day he swallowed my baby brother whole.

In the dream I was surprised, because I hadn't known I had a baby brother, but Mom was crying and Dad was yelling, so I figured maybe I did. That dinosaur licked his chops. He looked sort of embarrassed, but he also smelled like rain, like possibility.

I woke up at 3:34 a.m. with the sheets twisted around me and a deep sadness in my heart about my now-eaten baby brother. But then I remembered it was a dream, that I was an only child, and the grief of losing my imaginary sibling left me as easily as it had come, floating away in the dark.

What I couldn't shake, though, was the waking memory of Eph's kiss.

My fingers flew to my lips. I pushed at them with my index finger.

These lips these lips.

I thought about that dinosaur's heart, and how it simply *wanted*. The type of want that made you ravenous, made your eyes wild, made you want to tear into things, rip them apart with gnashed teeth, how you'd do anything to fill that hunger—anything to make your heart stop needing, stop wanting.

I tried to fall asleep again but ended up staring at the clock next to my bed, until I gave up, picking up *On the Road*, the dream heavy around me.

The next thing I knew, Ford was meowing plaintively in my face, his breath fishy. I peeled open a sleep-crusted eye.

11:38.

CRAP. I shot up. I had slept through my alarm, probably because of the dinosaur dream and the fact that I was reading a not-so-great book for most of the night and because of the kiss.

My first kiss.

I replayed every part of last night at the thrift store—Eph being so tall, and the kid with the lollipop-stained lips running by, and how I tasted mint, and how it was both horrible and marvelous.

The whole subway ride home had been profoundly weird. I was squeezed in next to Eph, but he was leaning forward on his knees, emanating serious no-talk vibes. But the possibility of silence alongside the kiss—the kiss!—was too enormous, so I started manically asking him as many questions about *Watchmen* as I could without actually confessing I hadn't had time to read it thanks to Keats and Kerouac and school.

I didn't—couldn't—stop.

By the time we reached my street, he had resorted to monosyllabic grunts, and I was riding high on a tidal wave of verbal terror—pretty sure right then that even if a giant piano fell from the sky on top of me or the earth cracked open and swallowed me whole, I still wouldn't be able to stop my astute cultural analysis of a *Watchmen* character compared to the different actors who'd played Batman over time. ("More Christian Bale, less Michael Keaton." What was I even *talking* about?)

Maybe the kiss wasn't weird for him. Maybe it was like he said: not a big deal. Maybe it was only a big deal for me because it was my epic first kiss—the stuff of songs and movies—and for him it was a favor for his pathetic, unkissed friend.

And now my first kiss was over, which was a relief. Better weird and awkward with Eph than weird and awkward with Keats, right?

Only I wasn't quite sure how to answer that.

I needed Audrey.

I didn't have her anymore.

Her absence felt like matter—something heavy and dark sitting right behind my sternum.

I picked up my phone to text her and then remembered how ugly I'd been to her in the hallway when I'd asked her to pick me, how we'd ignored each other every time we passed in the hallway the subsequent four days. I dropped the phone back on the bed and flopped down next to it.

Ford jumped up and onto my chest, happily kneading my rib cage and breathing fishy breath on me. I needed to get in a better head space for my date with Keats, and sleeping another hour with my stinky cat would have been perfect, but the new red boots were calling.

"Sorry, buddy," I said, reluctantly pushing him off. He nipped my arm.

I still got to Soho twenty minutes early. But maybe that wasn't so surprising, since I always leave for places early, perpetually worried I'll end up on one of those trains that gets stuck in a tunnel and I'll have to crawl my way aboveground with only my wits and the Mole People to guide me.

I decided to kill time at the McNally Jackson bookstore. Walking in and seeing the bright colors of book covers and the light wood floors, my heart slowed into a comfortable rhythm. Home. Books were home.

I started toward the mystery section, hoping to find a copy of *The Talented Mr. Ripley*, and rounded the corner so quickly, I plowed into Eph's dad, George, in front of the travel section.

"Oh, Mr. O'Connor!" I said, blushing. "I'm sorry!"

He ran his hand distractedly through his thick black hair. "Penelope, good to see you," he said, looking over my shoulder. "Is Eph here?"

George had this frown on his face, like he had eaten something he couldn't decide was rotten or not yet, but was veering toward probably spoiled. Had Eph told his dad about the kiss?

"No," I said quickly. "Only me, getting ready to go on a date. With a boy. Keats." I wasn't sure why I felt the need to add all that.

"Of course," he said, exhaling, just as a pert, freckled young woman came up behind him. Her tidy ponytail swayed as she handed him a steaming cup.

"Darjeeling with a little milk, just like you like it."

"Um, thanks, Annabeth," he said, blowing absentmindedly on the tea.

"So I bet Mrs. O'Connor is glad you didn't have to work today after all," I said, trying to sound helpful.

George sipped his tea and winced. "Actually, I—I mean *we*—are working . . . taking a little break from exhibit planning."

"Oh," I said, wondering why he was taking a break all the way downtown when the museum was all the way uptown.

Annabeth put her hand lightly on George's elbow.

"Oh, yes, I'm sorry—Penelope, this is Annabeth Miller. She's been helping out at the museum while she finishes up her dissertation. Annabeth, Penelope is a family friend, and one of my son's favorite people in the world."

"Hey," I said, extending my hand. "I bet you know my dad, Dr. Marx?"

She flinched, her smile fading; then, just as quickly, she

recovered, shaking my hand enthusiastically. "Totally!" she said. "He's brilliant."

"Um, yeah, thanks, I guess?"

We all stood there awkwardly, George focusing intently on his tea, Annabeth still smiling but now humming an anxious tune under her breath.

"So, I have to go," I said, holding up my wristwatch, even though I still had at least ten minutes to burn.

George seemed relieved. "Good to see you, Penelope."

"Yeah, you too. And nice to meet you, Annabeth."

She nodded, her lips pursed in a tight smile, and I walked as quickly out of the store as I could without actually running. Halfway down the sidewalk, curiosity got the better of me, and I backed up and peeked through the window.

George and Annabeth were exactly where I had left them. His back was to the window, but I saw Annabeth, and she was *not* happy—her face red and scowling, her hands gesturing furiously as she mouthed something.

I've always been crap at lip reading, and I was worried Annabeth would see me spying from outside, so I pulled back. But whatever she was saying, I was pretty sure it was angry and very sure I shouldn't have seen it.

I headed to the coffee shop, my new-old red cowboy boots clicking on the sidewalk, feeling queasy about what I'd witnessed. I stopped outside the shoe store next to Cafe Gitane and studied the boots in the window, wondering if I should text Eph or call him and tell him what I saw or make sure everything was okay with his parents.

But I thought about last night, and everything Eph-related switched back to weird mode in my mind, so I decided to shelve the whole thing, at least for now. Keats—it was time for Keats.

Cafe Gitane was dim and warm, with cozy blue-and-orange decor, and I felt like I was in Paris, or at least how I'd always imagined Paris to be. Audrey would love this place. The restaurant was tiny, so I saw Keats right away, sitting at a table, his curls even dreamier in the light and his dimples making me feel a little giddy. He was engrossed in a book, his chin propped up on his hand, his brow furrowed. Adorable.

"Hey, Keats."

He looked up from his book, smiled at me appraisingly, and stood, giving me a kiss on the cheek. His lips were chapped. "Hey, Scout. Cool boots."

"Thanks." I sat down, blushing, embarrassed at how much the nickname thrilled me. "Good book?" I leaned over to see the cover of what he was reading. *Fight Club* by Chuck Palahniuk. "Ah."

"Have you read it?"

"No, but I saw the movie with my friend Eph. He went through a period of being totally obsessed with it. I'm sure the book is better, though, yeah?"

"I've read it three times already. . . . I can lend you this copy when I'm done."

"Oh, thanks!" I said, entirely pleased by the assumption of future interaction on Keats's part.

"But you can't be mad at me if you don't like it."

"Never."

The waitress came over, bedecked in a cute little jumper, and Keats grinned all dimply at her, and the awesomeness of the previous minute evaporated. I wished my hair were chic and angular like the waitress's and that I had a pierced nose. But I reminded myself that Keats was with me, and instead of feeling bad that my hair wasn't that chic, maybe I should chill. Maybe the waitress admired me for being with Keats.

"More coffee," Keats said, handing the waitress his mug.

"A hot chocolate with skim milk, please. No whipped cream," I said.

Keats raised his eyebrows at me, smiling. "Doesn't that defeat the purpose of hot chocolate? Skim milk and no whipped cream? You're leaving out the best parts."

"But this way you can taste more of the chocolate," I said.

"Ahh, I didn't know I was going out with a hot-chocolate connoisseur."

"I have a PhD in hot chocolate." I felt a flush of pride that my banter wasn't completely terrible.

"How's Kerouac going?"

Crap.

I chewed on my lip.

His face fell. "Shit, you totally hate it."

"I'm not that far in," I said, trying to reassure him.

"You can tell me the truth."

I debated what to say. So far, it seemed like Sal and Dean were the human equivalent of those red-butt monkeys at the zoo—all chest-beating and gross. Nothing much happened in the first few chapters. And I was certain that if he were alive now, Jack Kerouac would be the type of dude-bro who would spread his legs so wide on the subway he'd infringe upon the legroom of the two adjacent seats.

"It's just that the guys are wankers, and I don't understand how anyone could like the book and not be a wanker—no wait, I didn't mean that. Oh, shoot . . ."

He looked stricken.

"I'm sorry, I didn't mean *you* were a wanker. Not at all. You're like the exact diametric opposite of wanker. Like a winker? Is that a thing? Like someone who gives nice winks or something? You're a really good winker. Oh, I'm so sorry," I ended weakly.

His shoulders relaxed a little. "No! Don't be sorry. It's me—it's just my ex, Emily . . ."

"The one in the picture in your room?"

He gave a rueful smile. "She always told me I made her read stupid things. She could be really cruel."

"That stinks," I said carefully, as the waitress returned, putting a mug down for each of us. Mine had a paw print on top, carefully created with powdered chocolate. When I took a sip, I burned my tongue.

"So please tell me you're at least reading something half-decent if you're not reading *On the Road*?"

"Well, I'm always reading and rereading Jane Austen. And I've been making my way slowly through *Watchmen* when I'm in the mood for something else," I said.

He furrowed his brow.

"You know, the graphic novel I was reading that day we met?"

"Oh, the comic book."

"Well, it's not exactly a comic book," I started to say, but he talked over me.

"When you get further into Kerouac, it's going to blow your mind. My older brother, Beckett, and I have been trying to figure out how to do our own Kerouac road trip ever since we read it last year."

I stirred my hot chocolate and tried to seem riveted.

"We're going to try to do it this summer. Beckett is researching the closest thing we can get to renting a 'forty-nine Hudson, so we can have the whole experience. . . ." He stopped, studying me.

"What?" I asked, my face flushing.

"You know, you're pretty cute when you bite your lip like that."

I melted, fields of white flowers unfurling like waves.

"So where'd you grow up?" he asked.

"Here. Well, mostly here. We lived in Ohio till I was six, and then we moved for my dad's job at the museum."

"Big change."

"Yeah, but as soon as I met Eph, I wasn't homesick anymore. It helped to have a friend."

"Eph, is he that tall guy with the brown hair you hang out with, the artist guy?"

I was surprised he had registered all that. "Yeah, he's one of my best friends and I've known him and his family for like forever, but we're just friends, you know? He's an old family friend. We don't date or anything—I mean, not that you asked . . ." Last night flashed through my mind and I felt a faint pang of guilt, but Eph had said it himself: It wasn't a big deal. *Chill, Penelope.*

Keats ripped open a raw sugar packet and poured it in his coffee. "Actually, I was going to ask," he said.

"That's funny," I said, feeling brave. "A few people told me you and Cherisse have a history—"

"Old family friend," he interrupted without missing a beat, and his smile was teasing.

"Fair enough," I said.

"Enough of her."

Fine by me, I thought, warmth filling my stomach. Keats wanted to be with me; he picked me. It was a miracle, this feeling of being chosen.

As the afternoon light faded, we talked and talked. And ordered two more hot chocolates and one more coffee (decaf this time).

Keats told me his first real concert was the National, which was so cool I couldn't stand it. It took ten minutes of prodding afterward for me to finally admit mine was Selena Gomez.

I liked the way he used his hands when he talked about something he loved—college football, Cormac McCarthy books, the movie *Clerks*, Arcade Fire.

He said he was addicted to Red Hots, had to order them online because they were hard to find, showed me a half-empty box in his coat pocket, close to the chest like a pack of cigarettes. No wonder he always smelled like cinnamon.

He told me the Washington Square Park brownstone where his family used to live was haunted, and when he was eight, his mom insisted they move because the ghost was hurting her chakras. Up until last month and thanks to Beckett's influence, he had covertly smoked a cigarette every morning and every night, along with an occasional joint, but he had finally decided to quit.

I told him how I thought John Hughes was a genius and that

he needed to watch *The Breakfast Club* stat, that "Fake Plastic Trees" was the saddest song in the entire world, that I hated the Flaming Lips. I said that the best place I had ever been was Costa Rica, on a trip with my parents, that I had seen a tiny poison tree frog there that was so exquisite, it made me cry, but that if I could, I would live in a mews in London, a place with flower boxes in the windows.

I told him the three things I liked best about myself: my handwriting, my eyelashes, and my ability to stand on one foot for extended periods of time.

We segued mysteriously into NYC pizza, and whether Di Fara's was worth the wait.

Me: Yes, a thousand times yes.

Keats: Overrated.

Keats leaned forward when I talked, his eyes focused on me, and I pulled out details of myself to show him. I liked how he asked for more.

"So, Scout, what are you going to be when you grow up?"

I shrugged. "Well, there's biology, but I don't really love it. I mean, I'm good at it, I know that."

Keats raised his eyebrows.

"That sounded braggy, I didn't mean it like that."

"No, you only brag about your handwriting and eyelashes and balance, I get it. Keep going."

"Hey!" I said, feeling like the best, most flirty version of myself. He grinned. "I don't care a ton about science. I mean, it's fine and all . . ." My voice trailed off.

"What do you care about?"

Besides you? I wanted to say.

"Words. I really, really like words."

He stroked his chin, sizing me up, and the silent focus embarrassed me, so I looked away, studied the cracked edge of my mug.

"Got it," he said. "A book editor. Because clearly you have a lot to say about how Kerouac could be better."

"No, I promise, I'm going to give it another chance!"

"I'm teasing you. You're cute when you blush."

I blushed four times harder.

"So, what are you going to be when you grow up?" I asked.

He told me how, starting with his great-grandfather, all the men in his family had graduated from Yale—there was even a wing of a building named after his family—and that Beckett was currently paving the way for a spot for Keats in his fraternity. His parents wanted Keats to pursue finance; Keats wanted to apply to the fiction program.

"I think my dad will disown me if I don't graduate with a job at Goldman Sachs in hand. But I have to follow my passion, you know?"

"Maybe you could do both?" I suggested.

"Do you think the fiction idea is lame?"

"No, not at all," I said, hurriedly shaking my head. "I told you, I love words."

"Emily thought it was a pretty pathetic excuse for a future degree."

I leaned across the table, wanting to squeeze his hand but not sure if I could touch him yet. "I think it's a really cool idea, and brave."

"You do?" He looked hopefully at me, his eyes clear and vulnerable and open.

"I do. I think it's pretty amazing."

He nodded appreciatively, dimples betraying how pleased he was. "You wanna get out of here?"

"Sure, yeah."

I watched him at the counter, asking for the bill. One plaid sock and one argyle sock peeked out between his jeans and beat-up Oxfords. He was so freaking cute it hurt a little.

When he came back, he handed me a Cafe Gitane matchbook, only it wasn't full of matches—instead it was a tiny notebook.

On the first page someone had written *Scout*.

Yes!

A smile started breaking through the clouds, and I turned to the next page.

Your nose.

My hand flew to my nose, but he shook his head. "Keep reading."

The way you bite your lip.

The next page.

The way you talk about words.

"The three things I like best about you," he said.

I felt all blushy and kind of a little bit frantic, so I tried to slow down my heart and all the blood coursing through me.

"Come on," he said, moving to the door. "Let's bust this joint."

As we passed the register, I grabbed another matchbook/notebook, sliding it in my pocket for Eph—he'd want to fill it with tiny dinosaurs.

Outside, it was a gray evening and chilly. We walked, not talking about which way to go first, and ended up strolling down Mott Street, the boutiques cozy and lit. We stopped in front of a building with a huge street-art mural on the side, a really cool black-and-white anatomical drawing of a rat.

"That's kinda creepy, but awesome," I said.

We studied it until Keats blurted out, "It's cold."

I took in his thin coat. "Why don't guys ever dress warm enough? You must be freezing!"

Keats grinned and clasped my arm in the crook of his elbow. "You're warm," he said.

We walked into Little Italy that way, weaving among tourists braving the cold and crowding the sidewalk, strings of white light-bulbs swaying over the street, and I couldn't imagine ever feeling cold again.

When we got to Canal Street, I beckoned him closer. "I have to show you something." I pulled him past vendors selling foreign fruits and vegetables, men with garbage bags of designer knock-off purses, everyone's breath starting to show in the chill. I turned and caught him watching me. I grinned. "Almost there," I promised.

I found the small silver food cart on Baxter Street, steam coming from within, and dug in my purse for a dollar, then handed it to the woman working, who poured batter into a honeycombed skillet. Keats leaned into the warmth of the cart, leaned into the warmth of me, and I felt his closeness, his solidness. In one fluid motion the woman opened the skillet and dumped out small, perfectly formed cakes, scooped them into a wax bag, and handed them hot to me.

"Mini hotcakes," I said, offering the bag to Keats. He tasted one.

"Oh man, you may have questionable taste in books, but that's good."

I teasingly elbowed him in the stomach, lightly, so I could feel him, and with one hand he gripped my elbow and squeezed it.

"How'd you find this place?" he asked, letting go and grabbing another hotcake, biting halfway through, the steam escaping.

"Eph showed me—his mom knew about it from one of her friends who used to live down here." I took a few of the mini cakes from the bag and popped them in my mouth, and they were sweet and warm, like pancakes, but light and easy, like goodness.

We meandered toward Chambers Street, companionably digging into the wax bag. When it came time for him to head toward his train and me to mine, I made him take the last three mini hotcakes. As I handed them over, he circled me with his arms, and I lingered there, against his shoulder, smelling pine trees and thinking, *Keats, Keats, Keats, it's finally happening.*

"I like you so much." The words came out of my mouth before I had a chance to stop them. So much for playing it cool. But Keats smiled the smile I was coming to know as his and his alone, the left side crinkling up a little higher, the dimple on that side a little deeper, his eyebrows furrowed.

He stepped back, held up the bag, and winked. "See you later, Scout."

I rode the train home as warm and light as the mini hotcakes, my burned tongue pressed raw and new against the roof of my mouth.

Santa Claus figurine
Santa Claus *statua*
Brooklyn Flea
Brooklyn, New York
Cat. No. 201X-14
Gift of Ephraim O'Connor

AS SOON AS MY ALARM WENT OFF THE NEXT MORNING, I SAT straight up in bed—awake and jingly and blushy with thoughts of Keats. I stretched my arms Ford-style, feeling happiness extending to the tips of my fingers, shooting out in beams of sunlight, and flopped back down with a contented exhale.

Being in love, or at the very least being in like, was waking up with spring inside me—everything chattering and blooming with blue sky and white petals.

My phone dinged, and my heart jumped.

> Thanks for yesterday, Scout. Having brunch with bro
> and parents today. Dad talking about b-school. It sucks.
> How's Kerouac? K.

Keats!

I flopped happily back down in bed, gazing at the leaves outside my window, the beginning of oranges and reds, a bright golden ginkgo yellow. It was Sunday, and I had never felt so pretty, so noticed, so delirious, like every part of me was light and perfumed and lovely.

I missed Audrey right then, wanting to tell her how liking Keats was a miracle, how it was everything Delphine had always dreamed of. I wanted to show her the matchbook notebook with his scrawled handwriting, and to tell her about the paw print on the top of my hot chocolate.

I debated calling Eph. But what would I say? *After I kissed you, the next day I fell head over heels with a beautiful boy?*

The social triangle was broken. So I scrolled through my phone contacts until I found the one I was looking for.

Hi Grace it's Penelope. Wanna go 2 the bklyn flea 2day?

Send.

As soon as I heard the whoosh, I second-guessed my decision. Even though we'd been at Nevermore meetings together, and I'd joined Grace and Miles at lunch on days I was brave enough to risk an Audrey-Cherisse sighting in the cafeteria, what if Grace and I weren't really hang-out friends yet? What if we didn't have anything to talk about? What if the silence was weird or I took a joke too far? Should I text her back and say "never mind"?

I conjured Eph, thinking what he would say about Grace, probably something like *Chill, Pen* and *If she's weird about it, you don't want to hang out with her anyway* and *Don't make things so fucking hard.*

Okay, okay, stop freaking out.

The phone dinged.

Yes! 11?

All right. Maybe I didn't always have to make everything so hard after all.

Perf c u there, I wrote, deciding right then that this was a reminder to take it all down a notch. Grace wanted to hang out; I wanted to hang out; done.

Keats liked me; I liked him; done.

Not everything needed to be hard.

I shoved out of bed and dug through my dresser for something to wear.

I pulled on Eph's gray sweatshirt along with black leggings and my Docs, tried to scrunch some Ellen-like waves into my hair, shoved *On the Road* in my bag for the subway ride to Brooklyn (I would persevere, for Keats!), and headed downstairs to grab a bite to eat.

A wrinkled bag sat on the kitchen counter, bagels spilling out, a trail of sesame seeds across the floor the only indication someone in particular had already dug into them.

"Dad? Is one of these for me?" I called out.

"Of course," he called out from the general direction of the living room.

I headed out to meet him, half a cinnamon raisin bagel already in my mouth.

"Darling daughter," my dad said, lowering his copy of the *Times*. "Just who I wanted to see."

"Mmm?"

"You joining your mom and me for a movie later today?"

"Where is she?" I asked, wiping a crumb from the corner of my mouth. I wondered if Keats liked bagels.

"Emergency coffee date with Ellen. But she'll be back by three for a movie."

"Is everything okay?" I asked.

My dad shrugged. "Not a clue."

I flashed back to George being weird in the bookstore, to Annabeth-with-the-ponytail touching his arm, and a wave of discomfort passed through me.

I kicked at the floor. "Do you know someone at the museum named Annabeth? She's working on her dissertation, I think?"

My dad furrowed his brow. "Huh, no, but you know me, I can't remember our neighbor's first name."

"True," I admitted.

"So, you joining your mom and me this afternoon? *Vertigo*'s on the agenda."

"I'm going to the Flea for a bit, but yeah, I can be back in time."

"Good. Adios, darling daughter. Until we meet again!"

Dad didn't seem to be worried about Eph's parents. Maybe I was making things too hard yet again.

When I got outside, the world took my breath away. It was stunningly, amazingly, beautifully fall outside, the sky the ridiculous color of a crayon. Glowing red and orange leaves littered the sidewalk, and I scuffed through them with my boots.

I loved the feeling of being in like. I loved the giddy feeling of being me today. I loved everything.

My phone dinged.

> Did you get my text? Did I offend you? K.

What? No! I stopped in my tracks, trying to type back as quick as I could.

> Yes! And no! And sorry! On my way to Bklyn. Can't wait to c u in chem.

I paused, trying to decide how to sign off, and feeling brave, not wanting him to doubt me, I signed *xo*, hit send, and waited.

> Ugh bklyn. Until tmrw Scout.

Okay, okay. There. I guessed things were okay now?
Another message ding, but this time it was Eph.

> U around?

I felt a rush of weirdness about the kiss. But it wasn't a big deal, per the other half of the kiss himself, a fact that exponentially increased the weirdness.

Weird: Eph wet his pants in second grade because the art teacher wouldn't let him use the restroom.

Weird times weird: Sometimes when Eph and I watched movies and he took off his hiking boots, his sweaty feet stank up the room so bad I actually gagged.

Weird to the third power: Eph hated reading anything other than graphic novels, comics, and *The Hobbit*—I think because reading was still challenging for him, a fact I totally got. But reading was pretty much the best thing in my life.

Weird to infinity: I watched him make two different girls cry at last year's spring dance, when they discovered he was dating them both at the same time.

I kissed that person.

Kissing Eph = weird.

(And good?)

No. Eph wasn't my dream boyfriend. Keats was.

Clearly, I needed a little time on my own to process things. *Flea w my friend Grace,* I wrote back. There. That should do it.

Grt c u there.

Dang it.

I was so busy fretting over Keats's message and Eph's message that I wasn't paying attention to where I was walking—and bam!—plowed right into someone.

"Watch it," the person said. I looked up.

That someone, unfortunately, turned out to be Cherisse. Even more unfortunately, she was with Audrey.

There's like more than one and a half million people living in the borough of Manhattan. One and a half million! Granted, Audrey lives within a ten-minute walk, but what were the odds that right there, right then, when all my newfound confidence was wobbling, when I was worried I'd hurt Keats's feelings, when I couldn't stop thinking about the feel of Eph's lips, that I'd run into the two of them?

The Bearded Lady's token was slacking off.

Cherisse was decked out in pinks and whites, like she'd just been weekending in the Hamptons. My lip curled, imagining what Eph would say about the getup—probably that she looked like an eighty-year-old socialite named Bunny.

"Hey, Pen," Audrey said, shifting uneasily, and I looked over at her, missing her something fierce.

Before I could answer, Cherisse straightened. "You should really watch where you're going, Penelope. I'd hate for you to walk into traffic because you were too busy looking at your phone."

I was pretty sure she wouldn't hate it very much at all.

"Sorry, Cherisse, I was texting Keats."

Cherisse wilted about two degrees.

Bull's-eye.

"You know how it is." I tried to giggle dizzily, like a girl in love, but it ended up sounding like I had just inhaled helium from a birthday party balloon.

Distracted, Cherisse started chewing on her nails, but Audrey frowned at me, and I immediately felt a little bad about who I was being.

"Um, what are you guys up to?"

"We're going upstate to see my gram," Audrey said.

"Oh," I said, thinking about how just a month ago I'd have been the person going with Audrey.

"Yeah," Audrey said quietly.

"I'm sorry—" I started to say, when Cherisse looped her arm through Audrey's.

"Aud, we *have* to go if we're going to get Balthazar croissants in the Grand Central food court and still have time to catch the next train."

I couldn't help it. "Are those vegan?"

Cherisse narrowed her eyes at me, but Audrey cut in. "They're for my gram."

I immediately felt small and unpleasant.

"Hey, tell your grandma I said hi," I said to Audrey.

"I will," she said, giving me a smile that felt perfunctory and empty, like she didn't really like who I was right then.

I wasn't sure I did either.

By the time I got to Brooklyn, and despite my efforts to the contrary, I was back to making things hard again. I definitely hated *On the Road*—I would finish it anyway because I always finished books and it was Keats's favorite, but *God*, Kerouac was the worst.

What if it hurt Keats's feelings if I didn't like it?

What if I blew it by not texting him back right away this morning?

Why did I stoop to Cherisse's level?

What if Audrey told her lovely grandma how ugly I'd been?

What if Eph wanted to talk about the kiss?

I sat on the steps of the school near the flea market, resting my chin on my knees and hugging them toward me. The smells from the food trucks floated my way: brick-oven pizza, pupusas, brisket, fried dough. I scanned the crowd for Grace or Eph. The Flea was crowded today—vendors trying to get as many sales as they could before the weather got cooler. There were booths with racks of old vintage coats and shiny pleather shoes, booths with hundreds of tiny plastic toys, booths with old wooden soda crates. There were also people selling sparkly dainty necklaces and ironic T-shirts with narwhals on them, candles made of beeswax, and wind chimes made of sea glass.

"Pen!" Grace sat down beside me, stretching her legs out and pulling a pair of quirky vintage red-framed sunglasses from her oversize polka-dot bag. "I love this weather!"

"Me too," I said. "I always think I like spring in New York best, and then every year fall rolls around, and I remember it's really the best."

"Agreed. Plus you can get apple cider in the fall, and that alone trumps most everything else. Want to start browsing?"

"Well, here's the thing. My friend kind of invited himself to join us. Sorry, I hope that's okay?"

"Sure, that's cool. I asked Miles if he wanted to come, but he's on a date with Starbucks Guy!"

"Really? Awesome! How'd it happen?"

"Miles finally asked him out. I think you inspired him. They're out now. Getting coffee from someplace other than Starbucks and walking the High Line. Miles is under strict instructions to secretly text me as soon as he gets a chance. I'll let you know what he says. Speaking of, how was *your* date?"

I filled her in on everything, including Keats wanting me to read *On the Road*.

She frowned. "Ugh, not my favorite."

"Right? I want to like Kerouac, but . . ." I trailed off.

"Here's the thing. If he's going to make you read his book, you should make him read a book you like. It only seems fair."

"Huh! That's a good idea," I said. I liked the idea of balancing the book scales. "Do you and Kieran make each other read things?"

"We're actually pretty much in sync, so we're usually reading the same stuff. Our only problem is trying to keep up with each other so neither of us inadvertently spoils things," she said. "We're both obsessed with this fantasy writer Terry Brooks—do you know him?"

I shook my head.

"He's awesome. This one time, Kieran finished one of his books before me, but because he didn't get my text about it, he totally spoiled the death of this *major* character—like *major*, but I won't say who, for when you read it. I didn't talk to him for like five minutes. It was our worst fight ever." She sighed.

"Five minutes?" I teased.

She blushed. "Yeah, I know. Miles is always making fun of us because Kieran's and my drama is not dramatic at all. He calls it 'dramatic minus the drama, which leaves *ick*.' But my last ex was terrible, and that drama was seriously not good, so I'm fine with ick. It's better than liking terrible guys and getting hurt."

I bit my lip, thought of Audrey's warnings about Keats.

"Besides, Miles has got a great guy right in front of him. Isn't Oscar awesome?"

"That Miley Cyrus thing makes me laugh every time I think about it."

"He's so deadpan, it's brilliant."

Right then I spotted Eph at the entrance and waved, then realized he didn't see me because all his attention was currently focused on some curvy girl with spiky punk rock black hair. She kept touching his elbow.

I rolled my eyes. What about the ethereal Mia? Was she not a big deal either?

Eph typed something into the girl's phone—presumably his number—and she gave a coy wave good-bye. As soon as he turned his back to her, I saw her give a silent squeal and delighted little jump up and down with her friends.

Eph was smiling, pleased with himself, but when he saw me watching him, his shoulders tightened up and Serious Face won out. He walked toward us, skateboard under his arm, his knit cap making him seem even taller than normal. I tried to shove any lingering effects of the no-big-deal kiss down way deep inside.

When he reached us, he scanned my outfit. "You know, someday I'd like that sweatshirt back."

The last time I saw him we had kissed, and *this* is what he had to say?

"Eph," I said, resisting the urge to point out he was being a jerk, "this is my friend Grace." Because she was my friend. I had a new friend. "Grace, this is Eph."

"Ephraim," he corrected.

I rolled my eyes, and Grace shook his hand.

"Rad shirt," he said admiringly, checking out her Hüsker Dü tee, and then, like some scene from some terrible frat movie, his eyes lingered obviously on her chest a beat too long.

Grace's face turned scarlet. I elbowed him in the gut, hard.

"Ow." He shot me a nasty look and I ignored him, pulling Grace with me down the first aisle.

"So how do you guys know each other?" he asked, poking his face over my shoulder.

"*Nevermore*," Grace said. I guessed the tone of her voice was the one she used when she was trying to pretend everything was all right. Ugh, Eph.

"What's that?" Eph asked.

"The literary journal—remember, I told you about that," I said, trying to regain my balance, our balance.

"No you didn't."

"Um, yeah, I did, remember? I was thinking you should send some of the dinosaurs to the journal for consideration." I turned to Grace. "You guys publish lots of cool art, right?"

"We do," Grace started, when Eph interrupted her.

"When did you tell me this? Was it in the middle of you talking about how *Watchmen* is just like *Hamlet*? Because sorry, Pen . . ." He pretended to yawn.

My bottom right eyelid began twitching. "I told you about it on the way to that vintage shop. Or was that"—I made finger quotes—"'not a big fucking deal' either?"

He flinched, and I felt momentarily victorious.

"Language, Penelope," he said, bouncing back smugly, and I scowled.

"I just want good things for you, Eph. I thought people should see your art."

"If I wanted people to see my art, I'd show people my art."

Grace glanced between us. "So yeah, I'm going to check out

these books." She practically ran across the aisle.

Eph whistled under his breath, watching her. "She. Is. Hot."

"What is wrong with you?"

"Uhhh, nothing?" He took off his cap and ran his hands through his hair.

The kiss sat between us like a particularly ugly hangnail. I knew picking at it would make the situation worse—a hangnail so red and sore your finger hurt more than it should for longer than it should—but I couldn't stop.

I crossed my arms. "Nothing? Really?"

"'Nothing? Really?'" he echoed.

My top left eyelid started twitching along with the bottom right. Great.

"So we're not going to talk about what happened on Friday?"

"What happened on Friday?" he asked casually, and my blood reached its boiling point.

"You kissed me!" My words came out sputtery and jagged, incredulous, clearing space around us with the volume. The bearded man standing behind the booth we were at chuckled, presumably at me, and I wondered if "accidentally" knocking over his table of button trays would get me arrested.

"You kissed me back," Eph said nonchalantly, picking up a particularly hideous red plastic miniature Santa, bringing it to the bearded man.

"Two dollars," the guy said.

Eph pulled out his wallet, the chain clipped to his dark jeans, handed the guy two singles, stood the Santa up on his palm, and offered it to me.

"I don't want *that*. Why in the world would you give me that?"

"It's cool?"

"Good luck," the bearded man said meaningfully to Eph, and Eph gave him a look that said *Right?* and everything in my vision went red and spotted.

I swatted at the Santa, and it tumbled to the ground, plastic clattering on the blacktop.

"Hey!" Eph said, bending down to pick it up.

"That kiss was a big deal for me!"

"Whoa, killer. *You're* the one who said it was weird."

"No I didn't!"

"Uh, yeah, you did."

I decided to pretend that hadn't happened.

I folded my arms across my chest. "And then you invite yourself to the Flea, sauntering in like you're the best thing since sliced bread"—he lifted his eyebrows at the lame insult, and I internally cringed but kept barreling forward—"and you're flirting with every single female in a ten-mile radius, sleazy old-school Captain Kirk–style . . ."

An amused snort.

". . . and then you ogle my new friend Grace and you don't even ask me how my date with Keats went and instead you buy me *that*." I pointed distastefully at the Santa.

"Trust me: At this point I'm sorry I bought you anything," Eph said dismissively.

"I don't think I want to hang out with you right now," I finished.

"Um, yeah. The feeling is mutual." He leaned over, stuck the

Santa in my purse's outer pocket, so its head was peeking out. "Tell Grace I said 'later.'"

I watched him angle through the crowd, knit cap a head above most of the people there, until I couldn't see him anymore.

The subway token lay under my shirt against my skin, a witness, so I pulled it out and off, dropping it in my bag, and shoving that Santa monstrosity in deeper so his stupid red face—why was his face red?—couldn't watch me.

When I found Grace, she was poring over a beautiful old book with intricate fairy-tale illustrations.

"Where'd Eph go?" she asked.

"We're not getting along."

"I sort of noticed."

"I'm sorry. He's not usually like that. *I'm* not usually like that. I don't know what's up with us."

Liar.

She nudged me and held up a book, a big smile on her face. "Have you read *Anne of Green Gables*?"

"About eight times," I said.

And we both said, "Gilbert Blythe!"

"Oh my God, I was so in love with him," Grace said. "Maybe you should make Keats read it, to balance the book equality?"

I laughed.

"So," she started, as she picked up a pink paperback of *Valley of the Dolls*, "can I be totally nosy and ask if you guys kissed?"

Birds stopped mid-sky.

Horns stopped mid-honk.

A baby stopped mid-cry.

I thought of Eph bending closer, his eyelashes fluttering, the taste of his lips.

Wait.

Grace meant Keats.

Grace asked me if I kissed Keats.

The world resumed moving—people talking, a baby screaming, a pigeon pecking for crumbs at the edge of the sidewalk, a car driving by blaring the Rolling Stones.

Of course. Duh. Chill. Making everything too hard yet again.

But then, a sinking feeling.

"No, we didn't kiss. Is that bad?"

"Nah. It took Kieran and me eight whole dates to even touch lips. When it finally happened, I was so freaked out. Things with my last boyfriend were really fast, but with Kieran, I didn't want to rush it."

"Really?" I asked.

Grace shrugged. "Yeah, I know it's weird . . ."

"No, no, it's not that at all." I wanted to tell her that knowing her made the night sky feel, if not crowded, at least a little less lonely—my star shining a little brighter with the company.

"Let's go get something to eat," I said instead. "My treat."

That afternoon, when I got home from the Flea, waiting for my parents to get ready for the movie, I thought about throwing the Santa away.

But some impulse in me couldn't go that far, so instead I crammed it in the back of a dresser drawer, behind all my sweaters where I couldn't see it.

Handwritten list
Tabulae manu scriptae
Helvetica Cafe
New York, New York
Cat. No. 201X-15

- Oatmeal
- Rosemary
- Cat Food
- Arcade Fire
- Heartbeats
- Tulips

THE NEXT MORNING AT SCHOOL, I WAS WALKING TO MY LOCKER,
when someone squeezed my elbow, and a thrill ran electric through me.

"Hey, Scout," Keats said, and I marveled again at the reality of
him wanting to be with me. My heart pulsed in my chest, like it was
trying to find its way to him.

"How are you?" I asked, leaning against my locker. I liked the
way he leaned around me when I did.

"I'm not feeling so good, you know?"

I frowned. "That sucks."

He grinned. "I don't think you're feeling so good either."

"What?"

"You know. There's been something going around, and I thought
you might have caught it too."

"No, I'm actually feeling pretty good."

He sighed. I decided I'd read it as an amused sigh.

"Scout, let me be frank: I think you should cut with me today."

Ahh—it *was* an amused sigh!

"Really?"

"Yeah. Wanna cut with me?"

I had never cut. If my parents found out, they'd freak, half because I'd never done anything grounding-worthy before, and half because they'd worry it was the first step on the path to being a delinquent. And I had a Spanish exam later that day and figured I should probably find Eph to make sure we were okay even though I wasn't sure we were. . . .

"If you don't want to spend the day with me . . . ," he started, his face falling.

"No, why would you think that?" I squeezed his hand gently. "There's nothing I'd rather do."

"Good," he said, giving me what I decided that moment was my official favorite Keats smile: the wry one with the eyebrow raise. Keats grabbed my hand, inclining his head toward the exit down the hall. "Let's go."

As soon as we rounded the corner, I saw Eph and Audrey talking. She looked surprised by something he was saying, until she met my eyes, and her face shifted, suddenly unreadable. She muttered something under her breath to Eph, and he turned, took in me and Keats holding hands, and his face darkened, chin jutting out.

Audrey squeezed Eph's arm before leaving, offering me a rueful smile. I lifted my free arm just a bit—not a wave, an incline, an acknowledgment.

The first bell rang.

"Keats, you met my friend Eph, right?" I asked.

"Yeah." He stretched his hand out to shake Eph's. "Good to see you, man."

Eph's nostril curled at "man," and I could practically hear the scoff as he shook Keats's hand. He turned to me. "Can we talk?"

"Now?"

He raised an eyebrow and I shook my head.

Keats nudged me. "It's almost second bell, Scout. We gotta go if we don't want to get caught."

Eph laughed, looking right at me. "*You're* cutting?"

"So?"

"So, that's not very you."

"Well, maybe you don't know me so well after all."

Eph tilted his head back, running his hands through his hair, clearly exasperated.

"Pen, I just want good things for you. That's all." I bristled at how he was parroting my words from the Flea right back at me.

The second bell rang.

Eph waited, irritable and tall and all broody like a thundercloud.

Keats waited, his face open and handsome and expectant and new.

I took Keats's hand and didn't look back.

We busted out the side doors and onto the sidewalk, merging with the rest of the world like it wasn't a school day, like we weren't students. It was gray and stark outside, the breeze tinged with an unfriendly edge, and my teeth chattered.

"So, that guy Eph is kind of an ass," Keats said as he looped his arm around my shoulder, pulling me close. "He looked like he wanted to beat the crap out of me."

"No . . ." I didn't know what to say, exactly. "It's not you. We're just not getting along—sorry you got caught in the middle of it."

"I don't mind. If you guys aren't getting along, it means I get more of you to myself."

I blushed hard, trying not to smile too much, and we walked down the steps of the nearest subway station, me still tucked into his side.

When the train came, we squeezed into the crowded car, finding two suspiciously empty seats next to a gray-haired woman in a frantically flowered dress.

After a few stops, the woman sniffed loudly, leaned over, and got close to my face: "I hope you have a terrible day!"

I rolled my eyes. "I should have known these seats were empty for a reason," I said to Keats, but he pulled me up and over to the other end of the car, glaring at the woman over his shoulder.

I was charmed at how chivalrous he was. This would not be a terrible day.

We transferred to the F at Rockefeller Center, and after a much more peaceable ride this time, got out at Second Avenue.

"Let's get coffee," Keats said.

I followed him along past a string of bodegas and restaurants and a hardware store and a Starbucks and a bagel store. I liked the way he held my hand and told me things: the time Beckett snuck him into a punk rock show, how his parents met at a fraternity party, how I should read Richard Brautigan after *On the Road* (okay, maybe not that one). We turned on Seventh Street and, somewhere between First Avenue and Avenue A, stopped in front of a small divey storefront labeled HELVETICA, a place I never would have noticed on my own. Maybe, I thought, it was like something from Harry Potter and only existed today, right now, just for us.

When we walked through the door, a small bell tinkled, and from behind the counter a tattooed, pierced girl with blue pigtails gazed up disinterestedly. "The back open?" Keats asked, and she grunted and returned to her *Village Voice*.

Keats led me between cluttered old thrift-shop tables with mismatched chairs. Lamps with kitschy shades threw light warmly around the room. If this coffee shop were a person, it'd be a little old lady with lots of secrets—like a spinster aunt who used to be a dancer in the circus.

As soon as I saw the back room, I gasped. It was covered with bookshelves from floor to ceiling. Hundreds of used books filled the space: old leather spines, cheap paperbacks.

"I love this place," I said to myself, but maybe I said it out loud because Keats said, "I figured you would."

He gave me that Keats smile. "What do you want? The usual?"

I raised my eyebrow.

"You know, hot chocolate, skim milk, no whip?" he offered.

Ahhh! Keats knew my "usual." "Yes, please . . ."

As soon as he left the room, I plopped down on a couch in the corner. Everything around me smelled musty, like when you open an old book and it smells like words. I rested my boots against the coffee table, watched halfhearted sunlight filter in from the one window, tiny dust specks lazily floating around me, and heard Keats talking with the coffee girl, heard her laugh—Keats could charm surly tattooed girls—and then the whistle of the coffee steamer. Old Depeche Mode started playing over the speakers. Keats must have talked her into turning on something.

I studied the books on the shelf behind me.

Lady Chatterley's Lover. It was an old pulpy paperback festooned with red roses and a sultry, cleavagey woman with lips parted, as if she were breathless. Lady Chatterley, I assumed. I flipped through the wavy pages—the book had clearly been dropped in water—and found a folded slip of paper tucked in the back.

I unfolded it, read the cursive script: *Sometimes I miss her more than I can stand.*

"You find one of the notes?"

Keats carefully placed our two mugs on the coffee table and settled right next to me on the couch. Thanks to the broken cushions he sank in perfectly close to me.

"The notes?" I took a small sip of the hot chocolate. It was unsweetened, and the roof of my mouth would again totally be raw after this, but I didn't care too much as the warmth trickled down into my belly.

"Yeah, people leave notes in the books here." He read the one in my hand. "Damn," he said, wincing. "That's hard-core."

I thought back to the photo from his room—the one of him and evil ex Emily—and I returned the note to the book and shoved the whole thing back on the shelf. "So there could be more notes in here?"

"Yep, most definitely."

I pulled out a copy of *Wuthering Heights*, held it up excitedly. "This is one of my absolute favorites. Have you read it? God, it's so terrible and romantic at the same time."

"Eh, lady writers, not really my thing."

"What?" Surely he didn't mean that. Surely I misunderstood him. But before I could ask him to explain, he triumphantly held up a brightly colored hardcover of *Love in the Time of Cholera* in one hand and a note in the other.

"Score."

He sat back on the couch, pulling me into the curve of his side as he unfolded the note.

He was warm. And he smelled like a Christmas tree. And I thought to myself: *I am with Keats, a beautiful boy, in a coffee shop filled with books. Don't freak out, Pen. This is a big deal.*

He handed me the note, nuzzled his head against mine.

I blew on the chipped edge of my hot chocolate mug as I read.

Oatmeal. Rosemary. Cat food. Arcade Fire. Heartbeats. Tulips.

"Grocery list, you think?" he asked.

"Hmm. Heartbeats on a grocery list?"

"Good point," Keats said.

I chewed on my lip, thought about the Bearded Lady and my NYC subway token, giving me luck even though it was currently residing at the bottom of my purse with the lint and a stray aspirin. "Maybe it's some secret coded message, from spies, you know? They're on opposite sides, but they met—in Paris—before they knew they were spies, and they fell in love, and now they have to meet secretly, all Romeo and Juliet like. So they write grocery notes with code words in them and leave them here."

Keats was watching me with an amused expression. "What does the list mean?"

"Well, she wrote it—you can tell by the handwriting. And she

181

wants to meet him after breakfast—oatmeal—by the Shakespeare garden in Central Park. Rosemary."

"The cat food?"

"Um, he has to bring some, in case there are stray cats there."

"Arcade Fire?"

"That's how he knows it's not some regular old grocery list. They first saw each other when an Arcade Fire song was playing, and her heart beat so fiercely, she said it was like tulips were blooming . . ."

I stopped talking, feeling a little dorky, but when I looked at Keats, he was watching me intently. His eyes were different—not amused, but soft and serious. He put his arm behind me and brought his lips to mine.

I closed my eyes, ready for dinosaurs to roar.

Instead I got Keats's chapped lips.

I pulled back, not sure what to do next, and Keats gave me a half-lidded sleepy smile, and he kissed me again, more insistent this time. It wasn't like when Eph kissed me, mint and salt and lightning and wonder.

This time it was chapped lips and a boy with a dimple as deep as a well, a boy who seemingly didn't like lady writers, a boy with his hand pressed against the small of my back.

Thoughts flashed through my mind: *This is different—this is for real—maybe I'm not doing it right?* But Keats's tongue slid into my mouth, and mine moved into his, and it was better then, my body relaxing into it, taking care of things for me.

At some point I felt myself crumple the secret spy grocery list in my hand and shove it in my pocket.

No one else came into the cafe, and the girl from the counter didn't bother us, so we stayed there for the next hour, occasionally talking but mostly kissing.

I thought about Eph only once, when Keats went to the bathroom. I stood up, stretching, and browsed the shelves. In a corner so high I had to stand on my tiptoes, I found an old, wrinkled copy of *The Hobbit*, its pages yellowed and rippled, like someone had spilled something on it. It didn't have any notes in it.

Without thinking twice, I pulled a scrap of paper from my purse and wrote *Eph*, the letters hard, leaving an imprint on the other side. But then I didn't know what to say after that—words not exactly working.

I heard the murmur of Keats's voice from the next room, talking with the girl at the counter, so I dropped the scrap of paper in the pages of the book, and then shoved the book back in its impossible spot on the shelf, where all the other forgotten secrets lived.

Keats came in, paused, looking at me, taking me in from top to bottom, and I didn't know what to do with my hands, felt them useless next to me. But then he stepped forward, strong and decisive and pulling me into a kiss, and both of us sank back down onto the couch like an exhale, like things held back and then released.

After a bit, when my lips started to feel bruised and puffy, we left, nodding at the waitress on the way out, shuffling on coats and walking into the cold air. Keats took my hand, and we walked through the East Village to Washington Square Park, watching skateboarders maneuver around, and I thought, *This boy. This boy, not anyone else. This one, holding my hand.*

We listened to a man play old ragtime tunes on a standup piano, right under the arch. We stopped at a food cart to get hot dogs and ate them outside, sitting on a wood bench, watching pigeons and kids flutter around, and we nestled together, and I thought, *This is the boy I pick.*

I couldn't calm my beating heart, couldn't stop my mind from racing through the possibilities.

Oatmeal.

Rosemary.

Cat food.

Arcade Fire.

Heartbeats.

Tulips.

THE FOLLOWING WEEK, I WAS IN A FULL-FLEDGED KEATS HAZE, MY lips puffy from consecutive days of near-uninterrupted make-out sessions.

He had surprised me the day after our Helvetica outing, offering to walk me home after school. On our way there, he made me laugh to the point of tears, his Mrs. Carroll imitation scarily perfect. He played the new National song for me, sharing one of his earbuds, his head nodding next to mine, in sync with the music. When we got to my stoop, the cool of the concrete steps passing through my jeans, we made out, entwined as scarlet leaves drifted magically in the air around us.

On Thursday, between watching teenagers break-dancing, some guy drawing caricatures, tourists getting lost, and locals walking their dogs, we sat on a wooden bench near Strawberry Fields in Central Park and made out some more, the trees bowing down around us like we were holy.

That Saturday, we walked from Keats's house to Battery Park City, the river glinting bright alongside us, and went to the Poets House library. I rested my head on his shoulder as he read me Jack Kerouac poems, the late-afternoon sunlight making me drowsy enough that I was able to tune out Kerouac and just listen to Keats's voice. It was a miracle, Keats next to me, the very fact of him liking me.

And Sunday we went to the Cloisters, orange leaves falling outside, holding hands inside while we studied the unicorn tapestries, my heart dreamy with the drug of pure like.

Keats was waiting for me at my locker Monday morning. He promised we'd go to the Strand after school. I spent the morning giddily imagining him pushing me gently against a shelf, his lips on mine, words around me, and by the time lunch rolled around, I could barely spell my name, already lost in the headiness of the afternoon's potential.

"Pen!" Grace called to me from down the hallway, and I blinked twice, rubbing my neck.

"Hey!" I said, sunshine spilling lazily out of me.

"Hey, you," she said, giving me an admiring look. "You are totally blissed out. Keats?"

I smiled, big and dopey.

She wrapped an arm around my shoulder, pulling me down the hall. "You're late for *Nevermore*. For that matter, so am I. Turns out we have a little more space to fill for the next issue, but it needed to go to the printer like yesterday. So we're getting pizza and reading. Unless you have plans with your Prince Charming?"

I shook my head.

"Follow me."

When we entered the room, May waved cheerily.

"No Emily Dickinsons or Walt Whitmans yet," she said. "But we'll find them!"

Miles was bent over a pile of paper, his Mohawk uncharacteristically and ominously flattened down, scowling. "Be warned, there are *a lot* of vampire short stories and poems with thorns and dark tears and bleeding roses today."

"Have you guys read *Twilight*?" Oscar asked.

Miles shot him a withering look, and Oscar shrugged. "It's really well done."

"I can't even," Miles replied, turning toward the wall and scowling.

I was just about to launch into questions about what Oscar could possibly find redeeming about *Twilight* when he winked at me.

"Man, you're good," I whispered under my breath as I sat between him and Miles.

He shrugged, settling back with a submission, stretching out his legs.

"Soooo . . . how's it going with Starbucks Guy?" I quietly asked Miles.

He snatched a submission from the pile in front of us, in the process scattering the remaining entries across the table. May frowned and reached over, straightening them into a neat pile.

"Gracie·told you?" His voice was petulant.

"I told Pen what?" she asked, sliding into the seat on the other side of Miles.

"About my date?"

"I told her the beginning but not the end," Grace answered.

Miles sighed unhappily and loudly, pretending not to notice the way May glared across the table at the noise.

"What happened?" I asked quietly.

"Nothing happened," Grace said. "Someone's being dramatic."

"I'm not talking to you." He gave Grace the hand and turned to me. "His breath smelled terrible."

"Oh?" I said, not sure how to respond.

Grace rolled her eyes behind him.

"And he talked nonstop about his training at Starbucks and didn't ask me any questions, and at one point there was actually a ten-minute soliloquy about the best pork chops he'd ever had. Turns out he hates E. E. Cummings—was only reading him that one time because he had to. It was awful and boring and not at all romantic. Total nuclear disaster."

"Oh no," I said, immediately thinking of my encounter with the dirty hot guy at Grey Dog. "Maybe he was nervous?"

"Exactly what I suggested. I don't think he's giving him enough of a chance," Grace said under her breath.

"What kind of romantic story is that?" Miles practically yelled. "'When your dad and I met, he couldn't stop talking about pork chops'? That's terrible!"

May made a harsh "shhhh" noise, and Miles gave her the finger.

"Classy," she muttered.

"I want sweeping romance; I want a kiss that takes me to other worlds. Is that asking for too much?" Miles asked.

"Settle for nothing less," I murmured, thinking of Vivien and Delphine's vow, worrying faintly for the first time that maybe it was impossible to keep. But this wasn't me and Keats we were talking about.

"It doesn't work like that," Grace said to Miles patiently. "I just think you should give him another chance. When I first met Kieran, I thought he was so boring, but—"

"That's because he *is* boring!" Miles said.

Grace's face froze.

Oscar raised his head from the manuscript, watching Miles, and May started twisting a ring on and off her finger.

"You think Kieran is boring?" Grace asked, her voice cracking.

"The only thing he can talk about for an extended period of time is *Game of Thrones*," Miles said.

"I like *Game of Thrones*," Oscar offered.

"He never wants to go out," Miles said, ignoring Oscar. "He only eats hamburgers."

Grace's eyes were watering up, but Miles was on a tear, not even looking at her.

"He likes college basketball, for God's sake!"

"Hey," Oscar said to Miles, tapping him on the shoulder.

Miles shrugged him off. "What did he give you for your birthday this year again? A Best Buy gift card?" He wrinkled his nose. "If that's real romance, no thank you."

Grace was crying now, her face red and stricken. She grabbed her bag and headed toward the door, looking back at us before she left. "Screw you, Miles," she said, the door slamming behind her.

Miles flinched, the color draining from his face, his furious energy disappearing with it.

Oscar stood up then, his chair screeching across the linoleum, and pointed firmly at Miles, then at the door. "Out."

May shot me a panicked glance.

Miles looked at Oscar, confused. "You're kidding again, right?"

Oscar continued to point at the door.

Miles turned toward May and me. "You guys know I didn't mean it. I'm just stressed. I'll find Grace and apologize, okay?"

"You need to go," Oscar said firmly.

Miles waited for one of us to say something, but I couldn't stop thinking of the look on Grace's face, how we shouldn't have seen it, how we were trespassing on the secret parts of her heart.

Miles snatched his bag, furious again, and stormed out.

Oscar and May and I sat in silence for a few minutes, until she stood suddenly. "I'm going to look for Grace. You guys should keep reading—we need to find something by tomorrow if the issue's coming out on time."

Oscar sighed and handed me the next submission on the stack, grabbing one for himself too, as May left.

The short story I was reading—"Wonder Wheel"—started with a guy riding the Coney Island Wonder Wheel at night, making out with a girl named Jena.

Even though I wasn't very hungry, I leaned over for a slice of pizza, blotted the grease off with a paper-thin napkin, and folded the thin triangle in half.

The narrator was angsty, spending a lot of time moodily staring at the rain through cafe windows, drinking his coffee black while he lamented the fact that he was attracted to Jena—that even though he found her "mean and shallow as a teenage girl's eye shadow dreams" (sexist much?), he kept returning to her "like a hardened moth to a passionate and cruel flame" (clichéd much?).

Irritated, I flipped to the last page.

The final scene featured the narrator riding the Wonder Wheel, alone this time, smoking a cigarette and staring poignantly out over the sea. He had broken things off with Jena, her cruelty "a dark blot of cancer seeping into him like mold," but once he'd lost her, he realized that he loved her.

I was ready to check "nope" on the reader report when my brain caught up with my eyes and finally processed the last sentence: *As the Wonder Wheel jerked to a halt at the top, he stretched his legs onto the aluminum seat and studied his mismatched socks, the weariness of life beating ceaselessly into him like a drum.*

No.

No.

No mismatched socks.

I dropped my half-eaten pizza onto a napkin and flipped to page one, reading more carefully this time.

The narrator had an older brother who taught him to smoke pot when he was thirteen.

His mother complained frequently of ghosts.

But most damningly of all, even though his father wanted him to work at Goldman Sachs, the narrator wanted to be a writer.

Just like Kerouac.

I flushed, like I had been caught red-handed at something, but Oscar was staring out the window and no one else was there.

My stomach gurgled guiltily, but how was I supposed to know? It wasn't like his name was on the story.

I hated the story.

I wanted to burn it to the ground.

But at the same time I also felt this weird sense of protectiveness for Keats's vulnerability, sitting there all plain and raw on the page.

The first bell rang, and I checked the "not sure" verdict on the reader report and hastily handed it to Oscar, and instead of recycling the submission, per our guidelines, I shoved it in my bag.

"Talk to you later," I said at the door, my hands tingling with, what? The theft? Borrowing? Not recycling?

"Later," he said quietly.

I practically ran out of the room.

The right thing to do would have been to throw the stupid story in the nearest recycling bin and not give it a second thought.

Instead I read it furtively under my binder in World History. It didn't get better with repeat reads.

After the final bell, Keats was waiting for me at my locker, smelling like cinnamon. I snuck a glance at his socks.

I tried hard to banish thoughts of moths flying into flames and shallow-girl eye shadow.

"Scout," he murmured, pulling me into a kiss.

I had a fleeting moment when I wondered if Audrey or Cherisse or Eph was walking by. What would they think if they saw us?

He pulled away, reluctantly, and gave me a sleepy smile—what I was learning was his post-make-out smile. "How are you, babe?"

Babe. Keats called me babe. *Forget the stupid story, Penelope.*

"To be honest, kind of crappy. Two of my friends got in a really ugly fight. Have I told you about Miles and Grace? I'm worried about them. So I'm mega looking forward to taking my mind off things. I mean, looking at books." I rubbed his arm, gave him what I thought was a super-cute, flirty smile.

"Ahh, that's the thing. My parents want me home early tonight—Beckett's in town for fall break and we're having some fancy family dinner with Cherisse's family."

Cherisse's family?

I waited for him to ask me to join them.

He didn't.

"Oh," I said finally, trying not to sound too disappointed, wishing I could shove Cherisse in a lake.

"You're totally mad, aren't you?" He ran his hand through his curls, searched my face.

"No, it's okay, you should spend time with your family," I said, even though I wanted him to console me about Grace and Miles, wanted him to at least confirm he knew who they were.

"You sure?" His expression relaxed.

"Yeah," I lied.

"Thanks, babe," he said, giving me a quick kiss on the cheek and jogging backward down the hall. "I promise I'll make it up to you," he called.

Gloomily, I headed toward the door. Once I was outside, I decided to take Columbus instead of Central Park West. The walk wasn't as pretty as passing by the park, but after the day's events, I wasn't in the mood for fall's show-offy colors.

I wondered if Cherisse and Keats were heading to his brownstone together.

I wished he hadn't bailed. I wanted to be with him, wanted to make out until my lips hurt. I wanted to talk with him about Grace and Miles.

Or, at the very least, I wanted him to be a little more upset about canceling our plans.

But to be fair, he hadn't seen the fight, probably didn't know how horrible it was to witness, didn't know it made me sad in a way that reminded me of Audrey. And he was going to make it up to me. He *wanted* to be with me.

And, I reminded myself, Keats wanting to be with me was surely better than no Keats at all. This was what relationships were: give and take, ebb and flow. We couldn't hang out every second, right?

I chewed on my lip, walking by the greasy diner Audrey insisted made you smell like fried food if you were even on the same side street, when I did a double take.

Miles was sitting inside, slumped in a booth.

I didn't particularly want to go in, but I couldn't leave him there, so I sucked in my breath and walked inside, wrinkling my nose at the smell of cigarette smoke (even though it was nonsmoking) and alcohol (even though it didn't have a liquor license) and fish sticks (those, at least, were on the menu).

"Miles?" I asked.

He glanced up, his eyes red and face puffy.

"How long have you been here?"

"Since Oscar shamed me so hard I couldn't stay another second at a place where people knew my name."

"What are you doing here now?"

He poked at his fries. "Sad eating. Grace won't answer my calls. But I wouldn't blame her if she never talked to me again."

I sat down across from him, thought about putting my bag on the floor, then thought better of it and held it in my lap instead. "Yeah, today was kind of ugly."

"I'm not usually that mean." He shook his head, then grimaced. "At least not to people I love. I don't know what came over me."

I chewed on my lip, thinking of the ugly Santa that Eph gave me, wondering if I could say what I wanted to say. "I think you really, really wanted Starbucks Guy to work. I think maybe heartbreak made you a little bit mean."

I looked over, hoping I hadn't overstepped.

"Yeah, maybe you're right." He looked wistful. "I kept imagining how we'd be the perfect couple—we're the right height for each other, and I've seen him read poetry books on break, which is so cool, and his laugh is perfect and deep, and even his handwriting is great. I give up." He dropped his head to the table and I worried about what he might pick up from the surface.

"No, no!" I said, pushing his shoulder until he lifted his head and looked at me, thank God. "You can't give up. He's totally out there—you're going to meet your dream guy, and it will all fall into place."

"I don't know, Pen. I'm starting to think that Grace might be right. Life's no fairy tale."

I fell back against the chair, thinking of the Wonder Wheel and thrift-store kisses and family dinners with Cherisse, then remembered this place could very well have scabies and balanced on the edge of my seat again.

Miles picked up a nearly empty bottle of ketchup and squeezed it so hard it splattered ketchup over the fries and the table, making a sad, sputtering fart noise.

Without thinking, I said, "Exsqueeze me," and then mentally cursed Eph.

Miles smiled a little, though, so maybe it was worth it. He offered me a fry, and I shook my head.

"Do you hate me too?" he asked.

"Why would I hate you?"

"Because I was being, as Oscar made a point of telling me later, the most unlikeable version of myself."

"He said that to you?" I asked, secretly impressed with Oscar's moxie.

Miles nodded.

"Well, maybe it wasn't your finest moment"—I felt suddenly self-conscious—"but I'm really glad to have you as a friend. Just because someone isn't at their best doesn't mean you write them off forever." As soon the words left my lips, I thought of seeing Audrey the day Keats and I cut, how neither of us knew how to even wave at each other like real people anymore. I thought about last night, how when I heard there was a new David Lynch movie coming out, I picked up the phone to call Eph before I remembered, a sky full of regret, that I still wanted to shove him over.

It was lonely being mad at people.

"Did you really mean that about Kieran, what you said about him being boring?"

Miles sighed heavily.

"No. He's not who I'd have picked for Grace—like, he's so quiet all the time, and he's super into all this weird online gaming stuff. But he makes her really happy. Ugh, I shouldn't have said that. I was so out of line. She's just so smug about it sometimes. Like she knows everything there is to know about dating and I'm some sorry person." He dropped his head in his hands.

"She's just worried about you," I started to say, then sucked in my breath, thinking of Audrey. I didn't want to think about Audrey. "Give Grace a little time to cool off. You guys have a lot of history. That won't go away. You may need to grovel for the next five years, but she'll forgive you."

"You think?"

"I hope."

"I'm glad you were born, Pen," Miles said quietly.

"The feeling is mutual," I said, meaning it. "But I can't sit here for one second longer." I pointed at the Department of Health grade on the door.

"Crap, it's a C?" Miles yelped. "I've never seen a place with a C."

"I feel like I'm going to get some obscure gastrointestinal parasite from simply sitting at the table. I'll take you somewhere with better fries. My treat," I said.

"Promise?"

"Um, yeah, as long as you promise not to ever come here again."

I helped him up, and we left the grossness of the diner behind, heading out into the cool autumn afternoon. It was getting darker earlier, fall taking over from summer, things letting go.

— **Handwritten fortune**
Fortuna manu scripta
72nd Street Station
New York, New York
Cat. No. 201X-17

THE NEXT DAY, AT THE BEGINNING OF LUNCH, MAY FOUND ME IN the hallway.

"Grace isn't here, and I couldn't find her yesterday," she said. "And Oscar stopped by her house last night and no one answered."

"Miles has been trying to call her too. He hasn't had any luck either."

"Not exactly holding my breath on him being the one to get through," she said dryly, and twisted one of the rings on her fingers. "I'm going to skip lunch and go check on her. Wanna come?"

"Sure," I said, grabbing my fleece coat and feeling another pang of missing my denim jacket.

"Cutting again?" a voice asked.

Eph was standing behind me, holding his bag, everything about him braced for a fight—straight-backed, chin sharp, eyes mocking.

"I don't have time for this, Eph," I started.

"We're not cutting. We're going to help our friend Grace," May interrupted, offended by just the implication of playing hooky. "We'll be back before lunch is over."

"Oh," Eph said, his face falling slightly, but I didn't feel pleased, just sad.

"I want good things for Grace," I said to him softly. "I need to go."

He stepped back, motioning for us to leave.

Grace's apartment building was on West Seventy-Second Street, almost near Broadway, so we walked quickly, not wanting to miss the next period. I noticed more bare trees, the way everything was hunkering down, getting ready for the blast of cold building in the future.

"Geez, what's with that guy? Getting all up in your business," May said. "Does he like you or something?"

"No!" I said quickly. "I'm dating Keats Francis—do you know him?"

"Oh yeah. But I didn't know he was dating anyone."

I frowned. "Well, he is. Me, that is. He's dating me." I was surprised by how short I sounded.

"I'm sorry," she said.

"No, I'm sorry. I'm just . . ." I trailed off, not sure how to finish.

"Me too," May simply replied.

Keats's canceling yesterday clearly had me on edge. But that happened. People canceled plans all the time.

But to cancel to hang out with *Cherisse*? Gross.

I thought of Keats, the way he'd kiss me at the spot behind my ear and give me shivers.

I needed to get over him canceling.

Get over it, Penelope.

"I'm really worried about Grace," May announced, and started chewing on her nails.

"Hey," I said, stopping her gently. "It'll be okay."

"I know, it's just . . . Kieran is so good for Grace. And it took her so long to see that. I hope this doesn't change anything. Ugh, I could literally strangle Miles."

"I thought Grace was super into Kieran?"

"She is. But when she met him, she was still with her ex Joe. He was a drummer in a punk band called the Migraines—the name wasn't metaphorical—and except for the occasional decent drum riff, Joe was literally a waste of space. Grace was always trying to make herself 'cool' enough for him—she got her nose pierced on his request and was on all these stupid weight-loss diets because he told her she was chunky."

"Wait a minute. Grace? You're talking about *our* Grace?" I couldn't imagine a version of my friend where she wasn't calm and happy and 100 percent confident in who she was.

"Yeah, and then there'd be the monthly freak-outs when she discovered he'd hooked up with someone else."

"Ugh, that sounds like the worst. Why'd she stay with him?"

But I didn't get to hear her answer, because as soon as we turned the corner to Grace's building, we nearly ran into Grace and some guy, stopped on the sidewalk, making out.

"Grace?" I asked uncertainly, more than a little embarrassed.

"Kieran!" May squealed, running forward as Grace and the guy reluctantly pulled apart.

Kieran wasn't what I expected. He didn't have Grace's rockabilly style, or Miles's weary hipness. Instead he was kind of schlubby, with thinning hair and a pale blond beard, baggy jeans, an untucked oxford, dirty white gym shoes, and, currently, a super-intense red face.

"She knew him before I did," Grace said to me, watching May disappear into Kieran's awkward bear hug. "What are you guys doing here?"

"We wanted to make sure you were okay."

A smile burst out of her like a symphony. "Kieran surprised me this morning. We talked yesterday afternoon, and then he took the twelve-hour bus ride from Buffalo—he got here at seven this morning."

"Wow, that's a long bus ride."

"And he has to get back on a bus this afternoon at four, so he can make an exam tomorrow," Grace said proudly.

As a rule Grace usually always seemed pretty happy. But around Kieran she was glowing.

She leaned against him. "Kier, I want you to meet my friend Penelope."

"Hey," he said, his voice so low and quiet I had to lean forward. "I've heard a lot about you. Good to finally meet you."

"Yeah, you too," I said.

He shoved his hands in his pockets, and for a second he looked uncomfortable in his body, like it was too big for him, but Grace leaned up against him, wrapping her arm around his waist, and he relaxed.

"Can't you stay?" May asked. "You can come to the *Nevermore* release this weekend," she said. "Kieran started *Nevermore*," she added for my benefit.

"It's finals next week," Grace said.

Kieran's face screwed up, like he was doing mental math. "If it wasn't such a long bus ride . . . maybe if I left right after, I'd be back in time to study Monday morning . . ."

Grace interrupted him. "Kieran, no way are you missing finals for me. I still can't believe you came down today. I'm the luckiest girl in the world, you know that, right?"

She stood on tiptoes and kissed him, and he blushed and she beamed.

"We should leave pretty soon if we don't want to miss next period," May said, nudging me. "Kieran, can we all hang out when you're back at Christmas?"

He blushed again, and she happily hugged him, launching into a one-sided conversation about her latest copyediting dilemma. I could see the way he was truly listening, not just nodding for appearance's sake, murmuring in agreement with May.

At one point he burst out, *"Semicolons?"*

"I know, right?" May said.

"Copy-editor humor," Grace said. "By the way, thanks for looking out for me."

"We were worried."

"I'm okay now," she said. "It took a while, but I got here."

"It's pretty romantic that Kieran's spending twenty-four out of forty-eight hours riding the bus for you," I said.

"Yeah, it is, isn't it?"

I waited a second, trying to decide if it was my place to say what I wanted to say next. "Miles feels really, really bad."

She sighed. "I know. He keeps texting and leaving me messages. I know he didn't mean it. It's hard sometimes, though, to see him being all impossible about things. It reminds me of how I used to be, and how unhappy I was," she said, her face dark. But then she let out a relieved smile, like she'd narrowly escaped something. Maybe she had.

"I'll call him later today," Grace added. "But I figure it can't hurt for him to sweat it out a little longer. Patience is not his strong suit. He could use some practice."

I laughed. "You don't say?"

She hugged me. "Thanks for coming, Pen. See you tomorrow?"

"Yeah, and enjoy the rest of the afternoon with Kieran."

"Oh, I will," she said, wiggling her eyebrows. "Trust me."

After the final bell, Keats was waiting for me. He looked tired, distracted.

He gave me a kiss, lips chapped.

Eph's lips flashed through my mind—smooth—and I pushed the thought away.

"Hey, Scout. Sorry I had to bail on the Strand yesterday."

I thought of his Wonder Wheel story and felt immediately guilty, though I wasn't sure what exactly for.

"That's okay. It all worked out for the best anyway," I said, trying to really mean it. "How was Beckett?"

Keats frowned. "An asshole. He's bailing on our trip."

"What, no way!"

"Well, not totally bailing, I guess, but we're not going for the whole summer anymore. Instead we're cutting it back to two weeks so he can go to Bali with his white-trash girlfriend."

"Oh." I winced at the description.

"She's one of Emily's best friends," he added, as if that made it all okay.

"Oh," I said again quietly.

We started walking down the hall, and he was clearly still stewing, his face stormy.

"Well, at least if you're only gone for two weeks, we'll have more time together," I offered. "And it'll be awesome. We can go to Coney Island and watch movies in Prospect Park and go to the Big Gay Ice Cream store . . . ," I said, listing some of my favorite New York City summer things.

"You're missing the point," he snapped.

I stopped mid-sentence, mid-step, hurt.

He stopped too, his face exasperated. "Scout, I didn't mean that. Please tell me you're not mad."

"No." I shook my head, confused, feeling potentially teary, trying to push it back. "It's only . . ."

His voice softened. "Beckett planned this for me after Emily and I broke up. It was supposed to be our trip—no girlfriends, no baggage, just us on the open road."

"Oh," I said, realizing I was getting tired of Keats's history with this Emily person.

"Listen, let's go to the Strand today instead, yeah?"

"Okay," I said somewhat reluctantly, but then he leaned over and kissed me under my eye, right on my cheekbone, and even though his lips were rough, it sent a shiver up and down me. "Okay," I said again, willing myself to be more certain this time.

As we stepped outside, leaves were rustling noisily across the sidewalk.

Keats was immediately distracted again, his eyes on a group of people from school hanging out across the street.

"Do you know someone over there?" I finally asked. "We can go over and say hi if you want." I squinted. One of the people kind of looked like Cherisse, and I immediately regretted the offer.

"Nah." He started to flag a cab.

"We're not taking the subway?" I asked.

"No, I'm just flagging a cab for the hell of it," he said, irritable again.

"I get really carsick," I said apologetically. "I'm sorry, I thought I told you that before. I know it's a pain, but I'm all barf-a-rama in cabs." I smiled, trying to make light of it.

"You don't like cabs?"

"Um, no. I get really sick, like I just told you."

At that second Keats unbelievably, actually, literally rolled his eyes as he turned to walk toward the train, his back ahead of me, hands shoved moodily in his pockets, and I felt gross and sad because this was not the boy who'd charmed me at his party, because I hated his comment about white trash, because I hated his "Wonder Wheel" story even more.

I bit back what I was going to say and reminded myself that he wasn't mad at me; he was mad at Beckett. He was having a bad day. *Be an understanding girlfriend, Penelope.*

"I'm really sorry about your summer trip," I said, resting my hand softly on his arm.

He stopped, closed his eyes, sighed deeply, then looked at me, his eyes beautiful and dark. "I really appreciate that, Scout. I knew you'd understand." He wrapped an arm around my waist, and I settled into the side of him.

This was good. We just had a wrinkle. That happened.

But not more than four steps into the station Keats's face turned sour. "It smells foul in here. We should have taken a cab."

I wished I could kick Beckett in the shin.

Or maybe Keats.

We walked down the steps to the trains.

The platform was wild and too crowded, people pressed closely together in a way that made you worried about getting shoved on the tracks.

Keats and I pushed toward the end of the track, where there was space.

But sprawled out on most of the wooden bench was a large man wearing what could only be described as an elaborately woven dress made of plastic bags—garbage bags and deli bags and sandwich bags—all tied and tufted together. At his feet were an empty Yankees hat, turned upside down, and a sign that said *Your fortune for $1.*

"Ugh," Keats said, starting to head back, pulling me after him.

But I refused to move. Nothing about the afternoon was perfect right then: Keats was not perfectly charming, his lips weren't perfectly smooth, he was acting like a moody a-hole. The subway smelled like wet parts at the bottom of a dumpster, and the man in front of us was goofily grinning at me in a way that was definitely abjectly terrifying.

I wanted to fix it. I wanted magic and fairy tales, and maybe this was my test. I needed to see through the muck to find the happy ending.

I was going to fix it.

"Scout, what are you doing?" Keats asked.

"You'll see," I said, moving toward the man.

"Come on," Keats said from behind me, grabbing my arm. "You shouldn't give money to these guys. They could be scam artists."

I shook off his grip and stepped up to the old man, catching his eye.

He smiled. He was missing some of his front teeth, and the remaining ones were yellow, and his breath was stale and dank, as if all the subway stink was actually coming from the inside of him.

I felt my resolve crumbling, but I forced myself to step forward and gently hand him a dollar.

"My fortune, please."

He snatched the bill out of my hands and dropped it in the Yankees cap, then pulled out a dirty old tube sock from his side and began digging through it. A bunch of folded-up pieces of paper spilled out—all the colors of the rainbow, like Miles's Mohawk: a good omen.

I suddenly and desperately missed my subway token, still shoved in the bottom of my purse after my fight with Eph two weekends ago at the Brooklyn Flea.

The man pulled out a neon-green piece of paper and offered it to me, grinning his missing-tooth smile, and I smiled at him, because this was my New York fairy tale, this was my New York fairy godmother in disguise.

But then, as my hand touched his, he opened his mouth and screamed right in my face "Canada is *doomed to destruction*!"

I yelped, jumping back, my heart in my throat.

"Come on," Keats said, wrapping his arm hastily around my shoulder.

The man responded by hocking a giant wad of spit near Keats's oxfords.

"Fuck," Keats swore, and steered us down the platform.

A few tourists stared our way, trying to suss out who had caused the outburst. The man continued to yell about Canada, throwing in some choice comments about terrorists and amaretto and cats.

"God, I told you I didn't want to take the subway. I told you not to talk to that guy," he said.

"I wanted to make things better," I said.

He rolled his eyes again, and I thought about Grace's ex-boyfriend, how he'd made her feel bad about herself.

We waited for the train in an awkward silence, one punctuated only by periodic bursts of 9/11 hollering from the other end of the platform.

"Maybe we should head home?" I offered after a few minutes, waiting for him to disagree.

"Good idea."

But I just stood there, not leaving, wondering how to fix this.

"You're coming to the *Nevermore* launch party on Sunday?" I asked.

"Yeah," he said, glancing anxiously down the tunnel for the train lights.

I tried to remind myself that he was having a bad day. That liking Keats meant liking all of him—good and bad—and that he just needed some space.

But my stomach hurt, and I felt sick, even though we hadn't taken a cab.

While he paced the platform, I unfolded the green piece of paper, my hands shaking.

> *JESUS IS THE WAY THE MOON IS AT*
> *COLUMBUS CIRCLE 59TH STREET*
> *MOON LANDING FAKE 9/11!!!!!!!!!!!!!!!!*

I wanted my dollar back. I wanted my afternoon back. I wanted my fairy tale back.

I felt so embarrassed, and as I watched Keats get onto the arriving train, barely waving at all, I bit my lip so hard I tasted blood—all to keep from crying.

Nevermore, literary journal
Nevermore, acta litterarum
Cafe Grumpy
New York, New York
Cat. No. 201X-18

KEATS AND I HUNG OUT THE DAY AFTER THE SUBWAY INCIDENT,
a sunny Wednesday, and everything seemed normal again. We made
it to the Strand that time, and even though I felt tentative from the
day before, he was übercharming, buying me an amazing illustrated
edition of *Moby Dick*, finding us a secluded corner in the poetry
section to make out.

To be honest, it scared me a little, how normal he seemed, as if
the day before had never happened. But maybe that was okay. The
subway incident had really sucked.

That afternoon, as we made out amid the comforting smell of
musty old books, I felt myself relax into him again, my body ease
into the shape of him. The way he kissed the spot under my ear, I
felt a little dizzy.

Maybe this was his gift, to make it all go away.

My gift to him: never telling him or anyone about reading his "Wonder Wheel" story.

By the time the weekend rolled around, I was wound up with energy and practically jumping with excitement about the *Nevermore* release party, like Beaker from the Muppets.

Mr. Garfield had arranged for us to take over the back room at a coffee shop on Sunday evening. When I showed up with several bags of cookies from a Little Italy bakeshop in hand, I gasped. Grace and May (the decorating committee) had transformed the place. There were a few rows of seats set up for the reading and small white fairy lights strung around the top of the room.

"So I'm thinking I'll turn the lectern over to Grace as soon as everyone's settled," Mr. Garfield said as I joined them.

"And I'll introduce you guys and Oscar," Grace added, nodding toward Miles, May, and me.

"Perfect!" Miles said, standing at complete attention, not teasing, not distracted, on his best behavior.

Though neither of them had said anything to the rest of us, clearly Grace and Miles had talked. Over the past few days, every time she suggested something, Miles agreed exuberantly. There hadn't even been any arguing when we had our first meeting for the next *Nevermore* issue. May, Oscar, and I had secret wagers on how long it would last.

I was glad, though, that things were, if not back to normal, at least closer to it.

"Where's Oscar?" I asked.

"Here!" Oscar ran in, his cheeks pink from the chill outside.

In his arms was a stack of printed journals, fresh from the bindery.

"Oooh!" Grace said, grabbing a few and handing them out.

"Our baby's all grown up!" Miles said.

"No typos I can see yet," May muttered, anxiously scanning the pages.

"What did you finally decide to use to fill that space? Did you pick the nature poems?" I asked, scanning the table of contents, double-checking that Keats's name wasn't on there.

It wasn't.

But someone else's was.

"We got some great art at the last minute," Oscar said to me. "Grace said you know the guy?"

I flipped to page seventeen.

There, in meticulous, amazing detail, was one of Eph's dinosaur drawings.

"Oh," I said automatically, because it took all my other little words away.

He had drawn two small brontosauruses, their necks long and calm, peeking into the old wooden attic at the museum where they stored the giant elephant skulls, light skimming in from one of the alcove windows. It was titled *Part I: Things Begin*.

Grace stood next to me. "He dropped them off when you weren't there. He also apologized for being an ass when he met me."

"He did?" I asked, unable to take my eyes off the image. Eph had managed to capture the wonder I felt the first time I saw the attic at the museum. The dinosaurs were clearly modeled after us—down to the Superman cape one of them was wearing. And it was all there: the sunlight, the sense of magic, the feeling I'd opened the wardrobe to Narnia.

I flipped to his other piece.

It was the last page in the journal and showed a solitary bronto-saurus, also in a Superman cape, craning his neck over racks of clothes in what looked suspiciously like a thrift store.

It was titled *Part II: Things Change*.

I pressed my fingers against my lips. I smelled mint; I tasted salt.

"You know, your friend's not so bad," Oscar said, admiring the image over my shoulder.

Before I could respond, there was a rough-lipped kiss on my cheek.

"Hey, Scout," Keats said.

I smiled, giddy with the journal, with Eph's art, with Keats at my side. "I'm so glad you could come," I said, handing him my copy. "Check out how gorgeous it is!"

Keats opened the journal, scanned the table of contents, an eye-brow raised.

"These are all that's in there?" he asked, his face not entirely readable.

I nodded carefully. "Yeah, that's it."

"Whatever," he scoffed, tossing his copy on a table without spending any more time with it.

I knew he was disappointed his piece hadn't been chosen, but I wanted him to be twelve-hours-on-a-bus selfless, just for a few seconds, just for me. "Um, what was that about?"

"It's . . . I don't know what I expected in the first place. It's only a high school journal—not exactly the *Paris Review*." He shook his head, like he was so above the whole thing he was in his own galaxy.

Asshole.

All my excitement about the evening and the journal and our work whooshed out of me. I hugged myself, stepping back.

"I'm sorry—I didn't mean anything by that, Scout." He tried to put his arm around me, but I jerked my shoulder away.

"You know, we worked really hard on this."

"Oh, damn, did I offend you?" he said. "I'm so sorry. I'm such an ass."

I realized three things then: One, Keats spent a lot of time asking if he offended me; two, I spent a lot of time assuring him he hadn't; and three, I wasn't going to this time.

He waited for me to disagree, to console him, but my face felt ugly and mad, and I couldn't say anything.

A flash of bright pink near the door caught our attention.

Cherisse, in her ugly neon-pink coat. Of course.

Keats sighed, stroking my arm to placate me. "Listen, Scout, I have to talk to Cherisse about something. I'll be back. But I'm sorry, 'kay? Emily worked on a literary journal too, and I think she kind of ruined me. I'm sorry I'm so messed up."

My face was motionless as he kissed me on the lips.

He sauntered over and gave Cherisse a kiss on the cheek. Ugh.

I turned and straightened the pile of journals on the table, not wanting to see one more stupid second.

"So you helped with this?"

I turned around. Audrey was standing there, her face unsure.

"Yeah." I nodded. "Yep. Yes."

"That's really cool."

"You got your hair cut," I said, pointing to her new shoulder-length angular bob. "I like it."

"Thanks . . . It's a change, but a good one, I think."

We fell into silence, until she perked up. "Oh, and I'm all set for the French Club trip to Paris this summer. I'm finally going!"

"You are? That's awesome!" All my muscle memory told me to reach out and give her a hug, but I stopped halfway, remembering what had gotten us to that moment, and stood uncomfortably.

"How's your grandma doing?" I finally asked.

Audrey's face fell into sadness. "She's having a hard time. She misses my grandpa a lot lately."

"Oh, Aud, I'm sorry."

"She's told my mom a few times that they still talk every night. Mom's kind of freaking out."

I chewed on my lip. "Maybe he does visit her? They did really love each other."

Audrey paused, her expression relaxing a bit. "Yeah, they did, didn't they?"

I thought back to the first few summers we visited the lake house, and how after our mandated nine o'clock bedtime, after we could hear Eph's soft snore, Audrey and I would sneak down the steps and watch her grandparents slow-dance, Billie Holiday or Bing Crosby crooning in the background. They were so in love.

Audrey shifted, tugging on a front strand of hair, not long enough to twist around her finger multiple times anymore, and I wondered again how we'd gotten so far from who we used to be.

"So did you see Eph's stuff in *Nevermore*?" I asked.

"Don't tell me you guys published his Teachers Farting series," she said, referring to the caricatures Eph had drawn of all our sophomore year instructors doing exactly that.

"Oh God, no." I paged through a copy and held it out to her, pointing to the first drawing. "Here."

Her eyes lit up as she took in all the tiny details, and I imagined she was feeling the same burst of awe I felt when I first saw his small magnificent worlds.

"Wow," she said. "That's really amazing."

"Turn to the last page."

Audrey let out a small sigh of wonder. "God, his mind is so freakish. But in such a good way, you know?"

"I do," I said.

"Is he coming?" she asked, scanning the gathering crowd.

"Maybe, I don't know."

"I hope so. I want to congratulate him. I haven't seen much of him lately since our, you know, weirdness . . ."

I cringed, but she seemed as awkward about it as I did.

"But I saw you guys in the hall a couple of weeks ago . . . ," I said.

"He was telling me about your fight, at the Flea."

"Oh."

"He felt bad."

"Seriously? He could have fooled me."

"Since when has Eph ever been good at showing his emotions? He's total crap at it," Audrey said.

"Did he tell you what the fight was about?" I asked slowly.

"He just said he was worried he messed things up at some thrift shop?"

"Oh." I didn't know what to say, so I chewed on my lip, thinking of the day Audrey and I became friends, the truck wheels tangled in her hair, how things get messed up so fast—past the point of fixing—and wondering if Eph felt that way with us. "Well, I'm glad you came. It's good to see you."

She shrugged. "Keats invited Cherisse, so I'm her wingman."

"Oh," I said, feeling the sting of it—Audrey wasn't here for me anymore—then wondering why Keats invited Cherisse to an event I invited *him* to.

Her face flushed, flustered. "But it's good to see you, though. I mean, I'm happy for you. And the journal is pretty cool."

Grace beckoned to me from across the room. "Pen! It's time to start!"

"I gotta go," I said. "See you around?"

"Yeah, see you around," she said with a small, rueful smile.

As Mr. Garfield welcomed everyone, I saw Eph duck in the back, tilting his head at me. I felt a rush of relief that he'd come, then remembered that he probably wasn't here for me—he was here because his art was in the journal. Mia floated in after him, tall and celestial and glistening and ethereal, and I glanced down at my beat-up Docs, my legs in black tights, and felt stumpy.

Grace stepped to the lectern, introducing me, Miles, Oscar, and May, and welcoming the first reader.

As people shared their poems and short stories, the ones we'd fallen in love with, I tried to pay attention.

But my eyes kept shooting around the room.

Keats was sitting with Audrey and Cherisse, and I couldn't help but notice the way he leaned in and whispered loudly to Cherisse throughout the whole reading, how she tipped her head coyly, how he rolled his eyes when someone shushed them, how they were distracting even from four rows away.

NoNoNo.

And then there was Eph. He and Mia were rapt at the readings, her head leaning against his shoulder. At one point she leaned up and gave him a kiss on the cheek, and they were so tall and pretty together, my heart panged.

I looked back at Keats, narrowed my eyes, squeezed the edge of the chair, and focused any potential soul-mate energy into psychically channeling *SHUT UP* his way.

It didn't work.

By the time the last contributor finished reading, I was way past furious. Everyone stood and clapped, but I couldn't even start, my hands clenched tightly against me.

Eph and Mia walked over, Eph hanging back a few steps.

"Pen, the journal is amazing," Mia said, genuinely happy to see me. Of course she was.

"Thanks," I said, turning away from Cherisse's loud fake laughing at something Keats told her. "Did you see Eph's stuff? It's amazing," I said as I turned toward him. "Seriously. I loved them."

Eph kicked the floor, hands shoved in pockets. Even though it was dark, he might have been blushing.

"It's no big deal," he said.

I was so relieved we were talking without fighting, that the physical matter of him was standing next to me, I grabbed his sleeve. "Sometimes, things *are* a big fucking deal. And these pictures are. They're phenomenal."

He raised an eyebrow. "Not frakking?"

"Nope," I said, smiling at him. "Definitely not."

Keats came up from behind me, sliding his arm around my

waist, pulling me close. "Hey, Mia, Eph." Mia waved at Keats, and Eph gave a curt nod. "Listen, Scout, you need to stick around here much longer? I thought we could go back to my place."

I couldn't meet his glance; I was afraid of what I'd do. Instead I lifted his hand off my waist and stepped aside. "I'll talk to you tomorrow, all right?"

"You okay?" he asked, trying to pull me close again. I held up my hand.

"I said *tomorrow*."

He held up both hands, giving Eph and Mia an indignant *Can you believe this?* look.

Eph ignored him. "Everything all right?" he asked me.

"Yeah," I said. "I gotta go help Grace and Miles."

Keats waited for a second, then rolled his eyes and walked to the exit. Cherisse was already gone, I noticed with no small degree of satisfaction. Audrey must have left with her.

When I looked back at Mia and Eph, she seemed concerned, and Eph looked like he was fully prepared to mow someone down.

I could tell by the jut of his chin he was about ready to say something I probably didn't want to hear, so I held up my hand.

"I'll talk to you later, yeah?" I turned toward Mia. "Thanks so much for coming."

All seven feet of her leaned down, a goddess bestowing me with her mortal presence, and she pulled me into a warm hug.

"Ephraim is so proud of you. Me too!"

Crap. I couldn't completely hate her.

"Honey, I'm going to go grab my coat. Meet you out front?" She gave me a soft wave and walked toward the door.

"'Ephraim'? 'Honey'?" I said.

He grimaced and shrugged into his fleece pullover. His hair stood up from the static energy. Without thinking, I stood on my tiptoes and smoothed it.

He looked surprised I'd done it.

I was surprised I'd done it.

"So, you going to come out and celebrate with us, Penelope Marx? Coffee shop closes in a half hour," Miles said from behind, his mouth full of cookie.

I grinned, shrugging into myself with glee. "Um, heck, yeah!"

"I love this girl—don't you love this girl?" he asked Eph.

I blushed, immediately looking for Eph's reaction. He smiled awkwardly.

"Yeah, I do," he said quietly, so quietly Miles didn't hear it, so quietly my heart leaned forward to hear it.

"Hey, Eph!" Grace said, joining us, May and Oscar following behind, as giddy and proud as I felt.

"Hey," he said. "Good to see you, Grace. The journal is amazing."

Oscar stepped forward, shaking his hand. "Wait, you're the dinosaur guy? Those blew me away. Tell me you've got more for our next issue. Maybe you could show them getting on the ark with Noah?"

Eph froze.

"Dinosaurs weren't on any ark . . . ," Eph started, and Miles leaned over.

"He's messing with you. It's his thing. Don't engage."

Eph's face relaxed into an appreciative grin. "Nice one."

Oscar nodded at the compliment.

221

"Hey, wanna come celebrate with us?" Grace asked Eph. "Your girlfriend can come too."

The word "girlfriend" immediately bothered me.

"I've got plans, but thanks. And yeah, we can talk," he said to Oscar, and they shook hands again, all cool-guy nodding, before Eph waved to me and left.

"Hmmm," Miles said loudly over my shoulder, watching him leave.

"No," I said. "It's not like that."

"I'm just saying . . ."

"You're not saying anything!"

He grinned.

"Celebratory churros at Coppelia?" May asked.

"Yes!" Grace said, pulling on her coat and scarf.

As we walked out the door, Grace yanked May's and my arms, her face surprised, and pointed ahead of us.

Oscar was talking animatedly and Miles was listening, rapt, periodically and affectionately nudging Oscar on the arm.

"That's amazing," Miles said to him.

May's mouth dropped open. I spun to Grace.

"What is that?"

"When did that happen?" May asked.

"How did it happen?" I asked.

Grace threw her hands up. "I have no clue!"

Miles looked over his shoulder to see if we were coming, and I can only imagine how the three of us appeared right then, stunned, mouths hanging open.

He stuck his tongue out at us and leaned closer to Oscar, and we all followed them into the early evening.

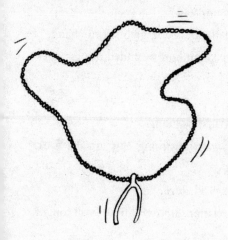

Gold necklace
Monile aureum
New York, New York
Cat. No. 201X-19
Gift of Keats Francis

ON MONDAY, KEATS WAS WAITING FOR ME IN CHEMISTRY, GIVING
me what was clearly meant to be an übercharming boyfriend smile.

I ignored him and sat down, pulling out my chemistry book and flipping to the day's reading.

I was tired from last night. After saying good-bye to Grace, Miles, Oscar, and May, I went home, ready to happily fall asleep thinking about the journal. Instead, I couldn't stop fixating on Keats's crappy behavior: his attitude when he discovered his story hadn't been picked, how I could hear his and Cherisse's irritating whispered murmuring throughout most of the reading—how everyone probably could.

I must have fallen asleep at some point; my alarm jerked me up. But if I didn't already recall being awake at four, the bags under my eyes when I got to chemistry would have confirmed it.

"How are you, babe?" he asked.

I grunted, feeling distinctly unpleasant.

"Scout." He reached across the desk and grabbed my hand. "I was up all night feeling like crap about how we ended things yesterday. Let me make it up to you?"

"I don't know," I said.

Mrs. Carroll came in as the first bell rang.

"I know, I know. Last night wasn't my thing. But you are. You're my girl. Please?"

I had never been someone's girl before.

Maybe this was just what relationships were like—you fought, you made up, you made out.

I felt myself thawing. "My birthday is on Saturday. Want to come over and have dinner with me and my parents?" I asked.

"Celebrating the day you were born? The best day in the history of the world? Scout, I wouldn't miss it." He leaned across the aisle and kissed me in front of everyone as the second bell rang.

It wasn't until halfway through Mrs. Carroll's endless lecture on the Bohr model of the atom that I realized Keats hadn't apologized for last night.

On Saturday, when Keats got to my house for my birthday dinner, he was forty-two minutes late. I opened the door, anger making my breath fast, but he was clearly flustered, his cheeks red, his nose running.

"I texted you—where were you?" I asked.

"Sorry, I'm so sorry, Scout. Subway problems. You're totally mad at me, aren't you?" He stood hesitantly at the doorway, his chest heaving, and I wanted to point out that he should have left earlier, that in New York you *always* give yourself a subway-delay buffer when you're going somewhere important, but he was here, celebrating my birthday, a big bouquet of pink peonies in one hand, a small wrapped gift in another.

Let it go, let it go, Penelope.

"Come on in," I said.

He handed me the flowers and started to unpeel all his layers of clothing—hat, scarf, gloves, two coats.

"Is your young man here, darling daughter?" my dad called from the kitchen.

I rolled my eyes. "Get ready," I whispered to Keats.

He smiled, taking the flowers back.

"Hey!" I said.

"They're for your mom," he said, and I took his hand and led him to the welcome warmth of the kitchen.

The sweet smell of my mom's tomato sauce as it bubbled on the stovetop filled the room. The windows were fogged up, the whole place on the edge of being slightly too hot but somehow managing to be just right.

"Hey, Mom and Dad, this is Keats."

My dad put down a glass of wine and jumped up from his seat at the table, extending his hand to Keats's. "Theodore Marx. Nice to meet you."

"You too, sir."

"Please, call me Theo."

Keats nodded. "Sure, Mr. . . ." He stumbled, turning red. "I mean Theodore, Theo."

I felt myself thaw even more—there was something endearing

225

about a nervous Keats. "Here, Mrs. Marx, these are for you," Keats said, handing her the peonies.

"Keats, these are lovely. Thank you so much. Let me find something to put them in. Have a seat, guys." She started digging under the sink for a vase.

My dad began pulling out the dinner plates.

"I can help," I said, but my dad motioned me back to the table. "It's your birthday. The one day of the year you don't have to help out."

My mom started spooning fettuccini on the plates. "So, Keats, is your family from New York?"

"Um, yeah, my mom grew up on the Upper East Side, but my dad grew up in Greenwich, Connecticut," Keats said, twisting at a paper napkin. "They met between junior and senior year at Yale, when they were summering at Martha's Vineyard."

"Ooh, la-di-da," my dad said.

"Theo!" Mom said.

"Dad!" I said.

"Nah, it's okay," Keats said, settling in the chair. "We're pretty much as Waspy as you get. My parents' wedding party included both a Vanderbilt and a DuPont. But if it gets me early acceptance into Yale, I'll take it."

"Hmmm," my dad said.

I cringed. There were few things my dad liked to complain about more than Ivy League privilege and the benefits that came with it.

"Dad, Keats is super into college football," I said, cutting off my dad's counterpoint at the pass.

"Yeah, my dad and I went to the Rose Bowl last year," Keats said.

Mom put our plates down on the table, steam rising from each, and I reached for the bread basket and passed it to Keats.

My dad leaned forward, excited. "So you got to see OSU take Michigan to the bank?"

Keats grimaced. "Um, yeah."

"Don't tell me you're a Michigan fan," my dad said.

At this point Keats might as well have declared himself a creationist and a Republican, considering that after Ivy League snobbery and Michigan fandom those were the only two Theodore Marx deal breakers left on the list.

Keats cringed and nodded, and my dad grunted.

Time to change the subject.

"Mom," I said, wiping tomato sauce off the corner of my mouth. "Keats and his brother are planning to take a road trip for a few weeks this summer that replicates Jack Kerouac's trip from *On the Road*."

"Oh goodness," she replied. "Isn't your mom worried about you two boys doing that? What if your car breaks down or one of you gets sick?"

I cringed.

"Uh, we're still figuring that stuff out. But I think it'll be okay?" Keats said.

My dad, sensing an opportunity, jumped back in. "Keats, has Penelope told you about Willo?"

I shook my head imperceptibly at Dad, but he ignored me.

"You'll have to come to the museum event next weekend! It's going to be amazing. You see—"

"What's the museum event?" Keats asked me, cutting him off.

"Oh, a thing for my dad's work, no big deal."

"No big deal?" My dad slapped the table good-naturedly. "It's only going to be the most amazing dinosaur exhibit we've had to date."

Mom smiled, rolling her eyes. "He's so modest," she said to Keats.

Dad got that telltale crazy-professor expression on his face.

"Willo, the dinosaur everyone thought had a heart!" my dad proclaimed. "Of course, it was probably just sand at the end of the day, but Willo's very celebrity allowed us to mount the exhibit in the first place. The dinosaur circulatory system is fascinating. . . ."

It was just the beginning. Keats nodded politely as my dad steadfastly plowed over any of my mom's and my efforts to politely change the conversation.

Finally, when a ten-minute discussion of the wonders of the dinosaur circulatory system started to veer into the marvels of the reproductive drive, my mom abruptly stood up.

"How about cake?" she asked. "Theodore, come over here and help me with the candles."

"Sorry," I said under my breath to Keats. "When he gets going, it's hard to stop him."

"I thought we'd be in there forever," he said.

And it was weird then, because even though mere seconds ago I wanted to clobber my dad to get him to stop talking about Willo, I didn't want Keats to agree with me. I wanted him to tell me my dad was cool.

Because he was.

He was *my* dad. Sure, he wasn't old-time movie-star suave, and he was crap at picking up conversational cues, but when he talked about what he loved, his eyes glowed with pure magic. And I loved that about him.

I thought about saying something, but my parents dimmed the lights and began singing the opening bars of "Happy Birthday." There were seventeen candles glowing above my favorite type of cake, the one I'd had for every birthday that I could remember: boxed Funfetti mix with strawberry icing.

My parents sang, and Keats smiled, resting a hand on my knee.

His palm felt like five hundred tons.

When it came time to blow out the candles, I felt strangely empty, like I didn't have any breath left in me to make a wish, or any wish left in me to breathe. I thought about Eph's dinosaur drawing, the one in the thrift store, about things changing, and about how a year ago I wouldn't have been able to imagine celebrating my birthday with a handsome boyfriend.

And without Eph.

I didn't make a wish.

Keats declined a piece of cake. "Artificial coloring," he said, shrugging apologetically.

"Your loss," my dad said, cutting himself an extra-big piece.

Soon after, my parents retired to the living room, and Keats and I sat quietly in the kitchen as I finished my cake.

From his pocket he pulled out the small wrapped box. "Here," he said, pushing it my way.

"Keats, you didn't have to—"

"I *wanted* to," he said. "Happy birthday, Scout."

The present was tiny and exquisitely wrapped.

"Nice job with this," I said, trying to conjure up the girl I was a year ago, the one who would have given her left arm to have a curly-haired boy give her a beautiful little wrapped gift on her birthday.

"Clerk at the store," he said, smiling, and I automatically smiled back.

I opened the box. Nestled on a deep blue velvet cushion was a tiny gold wishbone charm on a gold necklace.

My first thought was, *I hate gold.*

My second was, *This was expensive.*

And then, *This is not me at all.*

"Wow," I said, pulling it out.

"Here, let me put it on you." He swept my hair out of the way and, without asking, took off my subway-token chain, which I had rescued from my purse after the launch party. He handed it to me, putting the new necklace around my neck.

I studied the subway token in my palm, the chain kinked, the coin tarnished, as his fingers fumbled with the tiny clasp, his warm breath against my skin.

"There," Keats said. "You're gorgeous, Scout."

No one had ever called me gorgeous before.

I slid my subway token in my pocket and fiddled with the tiny wishbone, sliding it back and forth on the chain.

It was my seventeenth birthday, and not only had I finally been kissed, I finally had what should have been my fairy tale, my John Hughes, everything-turns-out-awesome romance.

Only I wasn't sure I wanted it anymore.

The next day, after school ended, we took the subway to West Fourth and then walked to his brownstone.

I thought about the last time I was there, his First of October party, and how that night was perfect.

"Anyone home?" Keats called as he unlocked the door, and when no one answered, he took my hand and I followed him, the old wooden stairs creaking slightly. When we got to his room, I dropped my bag on his floor and put my coat and scarf on his desk chair. Sitting on his bed felt too forward, so I slid down next to it and stretched my legs in front of me, leaning my head back against the side.

He clicked on his computer, and the Flaming Lips started filtering through the room like a subtle headache, one that won't leave.

I *told* him I hated this band.

Keats sat on the edge of his bed and patted the spot next to him. "C'mere."

"I don't know," I said.

"We don't have to do anything you don't want to do," he said. "It's just more comfortable."

I rose, smoothed my skirt, and sat down next to him.

Without another word Keats leaned over and started to kiss me, slow and careful, starting at the exposed spot on the slope of my neck and moving up, until he kissed my eyebrows, the spot between them, the gold wishbone sitting against the pulse of my throat.

My fingers felt cold.

Keats moved to my lips and I kissed him back, returning to the familiar taste of his mouth.

His hands pushed my shoulders down, and I lay on the bed, and he was above me, kissing my collarbone, the hollow dip in my neck.

I raked my hands through his curls, the softness of them.

"Your hair smells good," I said, and he was sliding my shirt up halfway, running a hand lightly across my belly, and I shivered, and he was leaning down and kissing my stomach, gently.

"Keats," I said, and my skin was tingling awake, and I realized no one had touched my stomach like this before, it was new land that he was discovering, and he lifted my shirt higher.

I closed my eyes, letting him kiss me, letting go . . .

. . . and I saw:

Miles looking affectionately at Oscar.

Kieran's confidence around Grace.

The three freckles across Eph's nose . . .

My eyes shot open. I pushed out from under Keats.

"Do you want me to slow down?" He seemed so regretful that I wasn't sure what to say.

He traced my clavicle, and goose bumps rose on my arms. I bit my lip.

No. I needed to be sure about this. This, this was a big deal.

I stood up, straightened my shirt down, smoothed my hair back into place. As I did, my eyes fell upon the picture of Keats and Emily, still sitting on his bedside table.

He saw me notice it.

"Crap, I knew that was going to make you mad," he said, grabbing it and shoving it facedown in a drawer.

I frowned, pulled on my peacoat, looped my scarf around my neck.

Keats let out a weighty sigh. "Scout, c'mon . . ."

For the first time, the nickname was grating.

"No, I gotta go," I said, leaving his room, a terrible sneaking suspicion dawning on me with every step that took me farther away from him.

I liked the idea of Keats.

But I wasn't sure I actually liked Keats.

Silver necklace
Monile argentum
New York, New York
Cat. No. 201X-20
Gift of Ephraim O'Connor

THE EVENING OF MY DAD'S WILLO EVENT COINCIDED WITH THE first snow of the season—a much-too-early November snow, fat flakes sticking on shoulders and hair.

I walked up the front museum steps in my red cowboy boots, shivering and scratching my neck where the lace collar of my vintage green velvet sheath dress met my neck. I was sweating profusely, the armpits of the dress too tight, the velvet too warm. And I hadn't really thought much about the red-boots-and-bright-green-dress combo until I was halfway there. I was going to be the big, sweaty Christmas weirdo in the room.

I followed the line of people trickling in the main entrance: men with suits, women with fur-collared coats, benefactors and socialites and science people all mingling together.

Entering the main hall, I felt about two degrees better and calmer, because there was the familiar giant blue whale hanging above me. And the entire room was magical, dimly lit with blue lights, the underside of the whale glowing luminescent, the square glass windows reflecting turquoise.

I thought about how when my dad had first started working here, he'd come home every evening singing that old Beatles song to himself, the one about an octopus's garden. He'd pull me up and spin me around. "I work under the sea, darling daughter," he'd say, and when my mom came in, he'd let go and pull her into a waltz, dipping her crazily, not stopping until she laughed so hard she cried.

I'd forgotten that about my parents.

I searched for them on the dance floor, but my dad was on the side, gesticulating excitedly to an older man, while my mom talked to the woman with him—benefactors, I was guessing.

"So, there you are."

I spun around. Eph was standing behind me, being totally wrongly handsome—no, hot—in an old brown vintage suit, an indigo tie somehow working with the whole thing.

I nodded, feeling weirdly shy.

He self-consciously smiled. "Mom made me change out of jeans. I found this in my dad's closet. I don't think it's what she had in mind when she said to borrow something from his closet. But if the suit fits . . ."

I scoffed at the bad pun. "That's some Theodore Marx humor right there."

"What can I say, I have good taste." He kicked the floor in his scuffed boots, not making eye contact.

"Wanna go see the exhibit?"

When we got to the central room, it was packed, people

236

drinking from champagne glasses, chattering excitedly, enjoying the socializing, and not paying a single bit of attention to anything about the dinosaur circulatory system. I was glad my dad wasn't in the room. It would have made him so angry.

Eph tilted his head toward the main attraction, and when we got there, we leaned over, looking at Willo—the dinosaur with a heart-not-heart. Its skeleton was oddly curled in on itself, almost in the fetal position, its legs tangled, like it was disoriented, confused, trying to protect the brown clump in the middle of its rib cage.

"You know, it's actually concretized sand," an older man said passing by. "They were wrong. That's the whole point of the exhibit."

Eph gave an exasperated sigh, muttering something under his breath about people minding their own business.

Of course I knew the old guy was right. But that didn't mean I still didn't want to push him over, make him go away.

Because at that moment, standing next to that skeleton, more than anything I wanted that rusty clump in Willo's fossil to be a heart.

I wanted to believe that, even though this dinosaur had existed centuries and centuries ago, its heart had pushed and pumped blood through its limbs like mine, that there was something vulnerable and tender in its leathery skin, that something of that heart still remained.

"Your dad did a nice job with the exhibit, Pen," Eph said.

"Yeah, he did," I said, leaning on the railing, unable to take my eyes away from Willo.

"Hey, there's my mom."

Ellen was on her tiptoes, scanning the crowd, her red hair glowing in the light of the room, like she was one of the exhibits.

"Mom!" Eph called her over.

"Hey, guys. Happy belated birthday, Penelope! You and your parents still coming over Monday night to celebrate?" I nodded, and she turned to Eph. "Have you seen your dad? There's a major donor who wants to meet him. You think he's in his office?"

"I haven't seen him, but we can look," Eph said.

"Great. If you find him, send him down to the main lobby. I'll keep making the rounds down here."

Eph and I walked through the crowd until we found the private staff door in the back of the room. The noise of the party behind us dulled to a murmur as the door clicked behind us.

The ensuing silence of the hall felt unbelievably loud.

"So what'd you do for your birthday?" Eph asked over his shoulder.

"Keats had dinner with us."

"That's cool, that's cool," Eph said. He turned forward. "Yep, cool."

I frowned at his back. Since when did Eph use the word "cool" three times in a row?

"He got me a gold necklace. It was really thoughtful."

He stopped, dismayed.

"A necklace?"

"Um, yeah, a necklace?" I said, echoing his tone of voice.

"Oh," he said, face falling.

"But I'm wearing my good-luck subway token," I said, holding up the chain. "It goes better with my outfit anyway."

"That's cool." He stalked down the hall, his pace faster this time, and I sped up.

"What's with you tonight?" I asked.

"Nothing. You and Keats make up from the other day?" he asked, not looking at me.

"What other day?"

"The *Nevermore* launch."

"Yeah, I guess."

"Cool."

Five times.

When we got to George's office, it was unlocked but empty, the lights off.

"Not here," I said.

The corners of Eph's mouth curled, the start of a crooked smile. "Want to go to the attic?"

"We can't."

He raised an eyebrow.

"It's locked."

In one uninterrupted move he slid open the top drawer in his dad's desk and dangled a ring of keys in front of me.

"I don't want to get anyone in trouble . . . ," I started, but Eph was already out of the office, jogging down the hall to the stairway.

The second floor was pretty dark—the only illumination coming from the basic utility lighting marking exits and entrances—and we couldn't hear the sound of the party anymore, only the creaking of the building in the wind. We were in one of the older sections, where my dad's office was. Everything was wooden—the old drawers and bookcases, the doors and desks. My dad even had one of those crazy old iron moving ladders for his top shelves.

Eph cleared his throat. "Remember when I kept insisting there was a real dinosaur who lived here and roamed the halls at night?"

"Yeah," I said, looking guiltily over my shoulder for security guards. I was pretty sure they'd give us a free pass, but it was our dads I was more worried about. "It was one of the first things you ever told me. You know, I was scared out of my mind anytime I was here and it was the slightest bit dark outside. I was convinced the dinosaur would eat me. Or my dad."

"Nah," Eph said. "It was a friendly dinosaur. Lonely, even. The last of his kind."

I thought of Willo.

Eph stopped in front of a weathered wooden door, pulled out a long, old-timey key, and clicked it in the latch.

"Eph," I said, my voice faltering.

"Come on." He started up the steps. "We're trying to find my dad, remember?"

I sighed and followed him up the stairs, leaving the door open behind me. With each step my mood lifted a little, like I was a kid following Eph up the steps again.

But when we got to the top, we saw that the attic had been cleaned out: no more elephant skulls like in Eph's drawing and our memories, only empty windows casting an empty silver light across the battered wood floors.

"No!" I cried. "Where are the elephant skulls?"

"I guess they moved them," Eph said. "It's probably not great to store things up here anyway."

"Yeah, but . . ."

I remembered the first day we found them. We each picked one to sit in, Eph in his Superman cape, me hugging my knees, the bone structures so big around us, our own ivory caves, how you could almost feel the tickle of a ghost trunk brushing your neck.

"God, I hate change," I muttered, hugging myself against the cold coming from the windows.

"Pen, I have your birthday present," Eph said.

I turned, and he was standing in the middle of the room, and he was so absolutely, unremarkably the same Eph I had always known. But my heart clenched, skipping a beat, because he was also totally different, his eyes waiting, my breath catching, ghosts around us.

"Here," he said, digging in his coat pocket and pulling out a small rumpled brown bag.

I stepped forward and unfolded it carefully, sliding my hand in, fishing out the shape at the bottom. Dangling at the end of a thin, sparkly silver chain was a silver T. rex charm, its tiny arms bent in fury, its mouth open in rage—like the skeleton downstairs, like the imaginary dinosaur who roamed the museum halls at night.

I gasped. It was perfect.

"Eph, I love it."

My hands were so jittery I fumbled trying to put it on, so Eph stepped behind me, his hands steady against my neck, fixing the clasp. His fingers skimmed my neck, and a small exhale escaped me.

It fit perfectly above my subway token, resting across from my heart.

I was already half in love with this small, angry dinosaur.

"Penelope?"

"Yeah?" I whispered, watching the way the T. rex glinted in the moonlight, like he was absorbing it, coming into his own.

And then Eph stepped in front of me and met my eyes, pulling me toward him, his hands pressing firm and solid against the small of my back, and I curled inside him, like I was Willo curling into myself, like Willo holding my heart close, and we kissed.

There was roaring in my ears, wooden floors shaking, Eph in the moonlight, Eph's heart in my hands.

He traced the line of my cheekbone down to the hollow of my neck, letting his finger rest there, my heart thudding underneath.

And then I panicked.

Because this wasn't a fairy tale.

This was the solidness and messiness of Eph—real in front of me—the furious and tender parts of him, the taste of his lips and the jut of his chin, everything infuriating and everything magical, all the belches and tiny dinosaurs, everything I could lose with letting go.

I stepped back. "We can't do this."

His face furrowed in confusion.

"You're my best friend," I said.

"But, Pen, ever since we kissed in the thrift shop . . ." He shoved his hands in his coat pockets and studied the floor, kicked his boot against the wood, then looked up. "At first I didn't want to admit it, you know? But I can't pretend it's not there."

He looked at me, his eyes hopeful.

I was afraid to ask what he was talking about.

"I already lost Audrey," I said. "What if things get messed up? I can't lose you too."

"This is different. This is inevitable." God, his smile was crushing me.

"What about Mia?" I asked. "Or Autumn or the punk rock girl at the Flea?"

242

"They're not you," he said plainly.

"Oh," I said, my voice small.

"Pen, here's the thing: I fucking love you," he said.

The beautiful words hurtled toward me with the momentum of a meteorite, fierce and terrible and un-take-back-able.

I wanted to shove him in the chest, to stuff everything back in his mouth, to stop this nonsense right now. Because what if Eph broke my heart? What if I broke his?

(But then there was this: What if I stepped forward, what if I took his hand, what if I said it back? What if there were stars falling and orange embers dancing in the air around us and our eyes burned with smoke and our feet hurt from the heat and around us dinosaurs were roaring in pain and we curled around each other, keeping each other's heart safe?)

I opened my mouth and nothing came out.

We stood there in silence, Eph's face falling by the second.

"You're killing me here, Pen," he said, his shoulders falling, his face broken.

I shook my head.

At that moment the door to the attic creaked open. Two people stumbled up the steps, lips locked as they tripped up—a woman's giggle, a man's grunt.

Eph registered it at the same time I did, and a soft cry escaped his lips—he was a boy again—and I gasped.

It was George.

But he wasn't with Ellen. He was with Annabeth, the lady from the bookstore.

George squinted at us, Annabeth swaying against him.

"Eph?" he asked, his voice slurred.

Eph's whole body tensed.

Annabeth hiccupped. "Is that Penelope? George and I were in such a fight last time we saw you, I'm afraid I wasn't very friendly. . . ." She giggled, hiccupping, and tried to snuggle against George, but he jerked away, leaving her tottering.

Eph's eyes were big when he looked at me. "What does she mean, the last time you saw them?"

"Nothing," I stuttered. "I saw them once, it was just . . ." My arms fell helplessly to my side.

"Fuck," he mumbled, shoving hair off his face, pressing his hand hard against his forehead. "Fuck, fuck, fuck."

I stepped toward him, but he only winced and put his hands up between us, taking a step back, a step away from me.

Annabeth seemed to wilt without George's support, so after ten seconds or four hours of no one saying anything, she left, propping herself against the stair railing as she sidestepped her way out of the attic, the click of her heels fading.

"Eph," George said, walking toward Eph, trying to embrace him.

But Eph pushed him away—hard—and George crumpled to the floor, beginning to sob, his elbows ajar. He held his head in his arms, bony shoulders cutting through the air, and his cries were sloppy, devastated.

I knew then that Willo had seen the meteor coming, had seen the fiery ball plummeting against the blue, and Willo froze, it was so beautiful, and then there was only the pain of change, a heart throbbing hard against the heat, how you could only save yourself.

Eph looked down once more at his dad, shook his head, and began walking to the steps, his back to me.

I couldn't move. I thought of losing Audrey, of Ellen's beautiful red hair, of holding Eph's hand, how things leave us and never really come back.

And then I made the biggest mistake of my life.

I let Eph go.

Tonka truck
Tonka *carrus*
New York, New York
Cat. No. 201X-21
On loan from Audrey Harris

I PUSHED OUT OF THE CROWD IN THE LOBBY AND STUMBLED
down the outside steps, looking for Eph on Central Park West and
again on Eighty-First. Trees loomed darkly across the street, and my
breath puffed out in front of me; my whole body started shivering,
my heart clambering, my arms jittering.

Too late.

He was gone.

It felt terrible, the way my teeth wouldn't stop chattering.

I dialed Eph's phone, but it went straight to voice mail.

I texted him. *Where r u?*

I waited.

I thought about his face as he said the words, the way it changed
when I didn't say anything back.

And then that soft, broken noise he made when he saw Annabeth.

I had messed up, big time.

His words echoed through me: *Here's the thing: I fucking love you.*

I said the words to myself, felt their clumsiness, the way they tripped over my lips.

I didn't even want to think about that, about what it'd mean for him and me and us. At that moment all I wanted was to find him, to wrap a fleece blanket around us both, to put on *Twin Peaks* Season One, to grab Sno-Caps, to let him rest his head on my shoulder, to tell him his parents would be okay.

I texted him again. *We need 2 talk.*

This time the response was immediate: *No.*

My hands shaking, I dialed his number again. No answer.

With a cry of frustration I hung up, shoving the phone back in my purse, and walked back to Central Park West.

I watched couples walk together, bundled against the cold, the earliest of small Christmas lights twinkling above them, parents swinging a toddler back and forth, a crowd of smokers on the museum steps, the sound of the gala streaming out every time the door opened.

My feet were anchored to the sidewalk, but my breath started to hitch, faster and faster, snagging on itself, fingers tingling from the cold outside, sweat beading on my insides.

I couldn't stay here. I didn't want to see my parents. Eph didn't want to see me.

My fingers tapped on the phone, shaky and imprecise. I had to keep deleting and rewriting, trying to get it right.

hi grace, u around?

I waited, teeth chattering.

> Kieran surprised me w another visit! Out w Miles and
> O!!!! I think it's a date! :) Come meet us?

Gravity failed me, no solid ground under my feet. I didn't want to be around my friends just now, but I knew I didn't want to be alone.

Ten minutes later I was on a ridiculously crowded C train, some dude's backpack pushing into my shoulder, a woman leaning against my hand as I held the pole.

I counted the stops until Keats's and excused my way to the exit, the street not the fresh breath I wanted but instead something petty and wet, the snow turning into sleety rain.

The four blocks to his brownstone felt extra long, and the tip of my nose was ice cold, eyes watering from the wind. I wanted warmth; I wanted assurance; I wanted to not remember how much I'd hurt Eph.

I rang the doorbell and stood under the yellow glow of his porch light.

Nothing.

I rang it again, keeping my finger on the button seconds longer, the shrillness echoing, until I heard feet pounding down steps, saw a shadowy figure pause in the window, heard the chain unlatch, the dead bolt click open.

Keats stood in the doorway. His face was flushed and his hair was a mess, his shirt untucked.

"Penelope?"

Not Scout.

"Can I come in?" I said, hugging myself in the cold.

He glanced behind him up the steps. "You know, now isn't the best time . . ."

My teeth started chattering again, and I tightened my shoulders against the cold. "Something really bad happened with Eph's parents, and I don't want to be alone. . . ."

I felt my eyes starting to tear up, and I stepped forward, but he blocked the door.

"Penelope . . ."

Again, not Scout.

"What's going on?" I asked, right as a female voice sang from somewhere in the house: "Keatsy, I'm getting lonely . . ."

Behind Keats, at the top of the steps, was none other than the worst person in the world: Cherisse.

She was wearing some silky piece of navy blue lingerie, a strap hanging over her shoulder, her hair tangled around her face, smile drowsy and content, until she saw me.

Both of us froze in place, Cherisse muttering, "Oh shit."

Even though I should have been surprised, the moment felt inevitable and perfect in a way, everything clicking into place.

Keats grimaced. "I can explain." He gestured to Cherisse to wait a minute and stepped outside with me, pulling the door closed behind him.

"Damn, it's cold out here," he said, smiling weakly.

I imagined my arms breaking off, legs snapping, all of me turning into pieces in front of him.

"See, I've known Cherisse forever, and something changed this year, and it's kind of really fucking intense. I wasn't sure if it was going anywhere, so I didn't want to tell you until I was sure . . ."

"Wait a minute. She's Jena?" I said, realizing I already knew the answer, that as much as I'd hated that Wonder Wheel story, it had come from someplace real.

"What?" He shifted from leg to leg.

Something cracked in me, and I mentally surveyed my limbs, not convinced they were all still attached.

"Why did you invite me to the party if there was already someone else? Why did you even like me?" I hated the way my voice sounded pathetic, all of Audrey's suspicions coming to fruition.

"What party?"

"*Your* party, the costume party."

He looked confused. "I didn't invite you."

An arm broke right off, more fractures spreading through my fault lines by the second.

"But the invitation, the one in my locker . . ." My voice trailed off, thinking back to the day I got it: Autumn/Summer/Spring yelling at Eph that she wanted to go, asking if I was "her."

Smudged ink on the corner: the blue of the pens he carried in his pocket, the blue of Eph's dinosaurs.

My heart split in two.

"I should go," I whispered.

"Can we at least hug it out?" he asked.

"Hug it out?" I asked.

I took in his eyes, his curly hair. I thought of the way he held my hand at the party, the way we talked in the moonlight, how he wouldn't shut up about Kerouac, how he brought my mom flowers and thought my dad was weird, the way his lips were chapped and dry, how he smelled like fire on your tongue, eyes watering, the way it felt to finally, finally have someone like me.

But how maybe that someone wasn't Keats.

Wile E. Coyote always hung in the air for one second before he knew the world had been ripped out from under him, before he plummeted to the ground.

This was that one second.

"You should use lip balm" was all I could think to say, and I turned and walked away, leaving an arm, an ear, half a heart on the sidewalk behind me.

I woke up the next morning to a soft knock on my door. It was 8:43 a.m. My sheets were tangled, and they smelled like night terrors, hands clammy, the sweaty residue of fear. I turned over to the wall, hoping my mom or dad would go away.

Another knock.

"Pen?"

My body tensed with the familiarity of the voice.

I shoved off the sheets, trudged to the door, opened it.

Audrey smiled weakly at me, holding my jean jacket, moving forward like she wanted to hug me but then stepping back, unsure, and hanging the jacket on the edge of my desk chair.

Shame coursed through me, at how she'd been right about Keats, at how she'd been right about me.

My eyes filled beyond my control.

"Pen," she said, her voice so kind and sad and full of love for me, her eyes tearing up, and I couldn't stand to look at her for another second.

I folded my arms across my chest and studied my feet, the faint leftover sandal tan lines from the summer. "Why are you here?"

"Cherisse told me about last night. I wanted to see if you were okay."

"You can't have been surprised," I said flatly. "You warned me this would happen."

She flinched. "I didn't know Keats and Cherisse were hooking up. I swear, Pen, you have to believe me. I would have told you."

I shrugged hollowly, everything in me numb. I turned my back on her and dug Eph's old gray sweatshirt out of my dirty laundry pile, pulled it over my head, and slumped on my bed, not caring if I looked weird and gross.

Audrey picked up a framed picture on my desk. It was from Fourth of July last summer, when she and Eph and I spent the afternoon camped out on her roof, cooling off with ice pops until the fireworks started. Audrey and I were sticking our tongues out—bright red—and Eph was making *loser* signs with his hands, his lips as red as ours.

I pulled my knees against my chest and tugged my old green-and-white plaid blanket up to my chin, trying to make myself as small as possible. Ford padded silently into the room, gave Audrey a one-off glance, then jumped onto my lap and awkwardly kneaded my leg, purring loudly.

Audrey put the picture down and clutched her hands together, like she was trying to still herself. She cleared her throat. "I miss you, and I'm sorry."

I didn't say anything.

"I'm sorry for the whole stupid mess of us over the past two months." She swallowed, hard. "Sometimes it's not easy to be your friend. You have such high standards. Not that they're bad," she added hurriedly. "You believe in things so wholly, in absolute friendship and epic true love, and your heart is so amazingly big. I love that about you, Pen. But I'm not Vivien anymore. I don't know if I ever was."

Ford settled happily, purring so hard a drop of spittle fell on my blanket. I wiped it off carefully, so I wouldn't jostle him.

"And I guess, I was hoping, maybe someday, we could begin again? We could learn to be friends again?"

I didn't know how to respond—everything from the past twenty-four hours, the past two months, whirled around me like some stupid *Wizard of Oz* tornado, uprooting all I ever believed in. "I messed things up with Eph," I said, my voice crumbling, the sad words coming out of me, something held back now released.

"Oh, Pen," Audrey said, rushing to sit next to me, bumping Ford, who yowled, and pulling me into a big hug. "Do you want to talk about it?"

I shook my head, trying to hold back all the sadness in me and failing.

I rested my head on her shoulder and cried and cried, thinking about everything I'd lost: Vivien and Delphine, my unwavering faith in fairy tales and happy endings, the dream that was Keats, the reality that was Eph.

When I wore myself out, the sobs softening and easing into an occasional tear-filled hitch of breath, Audrey leaned across the bed, pulled something out of her bag, and held it out to me.

"Oh my God, is that the . . . ?"

She nodded, and I took the Tonka truck from her hand—the one that got tangled in her hair all those years ago, the one that started our friendship.

"You still have it?"

She nodded again, and I dropped my head against her shoulder without thinking, turning the truck in my hand.

"As soon as the nurse cut my hair, she handed it to me and I kept it. I wasn't going to lose all that hair without something in return." She poked a finger out and spun one of the wheels, and we listened to it whir. "Of course, I didn't know I'd get you from that deal too."

"I wish we could go back to then," I said.

"We're not the same people anymore, Pen."

I thought about that truck whirring in Audrey's hair, how terrified she was, how it tangled and pulled, how she was trying so hard not to cry.

Be brave, I thought. *Be brave for the people you love.* "I'm sorry I got so mad at you for what you said—you were right, about me and Keats and everything. I'm sorry I made you watch David Lynch movies and that I have too many rules and that I make it hard to be my friend."

"I didn't mean all that, not really," she said. "Okay, maybe the David Lynch stuff, but, Pen, I was just hurt. And you know I don't think you're pathetic, right? Please tell me you know that. That was the worst part of all of it, that you believed I'd think that about you. I would never . . ." She shook her head.

"Thank you," I said quietly, realizing as she said it that I *did* know, that everything she had said that day had come out of love, out of multiple viewings of *Titanic*, of gleefully smelling giant bags of M&M'S, of August nights spent spotting fireflies at her grandparents' house, of slumber parties and whispered dreams, that all that history didn't just disappear, even if the people we'd been then no longer existed.

"But, Pen," she said, her voice quiet. "I can't *not* be friends with Cherisse. I'm not going to choose between you guys. I want you both, okay?"

I tried to figure out how to say what I wanted to say next. "I get that. But I can't be friends with her, Aud. Not with the Keats stuff."

She sighed. "I know. I just wanted my best friends to be best friends . . . I wanted everything to be perfect."

"I don't know what that's like at all," I said, nudging against her lightly.

"I'm sure you don't," she replied, smiling.

"But I get it now, what you were saying about bigger social circles and all that stuff. I met these guys, Grace and Miles, and it's like . . . well, it's like they know me already."

Her smile faltered, and I wondered then if we'd stay friends forever, or if we'd drift off into our new groups, and if maybe that was okay.

I didn't know what would happen.

I held the truck out to her, but Audrey shook her head. "Hold on to it for a bit. You need it more than me right now."

And I leaned over, gripping the truck hard, and gave her a hug, my arms moving on instinct, from history, letting go of all we'd lost, holding on to this small, fragile new thing we'd found.

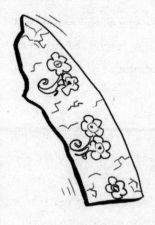

Pottery shard
Pars testae
Dead Horse Bay
Brooklyn, New York
Cat. No. 201X-22

AFTER AUDREY LEFT, I BRUSHED MY HAIR—KIND OF—AND CHANGED
into jeans, grabbing my dinosaur necklace and the Bearded Lady's
good-luck token, smashing on a hat and grabbing my coat.

"I'll be back," I called to my parents.

I ran as fast as I could the entire two and a half blocks from my
house to Eph's—it was so cold outside, I saw my breath in front of
me. I hated running. I felt like there were knives in my rib cage, but
I ran anyway, breathing hard, nearly knocking over an old woman
with a cart full of aluminum cans in the process.

"Sorry," I yelled over my shoulder, my legs pumping, until I
slowed to a stop in front of Eph's.

I rang the doorbell, heard footsteps, saw a tall figure peering
through the security glass. My heart skipped as the door opened,
hoping it was Eph.

It was his dad. George looked as if he had died sometime in the past twenty-four hours, dark gray circles under his puffy eyes, still wearing the same clothes he was wearing last night, the stench of sadness and alcohol coming off him like a cloud.

He wasn't dashing. He was broken.

"Eph's not here," he said, his breath stale.

"Oh," I said, not sure what to say next. George stared around me, not at me. "Will he be back later today?"

George smiled sadly. "No. He and Ellen left for her parents' house in Poughkeepsie at the crack of dawn this morning. They're not back until early tomorrow."

"Oh," I said, my shoulders falling. I shifted uncomfortably on the steps. "If you talk to him, will you tell him I stopped by?"

George nodded. "If you talk to him, will you tell him I'm sorry?" he asked.

I nodded solemnly.

George stepped back in, and the door clicked shut. I walked a block, glad I had Eph's sweatshirt on under my coat, that I was holding myself in what I still had of him.

My hands were shaky. I felt weird and jangly, all the energy from running over to his house not spent but building inside, making me feel twitchy and restless.

I didn't want to go home.

I texted Eph. *Call me?*

I wandered up the street, watching leaves crumble under my shoe, a plastic bag float around above me. It wasn't beautiful, it was garbage, and I hated that it was there and that some pigeon might get stuck in it, and I hated that I wasn't tall enough to reach it, and I hated that Eph was tall enough and he wasn't there.

I dialed his number. Straight to voice mail.

I stopped on the sidewalk, the wind around me so chilly my nose was starting to run, and I thought, *I don't know what to do. I don't know what to do.*

In a Jane Austen book this was when Mr. Darcy and I would stumble upon each other, our breath puffing sweetly in the cold in front of us, and we'd declare our love for each other, shyly, beautifully, purely.

In the world of Vivien and Delphine, this was when Jason North, the schoolteacher I had secretly pined after for years, would realize he loved me too, would run to the train station, trying to catch me before I slipped out of his life forever.

In *Titanic* this was when Leo would take my hand and we'd run until we found our happy ending or we'd die trying.

But I was standing alone on a New York City sidewalk that reeked of urine. My nose was running, and I didn't have a tissue, and I was worried a pigeon might strangle itself on that stupid out-of-reach plastic bag.

I wasn't getting a happy ending.

I didn't tell my parents what I'd seen in the attic at the museum.

I didn't tell anyone about what had happened with Keats.

Instead I got to school early on Monday and camped out by Eph's locker. I didn't know what I'd say about his dad. I didn't know what I thought about the kiss. I only knew I needed to see him.

Leaning against the wall, still wearing the now extremely smelly sweatshirt, I waited.

Grace walked by, did a double take, and stepped back.

"Not my locker," I said before she could ask.

"No, I was going to ask if you're okay?"

"Nope," I said, shaking my head and trying to smile, tears gathering. "Not at all."

"Want to talk . . . ?" she started, and then her eyes narrowed at something behind me, her breath sucking in sharply.

I turned around, instinctively dreading whatever was about to happen.

My instincts were right.

Walking down the hallway, hair shining and brilliant, her confidence parting the crowds in the hall like she was the ultimate Queen Bee, like she was Victoria's actual secret, was Cherisse.

Holding hands with Keats.

"Oh crap," Grace muttered under her breath, and she grabbed my hand, squeezing it tight. "What a complete bastard person."

Keats saw me and cringed, stopping abruptly in the hall.

Cherisse turned toward him, confused, and whatever he said to her must have involved me, because for one brief unbelievable human second an expression crossed her face that might have been shame.

"Pen, I'm sorry," Grace said, leaning around me and giving Keats and Cherisse the finger. *You suck,* she mouthed at them.

I giggled, even though I was crying. Keats looked stricken, but Cherisse was pissed, narrowing her eyes at both of us and spinning Keats around, marching him the opposite way.

For some reason it made me laugh and cry harder.

I wiped my face on my sleeve, the soft gray of the sweatshirt, hoping I wasn't simultaneously smearing snot all over it. "No, that's not it. It's fine. Seriously," I said, realizing as the words left my mouth that it was fine, that I didn't care about losing Keats.

She handed me a tissue and I blew my nose.

It was Eph who was breaking my heart, Eph who'd left an emptiness inside me that was as surprising and infinite and unknowable and terrifying as a black hole.

As if the realization had conjured him into being, I saw his long, slouched form round the corner and pause, taking in the scene in front of him. Me against his locker, blowing my nose and wiping my eyes, Grace huddled around me like she was protecting me from roving bands of blood-hungry Vikings, and walking toward him, holding hands, Cherisse and Keats.

It happened before I could say anything, a blur but in slow motion, too: Eph dropping his bag on the floor and racing forward like some superhero, straight at Keats, knocking him to the linoleum; Cherisse's hand whipping loose, her face opening to scream; and Eph's fist, pulling back, like grace, like the fury of gnashed teeth, landing a hard one right on Keats's face.

Cherisse's scream echoed through the hall, and people circled around them so I couldn't see what was happening, and Grace pulled me forward, elbowing through the crowd, and everything was sweat and adrenaline and noise and I needed to find Eph.

When we broke through, Mr. Garfield was pulling him off Keats.

Eph's eyes were wild, like he was ready to keep on fighting the whole world and every single person in it, but then he saw me.

A beautiful, horrible ache bloomed inside, all the nerves in my body tuned toward him, and I stepped forward, wanting to tell him

I was sorry about everything, that I believed him, that I loved him.

He met my gaze, and his face flattened.

He turned away.

Grace held my hand.

Mr. Garfield led Eph toward the principal's office.

Mrs. Carroll helped Keats up.

Keats moaned and cradled his nose.

Cherisse sniffled but still managed to fetchingly flip her hair, clutching Keats's arm.

Students muttered and whispered and laughed and dispersed.

The first bell rang.

Grace held my hand.

The second bell rang.

Grace held my hand.

And then my heart broke.

I dropped to my knees and cried, the most absurd girl in Absurd Town, the one who didn't know what she had until it was gone.

Eph was suspended for a week.

I didn't hear that from him, though. The seventeen times I tried to call him on Monday, he never once picked up.

Instead I heard it from Audrey, who stopped by my locker that afternoon, Grace and Miles on either side of me like bodyguards. She told us that Keats's nose was broken, that Eph should have been expelled, but that Keats had said he'd instigated it, which was one small point—the only one—in his favor, and that instead Eph was suspended for a week, and when he came back, he'd have to complete four weeks of community service.

Audrey walked me home after school, both of us quiet and cold, and she hung up my coat as I crawled into bed, Ford making himself as small of a ball as possible against my thigh.

That night I called Eph twelve times, sent him four texts. No response.

When I woke up on Tuesday, I couldn't bear the thought of going to school, my bedroom seeming much less fraught, so I told my mom I had cramps.

That night I called Eph eight times, sent him five texts. No response.

When I woke up on Wednesday, every time I thought of what happened at the museum, I burst into tears, so I told my dad I had a stomach virus.

That night I sent Eph two texts, called him twice. The second time I got a computerized message telling me the user's mailbox was full.

On Thursday I woke up to Ford bumping my head and purring.

I didn't pick up my phone.

I told my parents my heart hurt. I could tell I was pushing the limits of playing hooky, but I didn't care. I wasn't getting out of bed ever again.

On Friday morning there was a knock on the door, and my mom didn't wait for an answer, but entered the room and wrinkled her nose at the smell, eyeing the dirty piles of clothes on the floor.

Ford meowed loudly. Traitor.

"I'm not going to school," I said from under the covers.

Her head was tilted sympathetically, but her arms were folded across her chest—a strategic pose of both understanding (*I'm here with you*) and no-nonsense parenting (nothing was getting past those arms).

"Ellen called me late last night. I'm sorry you and Eph had to see that with George."

I closed my eyes, focused on the lack of colors behind my eyelids.

"Have you talked to Eph?"

I shook my head, miserable. "I think I lost him."

I felt her weight as she sat on the edge of the bed, smoothed the hair on my forehead. "Honey, do you remember the day you punched Eph at school and broke his nose? You were little kids and he lifted your skirt in front of everyone?"

I opened my eyes. "Yeah, his nose is still crooked."

"Do you remember what happened after?"

I didn't remember what happened, could only recall the stream of red coming down from Eph's nose, the animal noise he made.

"The principal called me, and I came down to pick you up, and you wouldn't talk to me. You kept crying and crying."

I didn't say anything.

"I thought maybe you were crying because you were so embarrassed. I kept telling you that it would be okay, that people change, that friendships change, and that if you didn't want to talk to Eph or be his friend for a while, that would be okay.

"And you started crying harder. Your face was all red and your shoulders were shaking so hard that it scared me, Pen, so I had you lie down, and I stroked your back to try to calm you down. I was really mad—I couldn't believe Eph had embarrassed you like that—but I was trying to be calm for you, and I kept rubbing your back."

I remembered the soft press of my mom's hand against my back, her whispers in my ear. *It's going to be okay.*

"When I finally got you calmed down enough to talk, you told me you were sad, but not because Eph embarrassed you or because you got in trouble for hitting him. Pen, you were upset because you'd hurt Eph. You said it made you cry to see him cry. And you were afraid he wouldn't want to be your friend anymore."

My breath caught, hurt blooming in me again.

"Things change, Penelope; people change. Sometimes you get hurt. And sometimes you're the one doing the hurting. You know, I look at George and Ellen . . ." She started chewing on her lip, and I realized I got the habit from my mom. "They're both hurting so much. But I have to hope that the love they've built through the years, and the memory of that love, will be enough to get them through, whether they stay together or not. I hope that even with all this craziness and change, something of what they had remains."

Her voice caught at the end, and that's when I saw that she was crying.

I froze.

I'd never seen my mom cry. Even when my grandparents died, she always had a parent face on, never once letting me see her break down or not be my mom. But there she was: not just my mom, but a person of her own, someone who chewed her lip and worried about people and loved her friends so much that seeing them hurt made her hurt. It was weird and vulnerable and kind of scary, learning your parents weren't just parents—that they were also people with breakable hearts.

The realization filled me with a crush of love, so I pushed myself up and hugged her shoulders, trying to hold my mom steady and safe, the way she'd always held me.

After a few minutes she drew back, sniffing loudly. "You don't have to go to school today, on one condition: Get out of bed and come bird-watching with me and your dad. We're going out to Dead Horse Bay."

"Don't you have to work?"

She shrugged. "You're not the only one who plays hooky. Downstairs in a half hour, okay?"

She kissed my forehead and left.

I lay there for a few minutes longer, miserable and sad, lonely and heartbroken, then pushed myself out of bed and to the shower.

After the ninety-minute subway plus bus ride, and then forty hushed minutes of my parents waiting to spot the kestrel at her nest while I fiddled with my dinosaur charm, sliding it back and forth on its chain, all my listlessness was mostly gone. My bones were restless.

"I'm going to go read on the beach," I whispered, holding up the copy of *Emma* I had shoved in my bag.

They nodded, shooting me relieved smiles (I was seriously cramping their bird-watching game), and I walked away, the tall grasses shushing around me, turning into reeds by the water.

I had heard about Dead Horse Bay before—the marshy area that had housed horse processing plants in ye olden times and had then been used as a landfill. It was now a weird stretch of beach where old bottles and leather shoe soles and the occasional creepy horse bone washed up at low tide. Ellen loved to wander there, bringing back old glass bottles for art projects, and Eph told me how he'd scavenge with her, the stretch of beach reminding him of something postapocalyptic—all the leftovers of lives long gone.

Yet despite everything I knew in advance, when I climbed the crest to the water, my mind blanked: no sadness, no anger, just the clean space of awe.

The beach was covered with bottles, a mosaic of glass where the tide had washed out—mostly browns and greens, the occasional cobalt blue and milky white. Mixed in were horseshoe-crab shells, indistinguishable pieces of leather, smooth driftwood, odd metal and plastic bits.

I began walking where the water met the shore. Even though the place didn't feel toxic—only dirty—I was grateful for the thick soles of my Doc Martens as I navigated the shards poking up from the sand, covered in deep ocean muck.

I wondered what the beach would look like when the sun was shining. That day was gray and cold, with a winter-ready sky, and everything in front of me felt as lonely as I did, all these broken pieces.

I stopped and examined a small round cylinder, the glass creamy white once I rinsed it off, the word POND'S on the side, and I realized it had once been filled with cold cream. I thought about the woman who might have used it, what her hands looked like, if she'd put it on at night before she went to bed, if she'd ever cried herself to sleep.

Using a stick, I dug a deep green bottle out of the sand. It was filled with dark black filth, barnacles growing around the edge, but it was the same shape and size as a soda bottle, and I pictured a girl my age drinking from it, the tickling of the fizz on the edge of the nose, summer blazing around her.

I shuddered as I walked over a miniature plastic baby missing its arms—way creepier than the Santa that Eph had given me—but I thought of *The Velveteen Rabbit* and wondered what had happened to the child who'd surely loved it when it was new.

I settled on the edge of an abandoned, spray-painted old rowboat. It sat under an old, dead tree, but people had tied bottles and pieces of glass from the branches, and the brokenness chimed above me as I rested my chin on my knees.

Nudging the sand around me with my boot, I uncovered a small shard of pottery dotted with blue flowers. I wiped it on the edge of my jeans, marveled at the detail of the leaves, the brightness of the petals.

Maybe it had been a sugar dish or a serving plate, a vase or a statue.

It was hardly bearable then, all these objects loved and discarded, the history left behind.

I wished I could go back to the time before I ever knew things could be broken.

I would find Eph there, take his hand, not let go.

We would close our eyes, hold on to everything fleeting and bright and shining, listen to the dinosaurs around us.

But instead I had this:

A broken piece of pottery in my hand.

Everything that remained.

As I sat there, watching gulls dive, listening to the shush of the reeds lining the beach, the lapping of the water along the shore, the clinking of glass, imaginary good luck and a dinosaur around my neck, I started to wonder if that was enough.

Handwritten list
Tabulae manu scriptae
New York, New York
Cat. No. 201X-23

THAT NIGHT, I DREAMED ALL THE DINOSAURS LEFT NEW YORK CITY.

They departed in waves and piles, flying and plodding, magnificent and terrible, each of them roaring in fury and sorrow.

And I let them leave.

When I woke at 4:13 a.m. on Saturday morning, my hand flew to my neck and found my tiny T. rex pendant right where it should be, rising and falling against my skin with each breath.

Maybe Keats and I would never talk to each other again.

Maybe Audrey and I wouldn't find our way back to being friends like we used to be.

Maybe Grace and Kieran wouldn't make it long-distance.

Maybe Oscar and Miles wouldn't fall in love.

Maybe Eph's parents would get divorced.

Maybe Eph would break my heart over and over.

Maybe I'd break his.

Maybe, in real life, there weren't happy endings.

But as I glanced around my room, sliding my dinosaur back and forth on the chain, I thought that maybe that was the point—that instead of happy endings, you get beginnings. Hundreds of little beginnings happening every moment, each of them layering into histories deep and tangled and new, histories you count on to remain, no matter what changes the world throws at you.

I knew what I needed to do.

I knew how to win Eph back.

I turned on a light and grabbed a pen and notebook, Ford squinting groggily at me from the end of the bed.

Chewing on the pen cap (proud for once it wasn't my lip), I started writing.

Welcome to the Museum of Heartbreak . . .

Once I started, I couldn't write fast enough to keep up with all my ideas. It was like I hit the memory jackpot. I chronicled history, scratched out things, made arrows and circles, created time lines, sketched memories, and it was totally my version of some crazy conspiracy-theory notebook, but that was all right.

I made a note to ask my dad about the museum attic.

I added an asterisk to the last item on the list, underlining it:

Ask Grace about Nevermore Christmas lights.

At some point Ford relocated from the end of the bed to my side, snuggling against my hip, not minding my jerky energy, purring until he fell asleep.

I reviewed my list, petting Ford distractedly.

And then I wrote more. The snow fell outside, bathing my room in an eerie not-quite-white light. It was like I was the last person on earth after a zombie apocalypse, but I wasn't sad . . . instead I couldn't stop remembering how glorious life had been.

I annotated my list, hastily writing descriptions next to each item, flipping back and forth between paper scraps.

By 5:07 the list was complete, and a layer of snow had made the world outside blankly silent and new.

Ford was in such a deep sleep he wasn't even purring, his front paw and nose twitching with some cat dream. I managed to edge my leg out from under the warm lump of his body without waking him. Victory.

And then I crept quietly around my room, collecting what I needed.

Eph's copy of *Watchmen*, the one that Keats first noticed, the one that made Eph go all fanboy every time he talked about it, the one I read because that's what you do for people you love.

The beat-up copy of *On the Road* from Keats, my teeth gritting in irritation from holding it again.

But also the note from when Keats asked me out in chemistry, and the little Cafe Gitane matchbook from our first date—the way he noticed things about me, the way I bloomed.

The found list from the book at Helvetica, how my lips were

puffy and bruised after making out, how his lips were chapped, how I learned I could be beautiful.

The Wonder Wheel story with its clichéd protagonist and mean, mean Jena.

The note from the creepy subway guy, crumpled and scary, and the gold wishbone necklace—how I never wore gold, how now that I thought about it, I was pretty sure Cherisse had the same exact charm.

The Tonka truck gleaming yellow, from the day we helped Audrey on the playground, the day our friendship began.

My old copy of *Anne of Green Gables*, the one that inspired countless hours of Vivien and Delphine stories, dreamy swooning, wistful sighing.

And, from the Dead Poets phone day, the bright flyer asking people to join the journal, like a gift from fate.

The first issue of *Nevermore* I worked on, the one with Eph's drawings—Mohawks and kindred spirits, a tribe, *my* tribe, the simple amazing miracle of words, the simple amazing miracle of someone calling your name at a party.

The crinkled dark chocolate Kit Kat wrapper—proof that the Holy Grail could be found.

A sheet of stickers—a starry night (or arts-and-craps project) paired with a black hole/dark night of the soul (or a boy wearing all black). The party invitation never meant for me, telltale blue ink on the corner, the luminous, luminous moon.

An old plastic Santa figurine from the Brooklyn Flea; how we both had days when, as Oscar told Miles, we were the most unlikeable versions of ourselves.

The red cowboy boots, and how he knew me better than I knew myself.

The gray sweatshirt I was never giving back.

A scrap of paper with a hastily sketched T. rex, the words *DONT BE ABSURD* scrawled below, the telltale hole of a bulletin-board pin now in the corner.

A shard of pottery—a bit of a life long gone, proof that even when things changed, something remained.

The Bearded Lady's most cherished possession: the subway token.

And mine: one tiny, furious silver dinosaur.

When I couldn't think of what else to gather, I placed the items in a winding line on the hardwood floor (except for my dinosaur—I wasn't quite ready to take him off), pushing the desk chair out of the way to make room. I arranged and rearranged, added placeholders, thought, moved things around again, stood on top of the bed to get an aerial view.

I began to label the collection.

I slowed down, remembering things. A few times I caught myself staring out the window at the snow coming down, but unlike the past few days, this time I didn't feel sad and lost, but rather dreamy and wandering, a tiny bit hopeful, definitely calm.

I wrote a note to Eph, one I would drop in his locker when he was back on Monday morning:

You are invited to the opening of the Museum of Heartbreak. Monday, after community service.

in the attic at the American Museum of Natural History. 7pm. There will be dinosaurs.

When I woke up that morning, the line of items and white cards curled around the room, wrapping under the desk, around the bookcase, along the edge of the bed, leading the way like a trail of bread crumbs.

Leading the way back.

Present Day

I AM IN THE MUSEUM ATTIC. EVEN THOUGH THE ELEPHANT SKULLS
are gone, I know their ghosts are here, can still catch the occasional
soft sigh from empty corners.

I make sure the key my dad gave me is in my pocket, remind
myself again to lock the door when I'm done.

Everything's ready.

Grace and Miles helped me string little white Christmas lights
around the ceiling and the gable windows, and it's so pretty, the way
they make tiny shadows on the wall. After they left, I taped a hand-
lettered sign neatly on the door: *Welcome to the Museum of Heartbreak.*

All the items my backpack could hold are now arranged on the
hardwood floor with their matching catalog cards—everything is in
its right place.

Seven p.m. The attic is chilly, and I'm glad I wore a thick sweater.
My neck feels empty without my dinosaur necklace and the subway

token, and my fingers keep wanting to twirl something, to fidget, but I try to just breathe, to be.

I know I will have the precise memory of this moment later, of the room listening around me, the subtle tap of my shoes against the wood floor.

But for now I concentrate on the past.

I remember how Audrey and I sobbed at the end of our first viewing of *Titanic* and how we watched it again, stopping it halfway through so Jack and Rose could have a happy ending; how we lay on the dock at her grandparents' house and tried to count the stars; how Audrey shines when she's talking about Paris.

I think of the way Grace's brightness is infectious, and how Miles takes longer to warm up, but when he does, his loyalty has the toughness of steel; how when I sit with them at the *Nevermore* meetings, I feel a warm sense of belonging I never expected to find outside of Eph and Audrey; how they accept not who I was but who I'm becoming; how I love them for the same reasons.

I remember Keats's hand moving through his dark curls and how I loved it so much; how he made me glow; how I don't like that he cheated on me or that I fell out of love with him or maybe never really loved him at all, but how without him, there wouldn't be a Museum of Heartbreak.

I think of my parents, how I get my worrying from my mom, my restless fidgeting from my dad, but how they love things like I do, dinosaurs and bird-watching and people—with their wholly, fully, marvelously ordinary love.

I remember Ellen crying, George ashamed, what they had, what remains.

And of course I think of you, Eph.

When we met, a tiny Superman putting his hand in mine, how you folded my fingers so gently around yours.

Watching your parents kiss, and later, your voice when you said you saw a real dinosaur, how we both wanted to believe it.

The red of the blood streaming down your face when I hit you, the ache of my knuckles for days after.

And our first kiss in the thrift shop, the freckles across your nose, salt water and mint, my lips meeting yours, the way our roots grow deep.

7:05, 7:10.

I don't know what our future will bring, but I remember.

I'm nervous and my armpits are getting sweaty, and it's 7:25, and I'm just starting to feel myself despair when you walk in, Eph.

You are stiff in the doorway, your hands shoved in your coat pockets, knit cap pulled down over your ears, your eyes taking in the room, the lights, the objects, what remains.

"Hey," I say softly, trying to ease you in.

"What's all this?" you ask, and I hear furious galaxies in your voice, the way broken things are crashing into each other.

"It's for you."

You don't move forward, your chin jutted out.

"An old Kit Kat wrapper? Thanks for that, Pen."

"No, it's a museum. A museum of us, of what got us here."

Your eyes narrow and your shoulders stiffen, but you step forward—one step, then another—cautiously taking in the other objects.

You stop in front of the note from Keats, the one asking me out. "Seriously?"

"Without it, we wouldn't have kissed, at the thrift shop."

You look up at me, your face unreadable.

"And this?"

"A pottery shard I got from Dead Horse Bay."

You wait.

"It got me thinking about all these things that are broken or gone, but how new things come too. . . ."

You lift the dinosaur charm, and I see the memory of that night cross your face—the way your world ended.

"Eph, I'm sorry I hurt you. I'm so sorry. I need you to know how sorry I am. It's just that what you said fucking terrified me."

You study the charm, then look up, the hint of a smile forming.

"Language, Penelope," you say.

I wave my hand, brushing it away, and step closer to you.

"The past week without you has been the worst ever. Since the night at the museum, my heart hurts—like it literally, physically feels terrible and achy and weird."

You wince, kick the floor again. "I'm sorry I sprang all that on you. And I get why you don't want to be with me, with Mia and Autumn . . . and with the way my dad is."

I can see you pulling into yourself, your face starting to harden, your shoulders stiffening.

"No, that's not true, not now. Please know that. You have to know that."

I start to put my hand on your arm, but I stop halfway, not sure if I've earned it yet. "Eph, look at me. Look at me. You broke my heart that night."

You scoff. "*I* broke *your* heart?"

278

I shake my head hurriedly. "Yeah, you did, a little. But so did Keats, and Audrey, and Grace and Miles and Oscar and May . . . and my parents and your parents . . ."

You wince.

"And I know I broke yours. And for that I am so, so sorry. But Eph, all that heartbreak? It got us here."

"Where's here?" you ask, and I see you when I met you, a small brown-eyed Superman, boldly showing me dinosaurs, telling me how the last one on earth lived in the museum, wandering the halls at night. But I also see you now, knit hat, bangs in your eyes, taller than me, handsome and familiar, kind and amazingly irritating all at once, and miraculously, cautiously, opening back up to me.

My heart beats underneath all these bones, and it is loud and awkward and real.

I walk over to you, get as close as I can, lean up against you.

What happens next, I know I will never forget.

"Eph, I miss you," I say, and I stand on my tiptoes, kiss you oh-so-gently on the bridge of the nose where I punched you, kiss you on the shoulders—once on the left, once on the right—where I shoved you, kiss your heart where I broke you.

"And, Eph, I love you." I kiss you on the lips, giving you all the sorrow and love and broken things I have in me.

"Huh," you say, holding me, pushing back to study my face, a slow smile growing on yours. "That wasn't so bad."

"Don't you mean it was frakking awesome?"

And then I take your hand in mine.

You don't let go.

Acknowledgments

This book wouldn't exist without Michael Bourret, who introduced Penelope and Eph, and Sara Sargent, who gave them their happy ending. You both get your own museum of heart love. Thanks to the entire Simon Pulse team for being excellent Museum of Heartbreak caretakers, in particular Liesa Abrams, Sarah McCabe, Mara Anastas, Mary Marotta, Lucille Rettino, Carolyn Swerdloff, Teresa Ronquillo, Christina Pecorale, Mandy Veloso, Faye Bi, and Karina Granda.

Big hurrahs to Lauren Abramo, for being a rights-selling ninja, as well as cbj Verlag, Scholastic UK, Sperling, and Pegasus for taking on *The Museum of Heartbreak*.

Adam James Turnbull, your art rocks, and I'm honored that you brought the Museum artifacts to life.

I'm so very grateful for the support of my writing partners-in-arms: Tracey Keevan, Nancy Lambert, Micol Ostow, Jenny Clark, Vim Pasupathi, Holly McGhee, Gary Giddens, and The Sweet 16's. Special shout-outs to Clara Leder, who is just as good at brainstorming ideas as she is at being a niece; Meredith Dros, for letting me glitter bomb her apartment; and Tara Felleman, for treating me to numerous celebratory margaritas.

Abundant and heartfelt thanks to all of *The Museum of Heartbreak*'s esteemed and kind benefactors, in particular: Deb Caletti;

Gayle Forman; Jim and Pat Leder; Steven, Tina, Clara, and Jack Leder; Penguin Books; Perigee Books; Patrick Nolan; Keri Smith; and Natasha Leibel.

To my amazing friends and family—you are all the good parts of Penelope, Eph, Grace, Mike, and Audrey, combined and multiplied to the infinite degree. Thank you.

Thank you to the real-life Willo, the Thescelosaurus who once had a heart, for inspiring parts of this story, and thanks to the amazing American Museum of Natural History in New York City.

And to all the readers whose hearts have also been flattened by the metaphoric meteor known as heartbreak: Hang in there—you're not alone. It will all pass, but in the meantime, build *your* museum (or write a book!).